DREAMS OF HELL
The Protector Guild Book 3

GRAY HOLBORN

Copyright © 2021 by Gray Holborn

All rights reserved.

No part of this book may be reproduced in any form or by any electronic or mechanical means, including information storage and retrieval systems, without written permission from the author, except for the use of brief quotations in a book review.

ISBN: 978-1-963893-02-1

Edits: CopybyKath

Design: DamoroDesigns

PROLOGUE, MAX

"Oh good, you're awake!"
My eyelids slid open, as I fought their resistance to the bright lighting in the room. Why were medical facilities always such an alarming, abrasively bright white with the world's harshest lighting fixtures? It's like they're designed to torture the patients being treated inside of them.

Greta, my favorite nurse, was standing above me, her gray hair as wild as ever and framing her petite, wrinkled face. Her smile lines were the deepest-set wrinkles of all, which somehow always made me feel warm in her presence, like she'd spent most her life smiling too hard, despite living in the chaotic world of protectors. She gave me hope that it was possible to find happiness in between the heartbreak that came with a life of fighting.

"We have to stop meeting like this," she said, with a clunky wink. The skin of her eyelids was so thin that I was half-convinced I could see through them when her eyes closed.

I sat up and immediately regretted it. My head felt like it was weighed down with bricks and I brought a hand up to massage my temples, scrambling to piece my life together. I ended up in this position—on a hospital bed with Greta looming above me all gargoyle-like—more frequently than I'd like. The injuries

I

were blending together at this point, and I couldn't quite place the circumstances that had landed me here this time.

"How long have I been out?" My voice was raw and grating against my throat.

Greta handed me a cup of water that I sipped down gratefully, relishing the feel of the lukewarm liquid as it slid down, soothing the ache.

She crossed her arms over her chest and sat down on my hospital bed, studying me with a mixture of amusement and worry. I had a feeling at this point that I was her most frequent visitor. I needed a punch card or something.

All at once, the amusement dissolved from her expression, replaced by a flash of crippling pity. "A bit longer than last time, I'm afraid. You slept for almost four days straight. Had us all worried sick. And I was half convinced your brother would burn this place down if you didn't wake up by today. I had to give him a sedative and force him to rest this morning."

Four days? I stretched back, groaning in relief when my head landed on a reasonably soft pillow. Had Greta gotten an upgrade since the last time I was here? And poor Ro, I really needed to work on getting my act together before I gave him an ulcer. Or worse.

But what the hell landed me in here again? I tried to think back, to cling to my last memory.

A string of images flooded my mind: freeing my hellhound, Ralph, breaking Darius out of the lab, running from Atlas, fighting the werewolf, and then—

Regret consumed me as soon as I landed on it.

"Wade," I said, alarmed by the agony I heard in my own voice. The sound of his neck snapping was suddenly all that I could focus on, the look in his empty blue eyes as he landed next to me.

"No." Tears clouded my vision as I looked at Greta, hoping she'd look at me, grin that caricature of a grin of hers, and tell me that he was doing great—in tip-top shape and already back to leading class and kicking ass. Or better yet, that it was all a dream—Darius, Ralph, the fight, all of it.

In that moment, all that I wanted was for her to rewind time or redefine it for me. But my stomach felt like it was wrapped into a tight, metal knot. And I knew; knew that when she looked at me, any hope I had of that knot unraveling would disintegrate until all that I was left with was a heavy pit, permanent and unwavering.

She dropped her eyes, fiddling with her long, sinuous fingers in her lap, before grabbing my hand. "I'm sorry, Miss Bentley. I'm terribly sorry—sorrier than I have words to express to you." She let out a long breath and shook her head. I focused on the way the wild waves of her hair climbed the air around her like gravity did not exist. Those wild strands were the only things holding me together. "This world isn't fair sometimes. And you've been through so much in your short time of living in it. Wade, well, he was as good as they come. It always seems to happen that way, doesn't it?"

Her voice choked up into a garbled mess at the end and I turned away from her, unable to watch as her glassy eyes brimmed over with tears, unable to witness and consume her grief for fear of drowning in my own.

I opened my mouth to ask the questions I needed to ask, but they were caught on the knot in my throat, in my chest, in my stomach—my whole being was a series of knots. It took everything I had to swallow back the sob.

We were protectors. It wasn't unusual for us to die young. And I'd only known Wade for a few short weeks, only interacted with him a handful of times. Why did I feel so empty at the thought of him no longer being in this world? I pushed my hand into the center of my chest, trying to rub out the ache that felt like it would forever linger there for as long as I lived.

"It-it's my fault," I sobbed, no longer able to hold back the wave of grief. "He was only out there because I ran, because I went after them—" My words crumbled into a mess of sobs, spilling from my lips in uncontrollable, unrecognizable sounds and syllables.

Me.

He was dead because of me.

He was there to try and save me, to protect me, and instead, he was gone, and I was here and everything about that felt wrong and broken and empty.

"Shh, shh girl, it's okay. It was nobody's fault. That is what protectors do. They protect. And Wade gave his life saving yours." Greta's bony arms pulled me against her, and she held me until every last tear was wrung from my eyes. "I knew him since he was a child, so understand that I know what I'm saying when I say that there is no other way he would have wanted to go. He died saving someone he cared for very much. That is a gift—a tragic, but incredibly beautiful gift."

I almost welcomed the pain throbbing in my head, in my body. I breathed a sigh of relief when it pulled me back under, lulling me to sleep.

※

At my request, I was moved into team Ten's cabin, occupying the room sandwiched between Ro's and Izzy's. I wasn't interested in socializing with anyone, not even them, but it helped a bit to have them so close, simply to be embraced by their proximity.

They left me to myself, mostly, coming in to sit with me now and again, or leaving me food and water when I couldn't handle their direct presence or company.

Eli had shown up to my infirmary room once while I was awake, to see how I was doing. But we didn't discuss anything of consequence, and I hadn't seen Atlas or Declan since the night the world ripped apart. I told him I needed to move out, that I needed some space. For a moment, he had looked like he wanted to argue, but he simply nodded and left. Ro told me he brought my stuff to my new room that very day.

A light knock sounded on my door. The knob turned and Izzy walked in. She studied my room briefly, her eyes lingering a bit too long on my uneaten lunch and pile of dirty laundry. Without a word, she sat down on my bed, her fingers threading through mine like puzzle pieces.

"It won't always hurt this much," she said, her gray eyes glazing over with tears. She'd known Wade for most of her life, and I hadn't even bothered to find out how she was coping. "The guilt, the sadness, it won't disappear, but it won't always take up so much room in your heart."

I felt my eyes brimming with more tears, and shook my head, frustrated with myself. I didn't trust myself to speak, so I squeezed her hand instead and nodded, hoping that all of my affection for her, all of my gratitude could spill through that pressure.

Her answering smile was enough to tell me that she understood how grateful I was. She'd been a surprisingly steady presence in my life, even more so the last few days. And I was struck, all at once, with how fortunate I was to have made such a good friend so quickly. I'd do everything I could to deserve her friendship going forward.

Her lips tilted in the tiniest grin as she cleared her throat softly. "Declan is here," she said, glancing at me with a tentative smile, like she wasn't sure whether or not to kick her out. "She wants to speak with you, if you're willing."

I bit my lip, not entirely shocked. I was expecting one of them to confront me eventually, to call me out for what happened. If I hadn't let Darius out, Wade would still be alive. I needed to hear one of them say it, and it might as well be Declan.

With a deep breath, I steadied my nerves, ready to own up to my part of the disaster.

Izzy led me to the front door, to where Declan was standing

in the bright sun, the light drenching her black hair in iridescent colors. She nudged me gently in my side. "I'll be just inside if you need anything. All you have to do is shout."

She waved shyly to Declan, her lips in a small grin, before she disappeared back into the cabin. I had no doubt that she'd be waiting just on the other side of the door, ready to catch me in my puddle of grief if I needed her to.

For a moment, I studied Declan in silence, watching as she stared up into the sky, her jewel-toned eyes as striking as always.

"I'm sorry I didn't come sooner," she said, her Irish accent like soft music. Slowly, she turned her head towards me until her eyes eclipsed the sun. "I thought maybe you needed some space before we talked."

"I appreciate that," I said, walking closer to her as I pushed my feet down into my shoes, my heels bending the back of my sneakers over in half. "How are—" I couldn't bring myself to finish the question. I knew the answer. I could see my own sadness mirrored on her face.

A fresh wave of guilt washed over me when I remembered that this wasn't the only person Declan had lost recently. Her cousin, Sarah, had been killed not that long ago. One wound was replaced by another, a stream made into an ocean.

"Walk with me? I have something I want to show you." She tilted her head towards the woods and I followed, tossing my sweatshirt on as we walked in silence. For a long minute, I let myself soak in the fresh air against my skin, the sound of the leaves rustling with each step. It had been days since I'd gone outside, since I'd felt the sun and smelled the fresh, warm scent of the woods.

"I didn't know that he followed me," I said, my words coming out rushed, no longer willing to be kept buried inside. It was the thing I'd wanted to voice to Izzy and Ro for days, but I couldn't bring my tongue to form the words—to make them real. "I thought he was safe at the house. I just needed to make sure Ralph was okay. I had no idea what was waiting out th—"

Declan stopped, gripping my face softly between her hands, her palms warm against my cheeks. "Stop."

I took a deep breath in, studying the curves of her face, the tension in her forehead.

"None of us blame you for what happened that night. Not even Atlas. And you shouldn't blame yourself either. You couldn't have predicted what would happen, what would be out there. And Wade chose to go running after you—that was his choice, not yours." She dropped her hands from my face, running them roughly over her own instead, like she was trying to erase the images of that night. "We all should have just been more honest with each other. We all made mistakes. Horrible, unimaginable, but completely avoidable mistakes."

I sucked in a breath, both relieved and scared. I knew what she was referring to, but I wasn't ready to talk about Atlas. I knew that it was my responsibility to report him. He had become the very thing that we hunted—was he any less of a monster than Darius? Or the creature that killed Wade?

I pressed my eyelids together, releasing a long, slow breath. I knew in my gut that Atlas wasn't like them. I just didn't know how to reconcile that with Guild teachings just yet. I wanted nothing more than to confide in Ro, in Cyrus—I was just afraid of what their response would be.

"Atlas and Wade were bound to a protector before," Declan said, the words falling out in a lilting rush. "Their father forced them to bind to a girl named Sarah." Her eyes darkened slightly, and I shivered as they pierced through me, revealing a grief and vulnerability I wasn't used to her showing. "She was my cousin."

I knew all of this already, but it was the first time Declan had willingly brought her up in front of me. I held my breath, waiting for her to continue. I grabbed her hand, offering her comfort in my limited capacity.

"And then it happened. What always happens," she said, frustration leaking through her words. She tightened her fingers around mine, like she needed the support in the way I'd needed

Izzy's. "She was killed. Wade and Atlas were almost taken down as well. Atlas was bitten that night. And then he transitioned."

The story spilled out of her quickly like an avalanche, the words chasing each other in a race to be finished. My heart beat rapidly against my ribs, like it was trying to escape the confines of my body. "Is he dangerous?"

I needed the answer to that question—needed to know if they were all protecting a monster—and I held my breath in the silence while Declan stared into my face, studying me.

"Yes and no," she said on an exhale. "He's gained control over the beast, for the most part. And he hasn't killed anyone. Eli and Wa—" she paused for a second, closing her eyes tight like the memory of Wade was clouding her vision. "We make sure that he's in control and we cover for him. But he wouldn't hurt you, and he wouldn't hurt anyone who wasn't a threat to him or the people he cares about. You have to understand that."

She squeezed my fingers, threading them deeper through hers, like she was desperate for me to believe her.

"Has he told anyone?" I dug my shoe into the ground, absently carving lines into the dirt as I mulled over the information. I knew what Declan wanted from me. She wanted me to cover for him too, to protect Atlas's secret. And I wasn't sure I could do that.

"No one but us."

We continued walking in silence, both of us processing the information. After a few minutes, Declan led me off the trail and I was momentarily worried that she'd brought me here to kill me —that if I didn't promise to keep the secret, she'd make sure I wouldn't be able to share it with anyone.

"I didn't understand why you did what you did," she said, shattering the silence as she walked up to an old, abandoned hut that was half hidden by trees and brush. "But I get it. You were protecting the hound—Ralph. He's a part of you in some odd way that none of us really understand. And because of that bond you were willing to do whatever it took to make sure he was safe."

My heart started racing at the thought of Ralph. I hadn't seen him since the night of the attack. On the few occasions we'd spoken, Cyrus swore that he wasn't brought back to the lab with Darius and the others, but I had no idea what happened to him. No one did.

"When Atlas and I were younger and needed to get away from the compound for a bit, we'd come hide out here." She pushed open the door, cringing as it let out a low groan. "It was a sort of second home for us over the years."

"Oh um, looks nice." I was shocked that the place was still standing but didn't want to hurt her feelings. Planks of wood were missing in various spots and the ground was more dirt and debris than floor.

She pulled one of her lopsided grins, teeth gently biting at her bottom lip. "It's not, not anymore. But we can fix it up."

I opened my mouth to ask what for when I was run over by a giant ball of black fur.

My eyes pricked with disbelief, and I threw my hands around Ralph's neck, laughing as he slobbered down my back. It was the first time I'd properly smiled in a while. I pulled away from him, checking every inch that I could see. That night, when we were fighting against the vampires and werewolves, he'd looked so battered and bruised. Part of me, deep down where I wouldn't let myself completely feel it, was afraid that I was responsible for his death too. But here he was, happy and giant as always, with his tongue lolling out of the side of his mouth like he was waiting to be thrown a giant ball to chase.

"You found him? He's okay?" I was laugh-crying now, and I didn't care if Declan saw the tear trails carving down my cheeks.

"I found him pacing along the campus boundaries that night. I figured if he was going to insist on staying close, it might as well be somewhere discreet, where he wouldn't be carted off again."

"Thank you," I said, staring up at Declan as she studied the dog, a look of conflicted trepidation on her face. I knew how she felt about him, about how she felt when it came to any of the creatures kept down in the lab. And I couldn't put into words how grateful I was that she didn't turn him in anyway.

"You can come here to visit him," she said, nodding. "But you have to promise you won't come without me. We still don't know much about hellhounds, and I'm not convinced he's exactly safe. He tore up a werewolf and a vampire that night. He's dangerous, Max. And you need to realize that." She scratched the back of her neck shyly before her eyes met mine again. "But he did keep you safe. And I do believe now that, at the very least, he's not a danger to you. Not intentionally, anyway."

I bit my lip, mulling over the words, recognizing what a sacrifice this was for her—how much her perspective had changed since the last time we'd spoken about Ralph. My heart filled with gratitude that she was willing to make this concession for me. And I thought back to her point—about how I was willing to risk it all for him because Ralph was now part of my family in some weird, confusing way. That maybe she was protecting Atlas for the same reason. The lines blurred sometimes when it came to people you loved. We just needed to get better at knowing when those lines blurred too far.

"I don't know how to feel about Atlas," I said suddenly. "About what he is. And I think he should tell somebody, at the very least Cyrus or Seamus. I don't know how they'd take it, but he's around a lot of protectors and it's a complicated issue." I let out a breath, trying to calm my racing nerves. Now was not the time to let my thoughts run away from me. "But as long as he doesn't hurt anyone, and you and Eli can keep him in check, I'll keep his secret. I don't like it, but it's what Wade would want."

Declan sat down next to me, resting her elbows on her knees. Relief flashed briefly on her face, and she watched for a while as Ralph hopped around, more like a playful puppy than a dangerous beast from hell. "Thank you, Max."

1
MAX

ONE MONTH LATER...

"Max, what the hell are you doing? Pay attention!" Ro tossed a dagger and I barely even blinked as it passed a few inches from my head, eliciting a grunt from someone—or something—behind me.

The room was a blur of motion and dust, but all at once the sounds and visuals of the fight just sort of blurred away, fading into black.

I turned around and watched as the werewolf he stabbed in the eye slid to the ground, crimson dripping into its dark gray fur.

How long did blood stain a wolf's coat? And when they transitioned back into their humanoid form, would the blood transition with them? They didn't really talk about this stuff in any of our hell theory classes. I had so many questions and uncertainties about the creatures we were supposed to hunt. I needed more answers.

"Max!" Ro was next to me, a blur of blond hair and blue eyes, as he shoved me out of the way just as the creature stood up again. He pulled a small double-sided axe, his new favorite weapon, from the loop on his black cargo pants. With a single, fluid motion, he swung, like he'd been practicing that motion every single day of his life.

And, well, he kind of had.

My eyes tightened shut as I heard the dull thud of the wolf's head falling to the ground, rolling to my feet. Yellow gold eyes and just enough fluff to look like an oversized domestic dog.

When I opened my eyes, I pushed all of my effort into looking everywhere but at the decapitated creature, but I saw it in my periphery anyway, cringing as I did. I knew this wolf wasn't Atlas. His wolf form was at least fifty pounds heavier and a tawny shade of brown, not this dull gray. I also knew that this wolf would have killed me if Ro hadn't stepped in.

But something had changed, and ever since I'd learned that Atlas was turned—probably on a mission just like this one—I couldn't quite look at werewolves in the same way.

I couldn't look at Atlas the same either, which was part of the reason I was shadowing and living with Alpha Ten, one of The Protector Guild's top field teams, in the first place. I needed space from the members of Six.

Ro was standing next to me, breathing out in heavy puffs, his blue eyes filled with condensed anger just waiting to explode. I knew him well enough to know that his anger was merely a disguise for worry. I looked at the smudge of blood across his face, trying like hell to ignore the globs that I felt across my own. Hunting wasn't exactly a glamorous day job. Everyone kept promising that, eventually, the gore and guts would feel no different at the end of the day than a mechanic's grease-coated hands. I wasn't entirely sure I wanted to reach that level of apathy.

"You want to tell me what that was about?" His forehead was damp with sweat and he wiped the blade of his axe against the fur of the very dead looking wolf. We were supposed to try and bring as many of them in alive as possible, but when push came to shove, that sort of mission was rarely possible. When you or someone on your team was being attacked, you had to take your shots when you could get them; otherwise, we'd be sacrificing far too many of our own just for the lab rats in the basement to get a new play toy.

I swallowed my disgust, frustrated with myself for feeling pity for the creature at my feet. Protectors were meant to kill supernatural creatures that escaped into our world from the hell realm. We were supposed to protect humans from beasts, not pity them. What the hell was wrong with me? If I kept doing this, it would be my head rolling around on the floor, not some random werewolf's.

"I'm sorry, I just spaced out for a second," I said, after what felt like too long of a silence. I loosened the grip on my dagger, breathing feeling back into my fingers. I scanned the area and exhaled a sigh of relief when I saw Izzy running towards us, her stormy eyes dancing with adrenaline, an ass-kicking grin plastered on her face. She was safe. Cyrus never warned me how much time and energy you spent worrying about the people you cared about in this work. It was one thing to put my life on the line, but it was another to stand by and watch as the people I loved did the same.

"Any others?" Ro asked as she reached us, scrunching her nose at the bloodied mess surrounding our feet.

And the blood. The Guild's dry-cleaning bill had to be fucking massive.

Seamus sent our team out after a couple of rogues were spotted about an hour outside of Guild headquarters. Typically, werewolves traveled in packs of ten or more, but three had been reported on the outskirts of our territory this week. It seemed like every day, they were growing more and more bold. And we still had no idea where this newfound bravery came from, or why the creatures we hunted were suddenly so interested in changing the direction of the chase.

"Jer and Arnell took out one outside, and Sharla, Mavis, and I got the other," Izzy said, her limbs still jittery with excitement from the fight. She was letting her short, black hair grow out, and she was now rocking a cute bob that was long enough to be pulled back into a ponytail. Her golden skin had a light sheen of sweat, but she otherwise looked like she could go ten more rounds with as many beasts as hell would throw at her.

I looked down at the one that Ro had taken out. That one and the two the others had taken out made three. We could go back soon. I tried not to make my relief too obvious. Two months ago, I was ecstatic at merely the idea of going on raids and hunting down every beast I came across.

But things were different now. And while I still went through the motions, I was more confused about our place in the world as protectors than I'd ever been before; and so much more aware of how fragile our lives really were.

Izzy frowned, glancing from the wolf, to Ro, and then back to me until her eyes narrowed like she was trying to peel back the layers of my thoughts with nothing but her own. "What happened here, anyway?"

I rolled my neck from side-to-side, avoiding a response. She knew what had happened, I could see it in her eyes as the adrenaline bled into her worry, into her fear.

Izzy and Ro were staring at each other, carrying on one of their silent conversations that seemed to happen more and more frequently these days. Sometimes it felt like a heavy, impenetrable glass had erected itself between me and them. I could see them, and hear them, but we were separate nonetheless; their silhouettes were just a bit out of reach, their voices just a bit muffled.

"We should get rid of Balto here and go find the others," I said, interrupting them and bending down to lift the carcass, pretending I was picking up a heavy, furry rug instead of a very dead, headless being. Try as I might, the illusion didn't quite hold as blood soaked into my clothes and onto my skin.

Ro took the body from me as Izzy skipped over to the head, grabbing it by a bloodied ear, not unlike how a child picks up a stuffed animal. I swallowed back the bile rising in my throat and followed them from the dark building.

As we left the now lifeless warehouse, I noticed a mattress tossed in one corner, with a few tattered blankets and an empty pizza box. A soft glow emanated from a lamp next to the bed, the shade covered with uneven stripes. The place wasn't exactly cozy, but there also weren't any cobwebs or dirt trails in the room. Whoever these wolves were, they were clearly on the run from something and had made a shoddy attempt at making this place feel like a home.

A home that we had invaded and murdered them in.

I blinked, pushing the tangible sympathy brewing in my gut as far away as possible. These days I seemed to oscillate between absolute bloodlust, wanting to go after each and every supernatural creature in the country, to a deeply unwelcome sense of shame and confusion. Part of me wished Cyrus had never brought us to The Guild in the first place. I missed our tiny cabin in the woods and our days filled with Netflix, sparring, and dreams of something more.

Cliche or not, ignorance really was bliss.

"MAX! MAX, WAKE UP." JER'S DEEP VOICE RANG IN MY EAR, and I pulled my head up, my pulse racing an erratic beat as I lifted my head from his shoulder. His dark reddish-black hair was getting long now and it swept against his brows in a heavy swoop. I watched for a moment as the lights from passing cars reflected off the strands, stuck in a weird hypnosis between sleep and waking life.

I inhaled, choking on his warm, woodsy scent. It wasn't a bad smell, but it also didn't make my heart race either. Still, it grounded me, brought me back to the car, to my body, to reality. Right now, it was enough. It was everything.

"Sorry," I mumbled, focusing on the feel of his leg pressed

against mine, on the steady lull of the road as Ro drove. I met his stare in the rearview mirror and cringed at what I saw. I hated making him worry, and lately it seemed that all he ever did was worry about me. I needed to stop falling apart, or at least I needed to create an illusion that I wasn't.

"Bad dream again?" Jer rested a hand on my kneecap, squeezing softly until I gently pulled away.

He'd made it clear that he was interested in moving beyond friendship, but I'd been lukewarm to the idea since that night. I had a feeling we needed to have a more direct conversation one of these days, as soon as I could muster the energy and the sinking guilt of disappointing another friend.

"That's it," Izzy chirped from the front seat as she craned her head around to look at me, dark hair falling over her eyes. "You've been sleeping like shit all month and you've been too focused on researching and sparring. We're going out tonight. We could all use a pick-me-up after today, you especially."

She had that don't-argue-or-I'll-fight-a-bitch look on her face and I didn't have the bandwidth to test her. I nodded, silently agreeing to do as she wished as I pressed my forehead into the cool glass of the car window, putting some much-needed space between me and Jer. It was easier to just go along with whatever Izzy had planned than it was to resist her. She was persistent as hell and obliging was the path of least resistance.

It'd been thirty-seven days since Wade was killed. And just as many days since I last slept through the night. Now, whenever I closed my eyes, I relived his last moments, watching as the vampire snapped his neck, and his lifeless body fell to the forest floor. The echo of that moment was trapped in my mind, ricocheting like a sadistic rubber ball. The sound of my scream, the smell of blood around us, the visual—god, that visual.

But more than the blood, it was the image of his lifeless blue eyes, crystal and unseeing that struck me to the core, making my knees give out and my eyes blur.

And when I didn't dream of his death, I dreamt instead of

him in a dim, dark room, screaming in agony as he thrashed around on a bed made of concrete and rags. He was always in pain when I had these dreams—and I knew he was in pain, because it was like I was too, like I felt his pain as if it was my own. The nights that my dream shifted to that cold corridor of stone walls, I woke up exhausted, drained. I might as well not have slept at all.

That meant I spent every night now, draining cups of coffee, trying to push off the nightmares for as long as I could, and woke up most mornings to Ro or Izzy rubbing my back as I came to, my throat raw from screaming.

"I'll talk to Cyrus," Ro said, his blue gaze steady and unnerving. He had a way of peeling me back layer by layer, until there was no way for me to hide from him. Brothers were annoying that way, even if they weren't related by blood.

It'd been weeks since I'd said more than a few words to Cyrus. I knew it wasn't his fault—what happened. But it was easier for me to be angry with him, to blame him for not protecting Ralph in the first place. Because otherwise, I was left with the cold reality that I was the one to blame, that Wade was out there that night because he was going after me.

Cyrus let me be angry, and for that I was grateful. He was giving me my space, spending most of his time cooped up in his brother, Seamus's quarters, studying patterns of various supernatural creatures, keeping the teams busy.

And damn were they busy. Six had been gone for over a month. I hadn't seen Atlas or Eli since I'd left the infirmary—and Declan had only been around once to show me the path to where she'd hidden Ralph. The next day when I woke up, they were all gone. They hadn't been back since.

I wasn't sure whether that was a good thing or not. I wasn't sure I could actually look any of them in the eyes, that we could just go back to training as scheduled. It was a lot easier to keep Atlas's secret when he wasn't around for me to trace every move, desperate for evidence of the monster beneath his skin.

"Thanks Ro," I said, too exhausted to say much more. If I was going out tonight, I'd need as much energy in my reserves as possible. "Can we pick up some coffee before we get home?"

"Always!" Izzy answered, even though she wasn't the one driving. "Cyrus still keeping you under lock and key?"

Lock and key wasn't as much of an exaggeration as it seemed. With so many hellbeasts breaching Guild boundaries, the entire campus was operating on extreme levels of paranoia. A ton of extra security measures and new teams were filtering in from satellite locations almost daily.

Cy was taking it to the next level though. It took Ro days to convince him to let me out with the team tonight. And then I balked, so the odds of him agreeing to let me into town again so soon were slim. I had a feeling Ro would be keeping the details of the raid to a minimum until after Cy agreed to let me out for a night.

In the weeks since the attack, I'd basically become a certified Rapunzel, and I'd lost count of the number of times I caught Ro and Cyrus arguing in hurried tones about a balance between keeping me safe and keeping me sane. I knew I should be grateful. They both loved me and wanted to protect me in their own ways. Which was fine, to be honest. I was happy to sit back and let them guide me towards whatever they wanted me to do—autopilot was about all I had energy for these days.

When we walked up to the local hangout, Vanish, less than three hours later, I repressed a shiver. The last time that I was here, I was attacked by a vampire and the hellhound who rescued me was captured and placed in a glorified prison. In a weird way, it was the catalyst that set me on the very precarious path I was on now.

"Just see how you feel after twenty minutes, okay?" Izzy whispered into my ear, her fingers clasped gently around my own, like she was my anchor, determined to keep me from floating away. "I think it'll be good for you to get out of the library and gym for a bit, to remember the fun parts of being a protector. It isn't all ass kicking and gore."

Vanish was a bar in town outside of Guild Headquarters that was owned by protectors. The entire strip was essentially here as a bribe to keep protectors occupied and entertained, so that more weren't persuaded to leave for another station somewhere else. The town itself was quaint, filled with both unsuspecting humans and protectors, whether active or not.

I nodded, silently agreeing with Izzy. I knew she was right, that I needed to get my mind off things for a night. If I wanted to win the battle of getting my life back, I had to begin the fight eventually. I tugged the edges of my silk dress down a bit, my nerves on high alert.

"Here," Jer said, handing me a fruity-looking neon-pink drink with a coy grin on his face.

"Thanks." I took a sip, relishing the feel of the alcohol as it burned down my throat like a dull fire. I was only eighteen—soon to be nineteen—but protectors didn't live by the same rules as humans. We were given permission to drink as soon as we started into heavy training. I guess they figured that if we were going to put our lives on the line, we deserved to let loose a bit while we were still able to. Members of field teams either retired early from burnout or died young during missions.

Glancing around the room, I relaxed. It wasn't a particularly full night, and the atmosphere was a lot more chill than the last time I was here. There were a few people dancing, but the music wasn't so loud that we couldn't have a conversation. If I were feeling more myself, I might even be enjoying the evening.

"Great," Izzy said, stirring her own cocktail around in small circles with a thin straw. "Reza's here."

Following her glare, I found Reza and Izzy's brother, Theo, in the corner of the bar, beers in hand as they danced. Theo had a giant, dopey grin plastered on his face and I had a suspicion it was because Reza was finally giving him the time of day.

Reza and her mother, Headmistress Alleva, had not-so-subtle

plans to get her to join Atlas's team. Now that Atlas was gone, it seemed that she was moving on, at least temporarily, to other options. Theo was completely in love with Reza, and I didn't entirely blame him. While she had a prickly personality, she was a badass fighter and absolutely stunning. Her long blond hair was pulled into a high, sleek ponytail and her thigh-length, cranberry dress made her large blue eyes pop.

Reza had been chilly towards me when I first arrived, but now with the guys gone, she no longer seemed to see me as a threat. Especially since I was no longer living with them or part of their team. This meant I was largely left alone, though it was still mildly entertaining to listen to Izzy huff about how now she was worried Alleva would bond her daughter to Theo.

Izzy wasn't close with her brother in the way that Ro and I were, in fact I'd really only seen them acknowledge each other on the one or two occasions they'd been forced to spar with one another. Still, even if they weren't best friends, I didn't blame her for not wanting a more permanent connection to Reza.

Bonds weren't exactly like human marriages, but they created unions stronger than family. Even if they remained platonic. So if Theo really did bond with Reza, there'd be no escaping the girl after graduation.

"I will not call her sister," Izzy mumbled, glaring over the lip of her drink, her usually jovial expression cast in shadow. "I'd rather die in a vamp attack than have to spend the rest of my life associated with her."

Frowning, I took a long sip of the liquid vacation, draining the glass. I knew Izzy was kidding, but it still rubbed me the wrong way, hearing her joke about a vampire attack.

As if reading my mind, Izzy nudged her shoulder gently into mine until our eyes latched onto each other. "Shit, sorry dude. That was a thoughtless thing to say, I didn't mean it. You know that, right?" She turned towards the bar. "Here, let me get you another one. I'm thinking it's a tequila kind of night, anyway. No more of this tropical shit Jer likes to order. We had a major win today and we deserve to celebrate like proper protectors."

I bit back my grin and nodded. Izzy was infectious and while I didn't spend much of my time these days smiling, almost all of the moments that I did were credited to her. She moved back to the bar, her hips swaying to the beat as she wove around everyone in her way, not sparing another thought or glance in Theo and Reza's direction.

"Want to dance, Max?" Jer's warm breath swept along the back of my neck, his hands glancing along my elbows like rough feathers.

I turned around and found myself less than an inch away from him, my chest all but smashed against his stomach. Shaking my head, I looked up into his hopeful eyes, so much more open and vulnerable than when we first met. "Not tonight, sorry Jer. I'm not really feeling the music. Just kind of want to sit back and chill if that's okay with you."

That wasn't entirely the truth. The last time I'd danced in this bar, it had been with Wade. And the idea of moving around, trapped in Jer's arms just did not appeal to me tonight. And honestly, maybe it never would.

A shadow of disappointment crossed his face, but he nodded, his jaw tensing a bit as he broke eye contact. My stomach lurched. I knew he wanted me to want him, that he wanted me to permanently join his team after I graduated. Hell, he probably was even thinking about initiating a bond with me. But I—I only wanted one of those things, and even that had nothing to do with him. Jer was a nice enough guy, but I couldn't force feelings I didn't feel.

"I'm going to the ladies' room," I said, offering a small smile as I took a step back from him. "That drink went right through me."

"A girl going to the bathroom solo? Alert the press," he said, trying to laugh away his disappointment. With a long sip of his drink, he nodded, face sobering up. "I'll be here, if you change your mind."

I pushed through the hall, my ridiculously high heels that were cute enough to warrant the discomfort clacking loudly against the fake wood floor. Stopping outside of a familiar room, I shut my eyes. My brain was flooded with images of walking through that door once before, of seeing Eli with a girl bent in front of him—the strange mixture of jealousy and fascination that filled me in that moment. Suppressing a shiver, I sped up and walked outside.

My breath came out in a long, steady hiss as I looked around the familiar alleyway. I wasn't sure why this was where I chose to find peace, the spot where I'd almost died. It was probably thoughtless of me to come out here, considering everything, but something about the isolation felt soothing in an unexpected way. Management must've added a few more lights out here since the last time I'd been around. Slowly, my feet carved a path until I landed on the exact spot I'd been attacked just a couple of months ago.

But I didn't feel frightened. Instead, a rush of excitement filled me, and I felt more awake—more alive—than I had in a while. Maybe I had a death wish? I ran a hand roughly over my face, trying to dull out my senses, until my throat cracked on a half-laugh.

"You didn't learn your lesson, then." A deep voice echoed around the cement walls. "Always meeting monsters in this corridor, it seems."

I knew that voice, felt it in my bones as it traveled through me. In a rush, I turned around, half expecting to be wrong, for some random guy to be standing behind me instead.

But there he was.

He towered at least a full foot above me, his raven-colored hair a bit longer since the last time I'd seen him. Scruff looked good on him, not that I should've been surprised by that. I wasn't sure the man could look bad even if he tried.

His brown eyes were a bit more guarded and emptier than I remembered, but they were still filled with that familiar, ethereal glow. I could hear my heartbeat pounding, unsure of whether it was from fear or something else.

"Atlas."

2
ATLAS

Her voice whispering my name stopped me in my tracks. I studied her, hardly able to believe that she was standing before me after over a month. An agonizing month where I had tried desperately to convince myself that I could forget about her, leave her behind forever, let her deal with whatever creatures were after her on her own.

Disappearing was easy at first, necessary even, but as the days dragged into weeks, it became more difficult. Max was the last one to interact with Wade, the last one to see him alive. Somehow, being closer to her felt like being closer to him in a strange, convoluted way.

She was wearing a dark dress that ended just above her knees, heels that gave her the illusion of height, so that she was suddenly only a head shorter than me. Her dark hair framed her face in thick, shiny waves that fell down her back.

Max was beautiful, that was nothing new, nothing surprising.

But what I wasn't used to was the darkness in her gaze. Her usually warm eyes that always seemed to be dancing with a hidden mirth, like the world was an exciting game that she couldn't wait to play, were dimmer than I remembered. Dark shadows under her lashes made it clear she wasn't sleeping enough, and she was significantly thinner than I remembered. The girl loved to eat, but it looked like she was wasting away now, like she was a shadow of her once larger-than-life self, her lean muscle now starting to fall away.

Her breathing was coming out in quick bursts, and I watched her pulse hammering against the smooth olive skin of her neck. Quickly, I took a step back.

The predator in me was familiar with these tells—she was afraid of me. The realization filled me with a disgust so strong I could practically feel it ripping at my seams. She knew who I was now—what I was—so I could never again pretend that I was nothing more than a protector when I was around her.

"What are you doing out here, Max?" I asked, trying to hide my relief and excitement at seeing her, as well as my disappointment that the same wasn't reflected on her face. I didn't mean to startle her. Hadn't even wanted to confront her at all. But when I saw her, wandering around again out here by herself, it was like I couldn't stop myself. She was a magnet, a goddamn forcefield. It was infuriating, if I was being honest.

"Where have you guys been?" she asked, straightening her posture like she could will herself into not being afraid, will her eyes into painting an illusion over what she knew lingered below the surface.

"We just got back tonight," I said, not answering her. We'd been in Europe, dealing with my father and sinking ourselves into mission after mission to drown out the fact that Wade wasn't with us. We needed time to readjust, to figure out how to be a team again. And my father—we had to deal with him.

And I—I needed to not be here.

"And the first thing you did was come into town?" Her dark, perfectly-sculpted eyebrow arched as she crossed her arms in front of her chest. I caught her eyes fling up to the night sky, and I knew instantly what she was looking for.

"Don't worry, Bentley," I said, trying to hide the disappointment from my voice, to ignore the sinking feeling in my stomach. "It's not a full moon." Her pulsing heartbeat quickened, and I bit back a smirk. "Not that I need one to transition, as you well know."

She turned around, running her fingers through her long, silky hair. Something was frustrating her, but it wasn't fear. If she was truly worried about her safety, she wouldn't show a predator her back. Especially not one as dangerous as me. I tried to ignore the flutter in my chest at that. I didn't want her to fear me, and that made me more uncomfortable than anything else. I pushed the feeling down, waiting until she turned around again.

"The rest of the team—Eli and Declan—are they alright?" Her voice wavered with anxiety, but she did a good job disguising it from her expression. I felt the acute lack of Wade's name, my chest constricting like I couldn't come up for air. "Why were you gone for so long? I thought—" she shook her head, dark eyes boring into me, but never quite looking into my own.

I took a step back, feeling momentarily like she was the dangerous one, the one capable of ripping my throat out by her teeth. Time danced on a wire, like one move could completely unravel me.

"It doesn't matter, we're back now. Eli and Declan are fine, all things considered." My tone dipped until it sounded cold, tinny, and I hated myself in that moment for not being better at disguising my moods. I was usually so much better at building these walls, but not tonight.

My father wanted us to stay in Europe; had demanded it, really. But we had work to do here. Max wasn't really part of the plan. On the flight over, we'd agreed to stay away from her, to keep her out of things. We were all still so raw from that night and Max had a way of drawing trouble to her. We all agreed that we wouldn't get sucked in, not again. Let Seamus and Cyrus assign another group to her guard duty, no matter how much the mere thought of that sent me into an uncomfortable tailspin.

But I needed to see her, needed to know she was okay before I could go back to pretending she wasn't there.

She nodded, and I knew the conversation was over. There was something guarded about her, like she'd constructed an entire shield around herself in less than a moment.

"Well, welcome home."

The words were hollow. Without another glance in my direction, she turned and walked back into the bar, using a little too much force as she slammed the door shut behind her. Every limb, every muscle in my body wanted to go after her, to force her to make eye contact and speak to me. Even if just for another minute or two. But I knew better, and that meant knowing it was better this way.

Satisfied that she wouldn't be roaming around out here by herself anymore, I went back to the cabin. Dec and Eli were hushed in a serious conversation when I walked through the door, both of them far too quiet when they noticed my presence. It was the kind of too quiet that made it abundantly clear that either I was the topic of their conversation, or they didn't want me to know the topic if I wasn't. They'd been having more and more hushed side conversations lately and I was trying hard not to let it get to me or make me feel like I was nothing more than an intruder observing their lives.

"Where were you?" Eli asked, his usually laid-back expression was hard and accusatory. I'd been pushing them away for the last few weeks. They were willing to let me for a while, but the last few days, they'd been taking turns keeping me under their watch. It was part of the reason I wanted to come back here. Somehow, I was under the illusion that surrounding myself with people and them with responsibility would give me a bit of a break. Or at the very least make me feel a little bit less like a prisoner. Apparently, I was wrong.

"I went into town," I said, tossing my keys on the counter and grabbing a beer from the fridge. Since we hadn't been around for a month, beer was about the only thing our kitchen was actually stocked with. "But now I'm back."

"Did you see her?" Declan was following my movements with

her eyes, trying not to let on how badly she wanted to know the answer to that question. It had become more than clear over the last few weeks that Dec enjoyed Max's company. It took a lot for her to make friends, for people to weasel in enough for her to give a shit about them. She wouldn't outright admit that she liked having Max around, maybe she even refused to admit it to herself. But since we were kids, she was one of the only constants in my life; I could read her like a damn book.

We hadn't talked about Max much over the last month. It was a weird agreement we'd all silently come to. But that changed on the way back.

I popped the tab off the bottle before taking a long, smooth sip of the amber liquid.

"I take it by your non-answer that you did," Eli said, his eyebrow arched in that smug expression of his. He was one of my best friends, but sometimes it took all I had not to punch him in the face. "Honestly, if we're all that drawn to her, I don't see the point in us fighting it. We'll be forced to bond eventually, might as well spend our lives protecting someone we don't actually hate. Better than getting stuck with Reza for fuck's sake."

There was a layer of bitter humor to Eli's words that I wasn't used to hearing. He told us a week ago that his father had spoken to him about bonding to Reza, but no matter how much we pushed the issue, he wouldn't go into the details. None of us were exactly keen on the idea of her joining our team, even if our team felt so much smaller now.

"You just want to fuck her," Declan said, her accent lilting in disgust as she slapped Eli in the arm.

Eli shrugged. "I wouldn't say no, if that's what you mean."

"You want to bond with her, fine," I said. I leaned against the refrigerator, studying them both. There was hope there, but there was also fear. "I'll be keeping my distance. Something is off about her. You saw the way that creature looked at her." The image from that night would be burned into my retinas for as long as I lived. The way that man picked up Wade, the way he stared down at Max with absolute focus and interest, and the way he disappeared into fucking thin air, leaving her unharmed. And I'm not convinced whatever draw she has is what you think it is. I don't think it's the start of a natural bond."

Wade was the one who had even put that idea into Eli's head in the first place, and now it was lodged there like dried gum. It would take a lot of muscle and scraping to eventually remove all of the traces.

"What, you think she's, like, evil or something?" Eli asked, straightening his posture in the shadow of a challenge. "Even you aren't that paranoid, Atlas."

I shrugged, not knowing how to answer that. As a werewolf, I didn't get to toss around labels like evil as easily as I might once have.

We all knew what I wouldn't say though. That collectively we weren't good for her. We'd already lost one of our own, and if I was going to stick around for Eli and Dec, and not go off on my own, I wouldn't be taking on anyone else's safety.

It was too much responsibility, and we were all too reckless. Too angry. And now, without Wade, too broken.

Max was better off with the members of Ten, even if it meant she spent an inordinate amount of time with that sniveling asshole, Jer, who'd looked at her like he was a lovesick puppy since the day she got here.

"She wouldn't want to join us again, anyway." Declan stood up, twined her fingers together until they cracked, and then walked slowly towards the doorway. "You didn't see her after she woke up. We lied to her. A lot. And she sure as hell doesn't trust us now—not that she ever did. She promised to keep your secret, Atlas, but she made damn clear she was doing that in honor of Wade, not for you, not for any of us."

Eli blew out a long, frustrated breath. He cared about the girl, more than he was willing to admit. And we both knew the odds of his father not pressing us on the Max issue were slim to none. I was willing to bet that his father would be pushing him to bond with Max before the year was out. "Whatever, man," Eli said as Declan made her way upstairs, two at a time. "I'm going to bed. This week is going to be hell."

They left me in the kitchen, where I stayed for almost two hours. I drank an entire six pack alone, telling myself I was throwing my own welcome home party. But really, I just couldn't bring myself to walk past his room without a healthy layer of alcohol dulling the pain.

3
MAX

Atlas, Declan, and Eli had been back on campus for three days, but other than the run-in I had with Atlas, I hadn't seen any of them. And I was trying like hell not to care about their recent arrival. In fact, I was doing everything I absolutely could to pretend they weren't back at all. I doubled down on my studies, spent more time sparring with Izzy and Ro, did everything I could to keep my mind focused on other things.

But that didn't mean the Academy wasn't glaringly aware of the fact that they were back. Reza, for one, had all but ditched Theo again, showing up to sparring sessions with her makeup pristine and every strand of hair in perfect order. Probably just on the off chance that Atlas would take over training us again.

Personally, while Alleva was a bit of a hard-ass and seemed to particularly dislike me, I much preferred having her preside over the sessions. She didn't fill my stomach with annoying flurries of anxiety. Any time she adjusted my position or joined the ring to spar with me herself, my skin didn't combust into thousands of prickling nerves that instantly took my head out of the fight. And I didn't have to worry about her turning into a giant werewolf out of nowhere.

I didn't think so anyway. My trust in protectors wasn't exactly high these days.

And, most importantly, Alleva didn't remind me of Wade, or of the fact that he wasn't here anymore. She was blissfully disconnected from every thought I had about the members of Six.

"Do you think they'll show up today?" Izzy asked, pushing open the wide doors to the gym. "I mean, Reza seems pretty amped up and convinced that they'll be sticking around. At least for a while."

"Yeah," Sharla added, pulling her dark curls into a tight ponytail. "Arnell said there was talk that they might be permanently transferring to the European Headquarters, since Atlas's dad is stationed there, but I guess that isn't happening now."

"His dad works at the European Guild?" I asked, annoyed that I sounded just a little bit too curious. "Why was he ever stationed here, then?"

Sharla scanned the room as we made our way back to the lockers. "Yeah, his Dad has the same job over there as Seamus has here. But they don't get along. Like at all."

"Can't imagine why," Izzy said, tossing her things down on the ground with a dramatic eye roll. "Atlas is such a fucking peach to be around most of the time."

Sharla bit back a laugh before her bright blue eyes grew serious. "Rumor has it that Wade's mother was a human."

"No way," I said, cringing when I realized how loud I was speaking. It was super taboo for protectors to procreate with humans. So much so that I didn't even know it was actually possible. "How do you know?"

Izzy shrugged, drawing my focus back to her. "It's kind of a poorly-disguised secret. Everyone knows, but no one really says anything."

"Wade also isn't the only protector born of a human, though." Sharla walked to one of the side mats, rolling her neck from side to side. Her blue sports bar matched the exact shade of her eyes, and between that and her perfectly clear, brown skin, she looked like she walked directly out of a freaking Lululemon ad. Seriously, the girl looked like a model, not like she could take down most people in thirty seconds flat.

But I knew her well enough to know that she wasn't a slouch when it came to sparring.

"Most are better kept secrets though," Izzy said, bending her left knee and then her right. "But Tarren, Wade's father, was ashamed of Wade and didn't want his birth getting in the way of his reputation. He started distancing himself from Wade when he was a kid. Until, eventually, he took the job at the European Guild and left him behind here. Out of sight, out of mind, I guess."

"And, because Atlas loved Wade," I said, my tongue halting briefly at the past tense, "Atlas stayed here to be with him."

"Yup," Sharla said, her usually warm and happy features twisting a bit, like she was trying to hold in her sadness but couldn't quite do it all the way. "Which is why so many people assumed that Atlas would head back there now. He hates his father, but now that Atlas doesn't have Wade as an excuse, it's unlikely Tarren will let him keep working here much longer. Protectors are big on legacy, and he'll want Atlas there to continue his."

"Plus," Izzy added, squaring off to spar with me first, "Seamus and Tarren are sort of frenemies, so I'm sure he hates that Atlas and Wade made besties with Eli. He'll want him out of here and out of that unit before Seamus forces a shared bond on them both."

I cringed at the thought of a forced bond. In my time here, I'd learned that it was the standard way to fold in protective networks. The number of female protectors was low and always declining. They were usually bonded to at least one, but occasionally two protectors to help enforce safety. They weren't romantic in nature, but it still grossed me out since I didn't grow up with the idea. That said, while people kept trying to drill it into my head that the bonds weren't sexual, it seemed that female protectors were almost always expected to bear children with their bondmates.

I'd already given Cyrus an earful about that though—protectors could do any kind of witchcraft they wanted with each other, so long as they kept their weird bond rituals away from me. Call me naive, but I was a big fan of free will and at least the illusion of choice.

I looked at Izzy, crouching low and putting my right arm out. In full Matrix glory, I gave a hand signal for her to try and take me down. I felt a small smile split my face as she responded, lunging forward. Sparring with Izzy, Ro, and the members of Ten was pretty much the only thing that made me feel alive these days.

And usually, I kicked ass. Seriously, not to brag, but in my months at The Guild, Izzy hadn't taken me down once. But when the gym doors swung open and I felt eyes digging into the back of my skull, I made the mistake of turning around. Which meant I instantly wound up on my butt, pinned.

A huge shit-eating grin flashed across Izzy's pixie-like face as she straddled me. "Holy shit. Holy fucking shit. I kicked ass." She jumped off of me, whooping around the gym to invisible fanfare, completely unaware that every eye in the gym was planted on the three figures who'd just walked in.

Atlas, Eli, and Declan wove around the mats without even looking at them, and while I could have sworn I felt them staring at me while I was fighting, they walked by us without so much as glancing in my direction. The three of them seemed different since I'd last seen them—darker somehow, more haunted. They were like three vengeful angels amongst us mere mortals. My mouth dried up at the sight of them.

"Atlas!" Reza went running across the gym towards him, her boobs bouncing in time with each step. "You're back." Without waiting to see if he'd catch her, she threw her arms around his neck, wrapping her legs at his waist. "I was hoping you'd be here today. Mother wasn't sure."

I looked away, my cheeks heating with embarrassment from the affectionate embrace. I didn't trust Atlas. Hell, I didn't even like him. So why did the churning feeling in my stomach feel distinctly like jealousy? I refused to be one of those girls.

While Reza was absolutely annoying sometimes, that didn't mean I wanted her to die. And I had a distinct suspicion that she had no idea that her body was coiled around a deadly werewolf; the very creature she was trained to destroy.

He stood there stiff as a board, the muscles in his back tensing. His back was to me, so I couldn't make out any expression on his face, but Declan and Eli both looked mildly amused at his discomfort, exchanging coy glances with each other as they watched him.

"Off," he said, his voice a low growl so deep that I wondered how I hadn't noticed the signs before—the tightly-wound predator just below the surface.

A look of disappointment flashed across Reza's face, her skin flushing with embarrassment. Whether they ended up bonded or not, everyone knew that they used to date. Well, Reza made it seem like they'd been dating, anyway. Which made it extra uncomfortable when everyone watched as she slid down his body, her long blond hair clinging to him with static. I actually felt bad for her. It had to be extremely painful for your boyfriend to come back after a long trip and not even pretend to be excited to see you. Even more so that it happened in front of a room full of peers. And knowing Reza, she would lash out at everyone else to help soothe the wound.

Probably me, if I was being honest.

"I wonder if she'll be transferred to their cabin now," Izzy said, her dark brows bending in the center as she plopped down next to me. "Since you're with us—" she shrugged, "I don't know, I'm sure Alleva will jump on the chance to shove her daughter under their roof." Her gray eyes slid to me as she bit back a grin.

"And just so you know, this interruption means nothing. I'm not even close to done celebrating the fact that I pinned you for once. Not. Even. Close."

I WALKED THE NOW FAMILIAR PATH IN THE WOODS BEHIND MY cabin. My mind was lost in a whirlwind of ranting as I finally let frustration seep into my bones that Declan, Atlas, and Eli all seemed hellbent on pretending like I didn't exist.

And I got it. Really, I did. I was a huge part of the reason why Wade was dead. And I didn't really want to be around any of them anyway. Atlas was a grumpy version of Teen Wolf, and the other two let me live under the same roof fully aware of his...affliction. It didn't sound like any of them had any idea as to how dangerous Atlas could be, which as far as I was concerned, meant that it was best if I just stayed away from him.

But the guilt, holy shitshow, the guilt. I was protecting Atlas's secret. It was a hell of a lot easier to do when he wasn't around, but now that he was—guilt clawed its way around my stomach, refusing to let go. What if he killed someone? What if he lost control and hurt Ro or Izzy or Cyrus? I didn't think he would ever intentionally cause any of the protectors harm, but didn't people deserve to know who they were sharing their campus with? There was a reason all of the creatures in the lab were heavily locked down and under constant supervision. It was a lesson I learned myself, the hard way.

I let out an exhale, as I picked up my pace. Maybe what I really wanted, more than anything, was for them to confront me. To blame me for what happened that night, for what happened to Wade. Maybe hearing them say it would give me a feeling of peace. If they ripped apart the final few strands holding me together, maybe I could start making sense of things again, go about the process of repairing whatever holes had eaten their way through my soul.

I turned up the volume on my earbuds, letting the loud, moody song wash away my internal grumbling until I reached a particularly tall mound of vines and twigs.

My face split into a big grin as I pulled back the shrubbery a few inches, hand swiping underneath for the cool metal handle as the rustling leaves blew a fresh, musty scent up my nose. I lifted the latch and pushed my way inside.

"Honey, I'm home!" I yelled, grin falling when the hellhound who lived here failed to greet me. Usually, he heard me coming from a mile away and would either run out to meet me, or pace excitedly on the large shag rug I'd procured for him. It was currently covered in a healthy layer of twigs and what looked like normal dog hair.

"Ralph?" I tossed down the large bag I snuck over, one filled with various fancy meats and vegetables from the cafeteria. Ro and I had been discreetly filling up tupperware during each of our meals over the last two days. Something we tried to do once or twice a week, depending on how much we thought we could get away with. Izzy took over the thievery when too many eyes were on us any given week, which had Ralph warming up to her real fast. Between our scavenging and collective attempt to fix up this cabin, Ralph had a pretty decent space to call home. "I brought your favorite. Duck! I swiped the last pound of it. You have no idea how many evil looks I got. This shit is a real hot commodity around hungry hunters."

I cringed slightly at the word evil. I guess technically most people would consider Ralph evil. He was a hellhound after all, from, well, hell. I put some of the food in a large bowl Ro swiped from Cyrus's cabin a few weeks ago. Ralph could hunt for himself, and he didn't spend all of his time here, but he loved when we came to visit.

"Seriously, where are you?"

I tried to disguise the hurt from my voice. Visiting Ralph was one of the few things that brought me legitimate joy these days, and I was big enough to admit that his lack of a sloppy welcome was pulling at my heartstrings in a bad way. Especially since my nerves and emotions were already so frayed today.

Leaving his food, I went out the back door.

Maybe he was out hunting for food now? I didn't get a chance to visit him last night like I'd promised, so it was also possible he was pouting somewhere out in the forest.

"Ralph? Raaaalph," I whisper-yelled, my hands cupping my mouth to help the words echo without catching the attention of anyone who might be wandering around out here. "Here, bo—"

My call turned into a very real yell when I felt the pressure of a hand wrap around my face. I planted my feet, moving my body slightly so that I could give my elbow enough space to dig itself into the groin of whoever was trying to attack me. Did they hurt Ralph? Is that why he wasn't here? Anger coursed through me at the thought of someone coming after him. I pulled my arm forward, ready to strike, just as I clamped my teeth down on my attacker's fingers.

"Ouch. Jesus, Max. Shhh, do you want the entire campus to come traipsing out here?" A sultry, smooth voice whispered against the shell of my ear before the hand dropped from my face.

I spun around, body humming with adrenaline, and met a pair of startling green eyes. "Declan?"

This was the first time I really had a chance to look at her up close since she'd returned, and she seemed so much harder than she had before, more exhausted. Her normally smooth, wavy hair was frayed at the ends and disheveled. The deep black strands coupled with the deep emerald of her eyes gave her an ethereal, wild look, like she was an extra in an apocalypse film. She studied me for a second, brow arching with a challenge. "Thought I told you never to come visit the hellhound unless I was with you?"

My hands met my hips and I took a deep, calming breath. Exploding was probably a bad move just now.

"Yes," I started, mentally trying to slow my pulse, "but that was before you just full-on disappeared. Not like I was going to leave Ralph out here alone for a whole month. That's neglect."

Declan opened her mouth to respond, but a giant black ball of fur came running towards us, ears flopping in the wind. Ralph skidded to a halt about a foot away, dropping a large, drool-covered red ball at Declan's feet, a self-satisfied grin on his face. Then, he hopped over to me and swiped his long tongue across my cheek before maneuvering my hands in the perfect position for some behind-the-ear-scratches. Ralph was seriously more overgrown puppy than a fiendish hell monster.

I stared at the red ball in disbelief before looking back up at Declan. I'd never seen it before and it wasn't the sort of object that just grew out here in the woods. "Did you—did you bring that ball to play with Ralph?"

Declan studied the dog as a small grin pulled at her lips. It was brief, and before I knew it, Declan's face was its usual walled-off mask, like she was made of sharp lines and granite. She shrugged, her eyes bouncing everywhere, everywhere so long as they didn't land on mine. "It's whatever. Thought he might be bored out here all alone and I needed some peace and quiet."

"Trouble in paradise?" I asked, letting my fingers get lost in Ralph's thick hair, while I picked out small twigs and leaves that were lodged around random tufts and mats. They didn't exactly have groomers for hellhounds, unfortunately, so he had to make do with bathing in the pond and my failed attempts at wrestling him with a large brush in hand.

Declan shrugged and scratched at the back of her neck, her long fingers getting tangled in a knot. I swallowed my grin when I realized that she looked about as wild and in her element here as Ralph did. With a heavy sigh, she dropped down on the ground and leaned back on her arms, her face tilted toward the brief rays of sun visible through the thick trees.

After a second, she finally looked at me, studying me from below, eyes narrowed and calculating. "You look fucking exhausted, Max."

I inhaled sharply before joining her on the forest floor, my bones rattled by my less-than-graceful landing. Why did people think it was okay to tell someone they looked tired? Like, gee, I had no idea that I was exhausted, thanks for informing me that I look like shit.

Declan tossed the ball from one hand to the other while Ralph tracked the movement, ready to pounce. He took off through the trees when Declan threw it aimlessly. It was a peaceful moment as we sat in silence, surrounded by a floor of dried leaves and dirt. For a brief second, I could trick myself into believing that all the anxieties and grief and guilt that plagued me all day, only to follow me into my dreams at night, were a thing of the past—nothing but a warped and distant memory.

"Reza's moving in and is redecorating like her life depends on it." Her eyes met mine for a second before turning back to the cluster of trees Ralph disappeared through. "I just didn't feel like being around while Atlas pretended to cater to every single one of Reza and Alleva's whims, simply because the path of least resistance takes minimal effort."

My lungs felt like they were cinching tighter at the idea of Reza moving in. The yellow room in Six's cabin was only mine briefly, but it still racked my nerves that it would belong to her now. I studied Declan, the small frown creating a shadow of sadness on her features. My stomach dipped. It wasn't just my room that Reza was redecorating. It was Sarah's, Declan's cousin.

While Six was gone, Sharla filled me in some on Sarah, since they were in the same cohort and grew up together. Sarah and Declan were close, so I couldn't imagine how it must feel, with Reza encroaching on that territory and erasing whatever small traces of Sarah were left in the cabin.

Would someone move into Wade's room too? Turn it into their own until, eventually, it was almost like he was never here —nothing more than a ghost lingering in the forgotten details?

The thought alone sent a heavy sinking feeling into my gut as

I dug my fingers into the loose dirt around me, desperate to ground my grief, no matter how literally.

"And does Reza have any idea that she's moving in with a werewolf?" I couldn't keep the accusation from my tone, even though I wasn't sure why I asked the question in the first place. As soon as it left my lips, I wished desperately to pull the words back in and swallow them. Did I want Reza to know? Did I want her to have a level of intimacy with the team that they'd never afforded me?

Declan's features hardened, making me realize that until then, she had more or less been sliding into a slightly more relaxed state here with me. The realization that I'd ruined the moment sent a new crack down my chest, joining the growing number of fissures I couldn't seem to avoid.

I gently nudged her foot with mine, waiting for her attention to fix back on me. I waited until her eyes landed on me, my heart stumbling a bit as it always did when she looked at me. Declan's eyes had their own kind of magic, not just because of their otherworldly shade that seemed so much brighter and more complex than everyone else's; but because down in their depths, I could see that she was swimming in a whirling pool of grief and anger. It was the one place that when you looked close enough, she didn't, or couldn't, hide her thoughts. Not all of them anyway.

"Hey, look, I'm sorry. I know that it's a shitty situation and that you all are stuck between a rock and a hard place. I know that it's not Atlas's fault that he was turned. And I don't blame you or Eli for wanting to have his back. It's just—" I huffed out a short breath and felt my cheeks heating with nerves, my own thoughts and feelings a jumbled tangle that I couldn't quite unravel. "It didn't feel great to be living in a house where you guys were constantly lying. And then, when I found out, it sucked being in a position where I had to help carry out that lie. In a weird way, I simultaneously wish that you had all told me immediately, but also that I never found out at all. Which is ridiculous and unfair, but it's the truth of it."

Declan opened her mouth, leaning in towards me just slightly, before settling back on her palms when I held up my hands.

"Just let me finish, okay?"

She nodded, her body angling towards me in focus, the swirling depths of her eyes suddenly still and illegible.

"It just sucked. And I don't exactly like Reza, but I also don't want her to wake up in the middle of the night to a werewolf ripping out her neck."

I pulled the sleeves of my sweater down, anxious for something to do with my hands. I could feel her sharp focus on me, and I shivered at the thought of being the object of her scrutiny. These days I was frayed and tattered—the fewer people to realize that, the better.

Of all the protectors that I'd met since moving here, Declan was the one who eluded me the most. It always felt like she was there while simultaneously being a million miles away. She could turn on the cheeky banter, just like Eli, but it always felt like it was her way of burying something else deep down. While Atlas at least pretended like he was trying to fit in, or at least blend in, Declan remained on the outskirts, a quiet observer of the world as it went on around her, like The Guild was nothing more than her own personal television program—and one that she was only marginally interested in.

"You weren't ever in danger in our house," she said, her voice low and monotonous, unreadable. "The wolf doesn't change who he is, what he believes. For the most part, he has control over the transitions, and when he doesn't, he makes sure he's isolated deep where no one would stumble on him. Atlas—he would never hurt you."

"But he attacked me before I even moved here. And he didn't exactly seem concerned about onlookers seeing him," I interjected, the words leaving my mouth without any permission from me. Not to mention that he'd shown up in all of his wolfy-glory in town the night that Ten brought me along to try and track him.

Declan straightened her posture, her face suddenly rigid and fierce. "What do you mean? He hurt you? Did he bite you?" Her eyes scanned from my head to my toes, like she could find the traces of Atlas's attack through my clothes.

My skin burned as her eyes carved their way over my body, and I hoped like hell I wasn't doing anything embarrassing like blushing as deeply as I feared I was. I wasn't sure why she affected me like this, but I hated it.

"No, but," I paused, recollecting the moment I first met Atlas. It was during my first kiss, before The Guild was more than just an entity I read about in Cy's books, and he'd interrupted it, pulling the local boy I'd been crushing on into an alley. "Well, I guess he didn't attack me exactly, but he attacked the boy I was with. Atlas, in wolf form," I added, awkwardly, "pulled the guy from my lips and dragged him away. It was in the middle of town and he could have been seen by who knows how many humans. And then, of course, there was the night he showed up in town and he and Jer got into a wrestling match."

Declan massaged her temples while she took in the story, her expression growing harder and harder to parse.

I was silent for a moment, eager for her response, desperate for some kind of justification and assurance that Atlas wouldn't *actually* hurt anyone, that he wasn't like other werewolves, that we could keep his secret and he'd be fine—everything would be fine. But then I got uncomfortable and antsy waiting longer than a nanosecond for her to thread together her response.

"And honestly," I said, nervously stumbling over my words, "he totally could have killed me if Ralph hadn't turned up and scared him away that first time he showed up."

Her head snapped up, her features cold and stiff with a layer of what I could only describe as dread. "That's why you're here now? That's why Cyrus agreed to help Seamus manage the field teams in the first place, isn't it?"

I nodded as Ralph walked back into view, a heavy line of drool dropping from his snout to the ground. His giant teeth were triumphantly clamped around the ball.

Declan stood up abruptly, absently dusting leaves and dirt from her black skinny jeans.

"I need to go," she mumbled, before turning around and leaving without another word or explanation.

"Okay," I said to her back. My voice was quiet, muffled by the breeze but loud enough for a protector's ears to pick up. I didn't even try to temper the frustration I was feeling. "Great talking to you too then."

Ralph pranced over, depositing a very wet, very slimy ball into my lap, ready for the next round of fetch.

4
DECLAN

I pushed through the front door, my mouth dry as sandpaper and ears burning hot as embers. "Atlas," I said, climbing the stairs three at a time. "Where the fuck are you, you fucking fuck?"

"Hey Dec." Reza slid out of Max's room and leaned up against the doorframe like she'd lived here her whole life. Her familiarity with the cabin made my skin crawl. "Anything I can help with?" Her voice was a purr and I shivered in disgust as she pouted her lips.

Why did she think that was cute or made her even the least bit likeable? She'd always been desperate for my friendship, like she hoped becoming my new best friend would be the surest way to get Atlas to fall in love with her. And since she'd moved in, I would have to put up with her climbing up my ass at every turn.

"No Reza," I said, folding my arms in front of my chest like I could shield myself from her attention. "I need to speak to Atlas. Now."

She bared her teeth, her frustration with me leaking out into a caricature of a smile. "You need to get over your hatred of me. My mother is already in negotiations with Seamus and with Atlas's father. The binding ceremony will happen by the end of the year, so the faster you get on board, the less awful it will be for all of us involved. It's not like you're exactly my first choice bff either, you know, but it wouldn't hurt for us to try and tolerate each other. Otherwise, one word to my mother and your aunt is going to double her efforts to get you to bond on the other side of the pond. Then you'll be off this team faster than you can blink."

My jaw tensed, the muscles grinding my teeth together as I forced myself to keep my mouth shut. Reza had always planned to bond with Atlas, but it was only recently that she'd set her eyes on Eli as well. But her mother pushing my aunt to negotiate my own bond? That was news to me. "You aren't a member of this team, Reza—"

"Yet," she interrupted, her thin brow arching, daring me to challenge her. She knew I couldn't. Not if I wanted to stay here with my team.

"Whatever, I don't have time for this shit. You aren't right now and that's what matters. I need to speak with Atlas and with Eli. Alone."

Huffing, she pushed off the wall and took a step back into the room. I caught sight of some of the changes she'd made. Alleva moved her in less than twelve hours ago and already Reza had taken down all of Sarah's things. I tried swallowing back the emotion that welled in my throat at the sight of her records and books haphazardly piled into a corner like it all belonged in a forgotten junkyard somewhere. The room didn't feel like hers anymore.

The closet was now spilling over with clothes and more training gear than any person could ever really use. Various weapons and knickknacks were littering the walls in a way that made this arrangement feel a lot more permanent than I hoped it was. Sharing my home with Reza would test every last ounce of patience I didn't have to spare.

"I see you've made yourself at home," I said, not bothering to keep the edge out of my voice. My cousin was killed by the werewolves who turned Atlas, and the room remained empty until Max's extremely short sojourn in the cabin. Now that Reza was here, clogging the atmosphere up with her vanity and power plays, I realized that having Max here was the best possible option for us. And my stomach sank at the realization that we'd completely blown that whole situation to smithereens.

Reza grinned as she slid her fingers along the door handle. "Unlike your last house guest, I plan on making this my permanent residence. Best get used to it. Atlas is in the office. Eli is fucking Sharla in his room." She glanced in the direction of Eli's room where, sure enough, I could hear some ass slapping and moaning. Reza's lip curled in disgust. "I'll make sure my mother soundproofs my walls this week. I refuse to have to listen to his revolving door of visitors every night."

She shut her door and I let out a relieved breath. It was a frustrating thing—not feeling comfortable in your own home. And since I learned that Reza would be moving in, I hadn't had a moment to feel at peace. Hanging out with Ralph and Max had been as close to relaxed as I'd gotten since we returned.

I pounded on Eli's door, unsurprised to learn that Sharla was back in his bed. Those two used each other for physical comfort all the time. And of all his usual pursuits, Sharla was the one I minded having around the least. She was at least a decent human being and didn't spend her time trying to weasel her way into our group like Reza did. They both knew that they were using each other to scratch an itch and it worked for everyone involved.

"Mate, not to cockblock, but you need to finish up quickly. We have business to discuss, and it can't wait."

"Aye aye, Captain," Eli shouted as Sharla burst into a fit of giggles.

The sound of furniture, or something equally heavy, knocking over signaled that they were ramping things up, so I backed away instantly.

Unwilling to wait however long it would take for Eli to show up before I confronted Atlas, I stormed my way into the office, slamming the door shut as soon as I was behind it.

Atlas was leaning back in his chair, staring at the ceiling like it held all the answers to life's big questions. Since we were kids, I'd lost track of the number of times I'd stumbled on him looking to the sky like this, all lost and desperate.

Usually, it inspired my sympathy, but not today.

"You're fucking mated to her, aren't you?" Frustration pinched at my insides, desperate to claw its way out.

Werewolves weren't like protectors. While protectors initiated bonds to encourage strength and protection, those bonds were often platonic and fully open to manipulation. But werewolves had a different physiological response to developing bonds: they lived in packs for protection and often mated to one person for life. It was an odd element of stability built into a typically chaotic and nomadic lifestyle.

Atlas dropped his legs down, his dark eyes meeting mine. Of all the guys, I was closest with Atlas. We grew up together and had helped each other through some pretty rough shit. And in all the time I'd known him, I never saw fear. Not the likes of which played out on his face right now anyway.

"What?" His voice was hollow, and I realized not for the first time how much losing Wade had taken a toll on him.

"Max," I said, settling into the other office chair. I massaged my temples, trying to calm the anger seething through my body. This was not something I should be angry about. It wasn't something he could control. Hell, until this moment, I wasn't even sure that protectors-turned-wolf even could mate. I took a long breath in and out before straightening back up, hoping my posture could convey the confidence I couldn't feel right now. "You're mated to Max."

He closed his eyes, spinning slightly on the axle of his chair. Atlas wasn't a fidgeter. That was usually Eli's M.O. when it came to covering nerves. "I don't know."

"What do you mean you don't know? And either way, why is

this not something you told us right away? You met her before she even moved here, Atlas?" The hurt leaked out of my voice before I could hold it back. "We're your team. We've gone up to bat for you throughout all of this shit you're dealing with. We've protected you at every turn. And you've been telling us constantly to back away from her, to sever ties? How the hell could you keep this from us?" My blood was boiling so intensely, I was surprised steam wasn't coming out of my ears. Hiding Atlas's true nature now was a fulltime job for us. We were not equipped to handle this though. This was new, terrifying territory. "What the fuck were you thinking?"

The door slammed open as Eli strode in. "Pleasure doing business with you Shar, I'll be sure to ring again," he hollered down the hall before closing the door again. His hair was all mussed, and he hadn't bothered to put a shirt back on yet. His shoulders were raked with fingernail marks and what looked distinctly like bites. He leaned back against a desk, glancing between Atlas and me, a shit-eating grin on his face like the damn cat who got the cream.

Eli was the most laid back of us all, but it didn't take much for him to read the room. "The fuck is up with you two?"

"Nothing," Atlas said, nostrils flaring slightly as he drilled a stare at me, silently begging me to drop it. "This isn't the time."

Yeah, the hell with that. This had carried on long enough. "Atlas is mated—as in werewolf mated—to Max," I said, sadistically pleased when Atlas's face flushed. Prick deserved to feel scrutinized right now. I was done with the lies. We deserved more, if we were going to have any chance at all of surviving as a team after Wade, we needed honesty and transparency.

Eli's shoulders tensed as he straightened up and stared daggers at Atlas. His usually playful eyes were suddenly devoid of all emotion and humor. "Come again?"

Atlas tossed a pen he was fiddling with onto the desk before he glanced up at us. "Look, I don't know for sure, okay? And even if it's true, I'm not going to do anything about it."

"Well, well, what would father dearest think of you being bonded to a mutt with no family history?" Eli said, venom in his voice. We both knew that Tarren was invested in bonding his son to the best possible female protector he could. When it came to the old families, bonding was a way to maintain power and to establish new strains of it. Hence why both Tarren and Alleva were hellbent on seeing a union between Atlas and Reza now that Sarah was no longer an option. Eli getting thrown into the mix was just the cream on top of that union, since Reza no longer had to pretend to give a shit about Wade.

Atlas's glare cut through Eli like a knife, and I stood by annoyed as they had their own, silent pissing contest.

"Could you even bond to a protector now?" I asked, voicing the concern as soon as it crossed my mind. "If you have a mate-bond, how does that work?"

"Believe it or not, Declan," Atlas crooned, his tone full of malice, "the werewolf that bit me didn't exactly leave me with a manual for how this whole thing works."

"He also saw Max before she moved here," I added, turning towards Eli and perfectly fine with throwing Atlas under the bus some more, just this once. "Apparently he wolfed out and attacked her boyfriend."

Eli chuckled in that way of his that made it clear he didn't find what he was laughing at even remotely funny. "Great. Just fucking great. How'd you even know who the hell she even was? And I thought you maintained control in your wolf form for the most part? You fucking attacked a human?"

Atlas shook his head, looking like he held the weight of the world on his shoulders. "I don't know."

I almost felt bad for pushing him on this issue. Almost. This was serious and we needed to know what we were handling here. He just looked so...lost. It made it difficult to come at him with guns blazing.

"So you just magically showed up to whatever hole in the wall Cyrus was hiding her in?" Eli cocked his head to the side. "No one outside of my father even knew where they were living. I'm not buying it, Atlas."

Atlas took a sip of what looked like water from the cup sitting next to him. Although it didn't smell like water from here.

"I can't explain it, okay," his dark eyes filled with legitimate confusion and a healthy dose of frustration. "Something just—drew the wolf there. It was like I could sense her somehow. For months after I'd changed, I would randomly wake up in different locations, with no clue how I got there. It was like I was searching for something but had no idea what. Like half of my brain was keeping something from the other half. And then," he shrugged, trailing off.

Months? He'd been waking up in random places for months? And hadn't bothered to let the rest of us in on that little pebble of information?

"You found her and attacked her boyfriend. Her very *human* boyfriend," Eli finished.

Atlas's lip curled and he shook his head. "He wasn't her boyfriend. And no one but Max and Rowan realized I was a fucking werewolf, obviously. But yeah, I found her, and the wolf got a little bit, I don't know, possessive, I guess. But it's not a big deal, we don't know much about werewolf mating. They aren't exactly forthcoming with their secrets or culture, let alone the fact that we know almost nothing about what gets thrown into the mix when a protector is turned into a wolf. But like I said, it's not a big deal. It's been fine so far—ignoring it, and her, to the best of my ability. So I'll just keep doing that."

He sounded so defeated, and my skin crawled with a weird mixture of pity and—jealousy? For some reason I hated the idea that Atlas had a real, supernatural connection to Max and that he had been trying to get the rest of us to ignore our own draw to the girl. But at the same time, this seemed to be wrecking him. It was hard enough trying to ignore whatever protective instinct I felt where Max was concerned, but I couldn't imagine how much more complicated that was for Atlas. He'd already lost so much, resisting this kind of pull must've been devastating.

"You're really going to just continue ignoring it?" Eli asked, scratching lazily at his jaw line. "Like just completely pretend that the bond isn't there?"

"I'm not going to pursue it, that's for damn sure," Atlas said, his voice gaining volume and edge. "I mean, don't you think it's a bit weird that we're all drawn to this girl we know nothing about? A werewolf, protectors, and a hellhound?"

There he went again, spouting his favorite 'Max is the devil's spawn' theory—preaching on and on about how we all had to keep our distance. I was beginning to think that he was just using this line of thought as a way to justify ignoring the mate-bond. That had to be a bitch to do.

"Hell, she's even befriended a damn vampire," he added under his breath.

I fought for control, digging my nails into the soft flesh of my palms. For weeks, I managed to forget that Atlas caught some lab vamp kissing her. That she'd...let him. And broken him out of his cell. Counting down from ten, I took slow, steady breaths.

"Something is off,' Atlas continued, "and I don't buy it. So yeah, I'm going to continue treating her like any other protector at The Guild and keep my distance."

For now. He didn't say it, but I felt the sentiment linger in the air. I had a feeling we were all going to lose that battle eventually. She would be all of our undoing.

5
MAX

I woke up to Izzy lurking over my bed like a proper B-movie stalker. She was still in her pajamas, but she was also wearing a bright pink party hat, her lips wrapped around one of those plastic things that unraveled when you blew on them.

While she looked ready to attend a kid's fifth birthday party, there was no mirth on her features.

"Nightmares couldn't even give you a break on your damn birthday, could they?" she asked as she scooched me over so that she could perch on the edge of my mattress, face the picture of maternal concern, so earnest that it made my heart ache.

"No rest for the wicked," I said, only half joking. I eyed the plate she was holding with amusement. "Chocolate cake? For breakfast?"

As if in answer to my question, Ro pushed his way through the room, a wooden tray balanced in one arm as he tossed a half smile in my direction. "Tried telling her that you weren't big on dessert, but she was adamant, so I brought this to help wash the sugar rush down."

He dropped the plate of fresh eggs and bacon, piled high enough that I was legitimately concerned the tray might collapse under the weight, onto my lap and stood back, eyeing Izzy's ensemble with amusement.

"Chocolate cake is a birthday must, no excuses." Izzy glanced at me out of the side of her eyes, a wicked smile forming on her lips. "That said, if you want to share some of it with me, that's completely allowed."

Exhaustion aside, it was a pretty good way to start a birthday, stuffing my face in my bed with two of my favorite people in the world. I was only feeling a little bit sad about the fact that Cy, Ro, and I wouldn't get to have our traditional celebration of steak and fries at the diner. Darlene would always warm up some apple pie for dessert and throw some twenty-year old decorations onto the wall.

After I stuffed the last bite into my mouth, practically bursting at the seams, Ro handed me two boxes.

His lips pulled down a bit at the side. "Cy dropped these off last night, said that he had business to take care of off campus today, but he wanted you to have them."

I tried to shove the lurch in my stomach down. Things had been strained between me and Cy for weeks, largely because I'd been pushing him away. But it still hurt that he wasn't going to be around for my birthday, especially since nineteen was a pretty big deal in protector culture. Historically, it was the year that angels from centuries ago, and protectors throughout the line, would begin to manifest their strongest powers.

The age was largely symbolic now, since modern-day protectors didn't have stages of power development—we were just stronger than humans, with longer lifespans and heightened senses—but it still stung that of all of the birthdays for Cy to miss, it was this one.

With a deep breath in, I shook away the mini pity party. If Cyrus wasn't around today, it was because he had something really important to do for The Guild. The stakes were too high these days for anyone to take chances, and all of the graduated protectors and teams were running on fumes trying to save lives.

I set the smaller, lighter box aside and tore into the heavy one. I glanced up at Ro, my smile mirrored on his face. A brand-new set of daggers and throwing knives, all lined with silver.

"Cy and I went in on these together," Ro said, picking up one of the knives and touching his finger to the tip. "Thought they'd suit you well, and you'll need the upgrade after graduation."

The handles were adorned with a beautiful sapphire material that fit my grip like they were made for me.

"Damn, you've got good taste, Ro," Izzy said, admiring one of the blades as she inspected it at eye level.

He grinned as I tossed my arms around his neck, hugging him just as he grabbed a dagger from my hand before I impaled us both.

"I have no idea what's in the other box though," he said, curiosity lingering in his voice. "Cy wouldn't fess up. He was afraid I'd ruin the surprise, I guess."

Overcome by curiosity, I ripped open the wrapping of the small box, smiling to myself at Cy's use of an old newspaper to cover the gift.

A small, black velvet box fell into my lap.

"Ooh, looks like jewelry," Izzy said with genuine excitement in her voice. "I wonder if he has good taste. It's always the quiet ones who do."

When I flipped the lid, I saw a small star locket and found myself grinning like a maniac. Cy and Ro always used to tease me about the small birthmark on my wrist, because it was shaped like a perfect little star. They used to pretend that I was an alien dropped off at Cy's door by a shooting star.

I ran my thumb over the smooth ridges, tears pricking my eyes when I turned it around. He'd engraved it with one word.

Family.

"Cy's not usually so sentimental," Ro said, his brows scrunched slightly. "Guess the move has him missing our old seclusion and lifestyle more than he'd anticipated."

"Open it," Izzy shrieked, her gray eyes dancing with the

morning rays shining through my window. "It's a locket, there's something inside."

I flipped it open by a small, almost invisible latch, and saw a picture of the three of us looking back at me. It was the only picture I'd ever been able to convince Ro and Cy to take with me. It was from exactly one year ago, on my eighteenth birthday. I'd learned it was a lot easier to get things I wanted when Cy had the guilt of a teen girl's birthday hanging over his head.

I blinked back the traitorous liquid threatening to spill over and handed the locket to Ro, a silent request that he latch the dainty necklace around my neck.

"Damn, he did really well," Izzy said as I dropped my hair back down around my shoulders, admiring the locket hanging above my clavicle. "Color me impressed. The old legend knows how to shop for a girl."

Suddenly, I wanted Cy here something fierce—I wanted to clear the air between us and apologize for taking my own angst out on him. I missed that feeling, the three of us bickering alone in a cabin, no responsibilities to worry about, no burdens to carry. Our world had shifted so quickly, and I was sick of it shifting me away from Cyrus.

Family. That's what mattered.

"Alright, that's enough sap," Ro said as he slid off my mattress and stretched. "What's the plan for the day? Vanish?"

My stomach tightened at the idea. Last time I was there, it hadn't exactly been an enjoyable experience. But I guess that part of the issue with being in a secluded location was that the options were pretty limited.

A giant grin split Izzy's face as she started bouncing on my bed like a little kid. "No way. Too boring. Plus, we were just there, and it didn't exactly seem to enthrall the birthday girl."

She shot me a grin and the tightness in my stomach melted away instantly.

"We're going to throw an impromptu gathering here with our

cohort and any of the teams that want to swing by. It'll be a day of movie marathons and hanging out. Chill, but fun."

It sounded perfect and I made sure to tell her so as I slid off the bed and stretched some. "I'm going to go for a quick run first, clear my head some and brush away the last vestiges of my sleep." And the nightmares that plagued it.

"Seriously," Izzy said, drawing out the word long and slow. "It's your birthday, we have the day off, and you want to work out?"

She looked legitimately offended, her lip turned up in disgust, which threw me and Ro into a fit of laughter.

All things considered, it was the perfect morning, the perfect way to start the most important birthday of my life.

But it was as I was carving my usual path through the woods, running with all of the energy that I could muster, my lungs pulling in heavy breaths of air, that my mood started to dip. I'd left Ro and Izzy behind, even with their offers to join me, because I'd wanted to push myself to my limits, to focus on my body and my senses.

The ground felt as firm as ever, the woods still had the same crisp, muddy scent that I'd grown to love, the sounds of birds and small critters rustling through the brush was as loud as ever.

My ankle caught on a low branch, and I watched in fascination as the bark carved a small red line into my skin. I waited with bated breath, to see if I'd heal more quickly than usual, half expecting my skin to instantly close up right before my eyes.

It didn't. The wound would be healed eventually of course, probably before I finished my post-shower run, but it didn't seem to be moving along the process any more quickly than usual.

I knew on a logical level that it was irrational to think that on my nineteenth birthday I would experience some instant transformation. Hell, it might not even be my true birthday if I was being honest. I showed up in a small bassinet outside Cy's door one day, newborn but no way to know how old.

Still, even though I knew all of this at a fundamental level, even though I knew that the age marker was more symbolic in modern generations, I couldn't hide the disappointment from myself. Part of me still believed that I'd wake up stronger, faster, that I'd heal quicker and have the sort of heightened senses comic book heroines had.

But I was just me, the same me that I was the day before, and years before, the only difference couched in the fact that, if anything, I was more exhausted than usual, maybe even less powerful.

Not wanting to stew too much in my disappointment, I made quick work of my run, enjoying the feel of my muscles pushing to their limits as much as I could. The day was relatively warm for so late in the season, no snow in sight, and I passed dozens of recruits wandering through the trees together, trying to soak up the morning sunlight and enjoy one of our few days off.

By the time I made my way back to Ten's cabin, I was in as good of a mood as I was when I left, any lingering disappointment about the anticlimax of turning nineteen abandoned in the woods.

When I reached the door, my lungs working overtime and burning with that intoxicating feeling that came with the end of a good workout, I noticed a stack of three boxes outside the door.

Taped to the one on top was a short letter.

M—

She would've wanted these to go to someone who would love and appreciate them as

much as she did. Happy Birthday.

D

I ripped open the top box, and felt my jaw unhinge. Packed neatly and with great care, sat the record player I recognized from Sarah's room. Not wasting time, I tore open the other two boxes, finding a collection of old records and some of the dusty novels that lined the bookshelves in the room I'd briefly inhabited. My hands shook as I ran my fingers delicately over the leather bindings, my lips whispering titles, both familiar and unfamiliar alike.

A feeling I couldn't quite decipher rushed through me, and my stomach tightened at the realization that of all of the people Declan could have given these precious objects to—the small reminders left behind by someone deeply important to her—she'd given them to me.

My thoughts churned at a speed I couldn't follow, as I thought back to all of my interactions with Declan. I'd been half convinced that she completely despised me half the time, as I'd been on the receiving end of her anger and frustration more often than not. But if she was willing to give me these—if she trusted me with such a precious piece of her cousin's memory—what did that mean? I didn't know what to make of it.

The rest of the afternoon went by in a flash, with Izzy insisting on decorating the entire cabin to set up for the evening movie marathon. After two hours, the living room and kitchen looked like a giant fairy had vomited glitter and streamers everywhere. To my surprise, everyone in Ten was equally excited about my birthday and that I'd be spending it there with them.

Considering birthdays had always been a relatively quiet affair back home, I was getting increasingly excited by the idea of celebrating with all of my new friends. And I was already looking forward to Ro's birthday next month. By dinner time, Izzy, Ro, Arnell, and Sharla had completely erased whatever bad mood I'd been in and, for the first time in a long time, I felt the outer pricks of legitimate happiness cracking through my grief.

"What do you want for dinner, birthday girl?" Izzy asked, her hand lazily swinging a bottle of beer around. "We should probably load up on carbs and greasy food. If you can't eat like shit on your birthday, what the hell is the point of life?"

As if on cue, a loud, dull knock echoed on the front door and Arnell reached out to pull it open. A giant, perfect smile spread across his face as he looked back at me. "This one's for you, Max."

Cy walked in, his eyes dancing around Izzy's decorations with a bemused, maybe even slightly terrified, look on his face. He appeared to be in better spirits than I'd seen him in since we'd arrived here and, unable to hold myself back, I ran to him, enveloping his lanky body into a hug.

He wasn't an overly affectionate guy, but I warmed when his arms wrapped around me, squeezing me gently. "Happy birthday, girl. Nineteen is a big accomplishment."

I wasn't exactly sure how simply turning nineteen qualified as an accomplishment, but after all of the close calls I'd experienced in the last few months alone, it made sense.

Pulling back from him, my nose caught a familiar scent—a scent that filled me with so much nostalgia I could've wept right there, in front of a house full of badass protectors.

"No way," I said, as I looked from his smug face to the paper bags he was holding in his right hand. "You didn't."

"It was a long trip, but who am I to start breaking tradition now?" His usually gruff voice was tempered with amusement as he walked into the room and made his way over to the long dining room table. "Ro, why don't you bring in the other bags from outside. Darlene made sure to include enough for all of your friends. And she made me swear on pain of death to tell you both how much she misses having you around on Saturday afternoons."

With that, he plopped the familiar white bag, nearly see-through in spots that were saturated with grease, onto the large, oak table.

My grin was so wide that my cheeks felt like they would crack from the pressure.

After heating up the servings, we all dug into the feast of steak, fries, mozzarella sticks, and apple pie, not one of us caring even a little bit that the meal had been prepared hours ago.

As we finished dessert, Cy gripped my shoulder in a warm

embrace that said all of the things that neither of us was any good at saying. Things weren't necessarily back to normal—how could they be when our world was going through so much turmoil? But we cared about each other, and we would always be family. And for now, that was enough.

In fact, it was everything.

6
MAX

More people than I thought would show ended up at the cabin, so that by the time eight rolled around, there were too many people with too much energy to continue a movie marathon. Instead, Arnell put on some music, and everyone scattered throughout the house to mingle and chat.

My mood was so high from dinner that I didn't even mind that we had to put movies on hold for a few days. I'd had a lifetime of movie marathons with Ro. But this was my first birthday party, the first time a group of friends came together to celebrate me.

"Enjoying the party?" Mavis asked, as he brought me over a fresh beer, popping the top off on his belt.

More guys needed to do that—let you see them prepare and open the drink. I'd seen too many movies to ever accept a drink from a guy without seeing it poured first.

Of all the members of Ten, Mavis was the one I was least close with. He was a lot more standoffish than the others, and I think part of it had to do with the fact that Mavis and Arnell had a bit of a romantic history. Which meant that he was taking a back seat to give Ro and Arnell a shot, which seemed wildly mature and sweet.

I nodded in response and took a sip of the beer. It was hoppier than I was used to, and I partially preferred Izzy's insistence on tequila and Jer's fruitier cocktails. "Thanks for this, and for being so cool with letting this happen here tonight."

He was a pretty quiet guy, so I had a feeling that Izzy's insistence on a party was probably not his favorite idea of the bunch. Things weren't exactly out of hand, but I doubted he could fall asleep early or read right now if he wanted to escape from the noise levels.

Mavis grinned, his black, narrow eyes full of laughter as he studied the crowd. "You kidding? I love getting to play fly on the wall for these kinds of things. Way quieter here than the bars, plus since we're on campus, people let their guards down more." He winked at me, pressing the lip of the beer against his own. "Not to mention that when I get tired, I'm just a crawl away from my bedroom and noise-cancelling headphones."

He arched his brow at me, staring at me out of the side of his eyes. His dark hair was tousled and shiny, like he'd just walked out of a salon. I'd never seen him looking anything but perfect. "Gotta ask though, if you're enjoying yourself so much, how come I keep catching your eyes wandering over to the door. Waiting for someone to show? We not enough for you here, Bentley?"

I felt my cheeks heat at his question, and I cleared my throat, distinctly looking away from the front door. "No, just trying to keep track of everyone," I lied. "You all are more than enough for me."

He winked before walking off, making a beeline towards Jer and a few of their friends. I hated that it was that obvious. And while I was grateful for everyone that showed up, I couldn't stop the small part of me that seemed hellbent one waiting to see if Declan, Atlas, or Eli would show up. Had Izzy invited them? Did it matter?

Plus, my stomach was still a confused mess from Declan's gift, and I was tearing my mind apart, trying to find a way to thank her for such a thoughtful gesture.

The door swung open, and my eyes latched onto a pair of cold blue ones.

Reza.

She arrived alone, but I saw Theo clocking every single movement she made as she strode through the room like she owned it.

"Had to come check out this cabin for myself," she said as she walked over to me and grabbed a beer from the tub at my feet. "Gotta say, it's decent, but I much prefer the aesthetic in mine. Too bad you screwed up that arrangement."

I knew she was fishing for information from me. No one really knew why I suddenly moved out of Six's cabin, only to immediately pop up in Ten's like some respawning videogame character. And the details of that night were under pretty strict guard. Seamus and Cyrus were probably the only two to really hear what happened the night Darius escaped and Wade died. Ro's response was to just avoid mentioning that night altogether. And the members of Six were the only ones to know all of the information—down to the final, terrible detail of Atlas wandering around on four legs instead of two on occasion.

I had a feeling that it drove Reza mad. She was used to having an inside scoop with her mother being headmistress. But even Alleva had limited knowledge of the events that night— even if she didn't realize the limitation of that knowledge in the first place.

"Yup," I said, the word drawn out as I popped the hard consonant, "too bad. Glad you're enjoying your stay with Six, though. I'm sure they're happy to have you."

I wasn't exactly sure if they were or not, and the smaller, pettier side of me was hoping like hell that they weren't. If Declan's gift was any sign, it seemed that she at least seemed to prefer my company to Reza's. I tried not to let that realization make me too smug.

"They are," she replied, tipping her drink back. Her usual confidence seemed tarnished somehow, though, and I glimpsed some rarely-seen insecurity peeking out behind her usually arrogant expression. "Doubt they'll show tonight though. This," she waved her bottle around the room, "isn't really their scene. Izzy slipped an invitation under the door this morning though, so I figured I'd at least check out your party as a representative of the group."

"How thoughtful," I said, biting back a much less grateful retort. "I'm sure your schedule is quite busy, so don't feel like you need to stick around if you have better things to do with your evening."

Her eyes dropped a bit at the corners as she surveyed the room. "Actually, I might stay for a bit, if that's okay?"

I opened my mouth, expecting to have to defend myself or end the conversation, but snapped my lips together so intensely that my jaw ached. She sounded almost sad, lost even maybe. And I recalled the tumultuous relationship she had with her mother, the way they engaged with each other during our sparring session over a month ago, and a wave of pity rushed over me.

Cyrus wasn't exactly warm and fuzzy when it came to parental material, but he was always encouraging and supportive. I had a suspicious feeling that Reza did not have that. And, despite what she wanted the world to see, it didn't seem like she was exactly having an easy time with Six either. Why else would she want to stay here, at a party for me?

"Sure, Reza," I said, taking another sip of my beer as I studied her. "You're welcome here for as long as you'd like."

Her eyes narrowed and I could almost feel her mood shift, the heavy wall erecting itself once again. "I don't know that like is really the word I'd use. But Atlas isn't home right now, and I don't think I can handle another night of staying in the cabin alone while Eli and Sharla have excessively noisy sex."

My stomach dropped, and it felt suddenly like an iron grip was closing itself around my chest. Eli and Sharla?

Thankfully, my face didn't give anything away, because Reza continued as if nothing changed. "I mean, I know she's here for now, but I'm sure it's only a matter of time before she shows up for another booty call tonight. And I'd rather not be there if she does." She paused, studying Sharla across the room. "Actually, maybe I can talk to her and see if they can just start meeting up over here. No sense in me being the only miserable one."

With that, she walked away, not so much as a goodbye or syllable from me, and made her way towards Sharla. Sharla, who was stunning enough to make a supermodel feel insecure. Sharla who was sweet, and warm, and funny. Sharla who was my friend.

I knew that there was nothing between me and Eli. Any start to that chemistry was battered away the night of our first kiss, and buried even further the night of the attack. But as much as I'd tried to ignore it, as much as I wanted to push the memory away, my thoughts flitted back to that night more often than I cared to admit. To the feel of his lips against mine, the way our skin came together and met, like we were two halves of a whole. To the way we discussed our childhood traumas and fears.

It was silly, really. I knew that Eli was a huge flirt, that he was well known for running through women in casual relationship after casual relationship. I was mostly just disgusted with myself for thinking that maybe we could have had something a bit different than that, a bit more somehow.

And Sharla was amazing. I couldn't compete with her, and I didn't want to. If she was with Eli, I would lockdown whichever annoying parts of my brain seemed determined to linger on him beyond the way it lingered on any other protector here.

I watched Sharla's smooth skin wrinkle in shock as Reza spoke to her, her eyebrows reaching so high up her forehead, it looked like they were legitimately trying to float off her face. I bit back a grin as the shock slowly melted away into a steely determination. I couldn't read lips very well, but judging by the ferocity in Sharla's crystalline eyes and the way Reza's nostrils flared in indignation, I had a feeling that Sharla wasn't taking any crap. She'd do what she wanted, when she wanted, at no behest to Reza's whims and fancies.

Suddenly, the room felt impossibly crowded and warm, so I finished my beer, grabbed a fresh one, and made my way out of the cabin for some fresh air. Winding my way around the perimeter of the house, I made it to the back. Ten had a nice bench set up that looked out into the woods, so I sat down, staring into the weave of trees so thick that I couldn't see a clear path. The night was chillier than it had been in a while, so I soaked in the breeze with relish, letting it soothe whatever heat and jealousy was coursing through my veins.

I tried mirroring Mavis's smooth move with the bottle top, but I was neither wearing a belt, nor did I know how to properly use something as leverage to lift up the ridged, sharp corners. I let out a puff of frustration and sunk back into the bench, my head tilted to the sky. We weren't quite as secluded out here on campus as Cy, Ro, and I had been back home, but the area was private enough that the stars were still bright. I watched them for a few moments, my hand growing cold from holding onto the bottle, as I drew invisible lines in my mind connecting different patterns in the sky. It was always a fun pastime for me and Ro when we were kids. A wave of nostalgia washed over me, and I found myself missing those days something fierce.

Why did we never realize how perfect a moment was until we were no longer living in it? It seemed like such a twisted irony.

"Need help with that?" A smooth, deep voice asked, and I shot up instantly, annoyed with myself that I hadn't heard anyone walk up.

"Jer," I said, letting out an exhale of relief, mixed with a chuckle at my own paranoia. "You scared me."

He grinned in that lopsided way that boys grinned, the kind that made them instantly more attractive and devious. "Not exactly the effect I was hoping to have on you." He sat down, his left knee brushing against my right, as he pulled out a keychain with a bottle opener and placed it against the lip of my beer until a gentle hiss filled the air around us. "What're you doing out here on your own? Not enjoying your party?"

I took a swig of my beer, studying Jer. There was an earnestness in the way that he looked at me sometimes, kind and open in a way that made me wish he set my blood on fire or made my heart skip a beat in the way that Eli and Wade had. Maybe if I let myself, I could grow to feel that way about him; maybe my body could learn to explode in goose bumps when his hand brushed against mine, or maybe my breath could learn to hitch whenever our eyes met across the room.

Movies and books made romance seem like it was all passion or nothing, but maybe it didn't really work like that. Maybe it had to grow organically, give you time to really sink into it.

"I just needed a breather," I said, smiling up at him, convincing myself suddenly that I would try my best to give him the chance he so desperately seemed to want. I wasn't entirely sure why he seemed so drawn to me, but Izzy seemed to encourage the match on occasion, and everyone in Ten seemed to trust Jer.

As if reading the decision on my face, he leaned in closer, until his eyes were close enough to see my own reflection in them. "I'm glad you're on our team, Max. I know it's been a chaotic start to your career at The Guild, but I think if you give us a chance, you'll find we might surprise you, and not in a bad way."

The way he leaned into the word 'we' made it abundantly clear that it wasn't Ten he was talking about. A questioning look crossed his face as he studied me.

I didn't pull away.

That was all the answer he needed, before he closed the

DREAMS OF HELL

distance between us, his lips crashing down on mine. His skin was so much warmer than mine, that I almost welcomed the contact if only because it scared away my chill. Tentatively, he licked the seam of my mouth until I opened in response, my tongue tasting nothing but the alcohol on his.

It wasn't a bad kiss. All things considered, it was probably perfectly adequate.

But no matter how much I wanted it to, kissing Jer didn't chase away whatever crippling chill had spread through my body the night that Wade died. I didn't emerge from the experience, the closeness, feeling suddenly alive again, or stop thinking about the way hearing that Eli and Sharla were together created a weird crack through my lungs, or a puncture.

After a moment, I pulled away, hoping that Jer had come to the same conclusion, that this probably wasn't going to be anything more than a friendship. Judging by the shy grin pulling up his lips, it wouldn't be that simple, that neat.

A soft rustle of leaves sounded in the distance, and I jumped away from Jer, like I was embarrassed or ashamed to be caught like this.

When I studied the area around us, as far as my eyes could see through the trees which, admittedly, wasn't far, I found nothing and no one in the distance.

Shaking the anxiety off, I took a long pull of the cold liquid, dreading having to do this right now. "I'm sorry, Jer," I said, the words falling monotonously to my ears. "I don't think this is a good idea. And I don't think that I'm in a place where I can give you anything but my friendship right now." I forced myself to look up at him, to have the courage to watch the disappointment lingering in his eyes—so out of place in comparison to what was there just a moment ago. "Is that—is that okay with you?"

His shock evaporated away until a kind, understanding expression took hold of his features. Squeezing my shoulders gently, he nodded. "Absolutely. Let's chalk tonight up to too much booze and getting carried away with the celebration—sound like a plan?"

I exhaled in relief and gave him a hug in gratitude. "That sounds like an excellent plan."

I didn't think this would make things weird in the house, but if it did, there was no use worrying about it until we crossed that bridge.

"Should we head back inside?" He asked, his breath coming out in visible puffs of air. "Kind of chilly, no?"

Pulling away, I realized that there was one more face I wanted to see on my birthday. Izzy's party was great, but I didn't want to return to it until I was restored with the proper energy for socializing. "You go ahead, I'm going to stay out here just a while longer, then I'll join you."

7
MAX

It was sort of ironic that one of the things I looked forward to most these days, one of the things that was almost always sure to put a smile on my face, was going to visit a giant creature from hell.

But Ralph had that way about him, and if anything could help me sort through the annoying emotions running through my body, it was a solo walk through the woods that culminated in being run over by a giant ball of fur and slobber.

I'd found my way to his spot so many times that it was almost second nature to venture through the dark to the small, abandoned cabin that we tried so hard to make habitable. It was honestly probably the only place on campus I was able to find without getting completely turned around or lost. Which, to be clear, was only because on the few occasions when I did just that, Ralph made sure to find me and guide me back home. Dogs were great.

When I reached the small hut, with slivers of moonlight shining through the branches and casting just enough light to highlight each step, I felt my anxiety about Eli and Jer and everything else just melt away.

Until it was right back again.

I swept the random brambles and leaves aside so that I could push open the door. Just like before, Ralph was nowhere to be seen. The stillness of the night sent shivers down my spine—it was quiet out here, too quiet. Something told me that this time Ralph wasn't off playing moonlight fetch with Declan.

The calm that stole over my body during my walk immediately dissipated when I heard what sounded like a scream far off in the distance. Did one of the students wander this far out? Had they encountered Ralph?

We'd been so lucky so far; even with all of the extra evening patrols, no one knew that he was out here. For as giant and bumbling as he was, he sure as hell knew how to keep out of the way and stay invisible when he needed to.

But what if all of that was about to change? Images of Ralph being carted back into the dim research lab flashed in my mind like a bad horror film. Getting him out of there, saving him from scheduled death, was the only good thing that came from that night. The thought of us ending back where we started sent a tremor of revulsion through my body. It couldn't have all been for nothing. The price was already far too high, impossibly high.

Running towards a screaming person by myself, in the middle of the woods, at night, was probably a bad idea. In fact, I was certain it was a bad idea.

But I took off chasing the noise anyway, charging through the trees like Tarzan, on the off chance that I could reach whoever it was that needed help, or help disguise Ralph in case my fears proved true.

There was something exhilarating about the way the wind whipped over my face, making my hair fly around me in an odd dance. I wasn't exactly in the best shoes for running, since I was dressed for a party, but I still relished the feel of my flats digging into the dried dirt, each step releasing a fresh plume of moss and something distinctly earthy. The woods here didn't exactly smell like the woods back home, but there was still something comforting in the familiarity. Comforting enough, that my heart pounded with excitement and determination, rather than fear.

I ran for what felt like hours, even though it couldn't have been more than a minute or two until I started to slow down. The screams had disappeared entirely, and I had no idea where to go from here. I fished around in my back pocket, looking for my phone so that I could call Ro or Cyrus and let them know that someone was out here and needed help.

My stomach dropped when I realized that my pocket was flat, my phone likely forgotten on my bed or on a random kitchen surface back in the cabin. I had one of my new daggers on me at least.

After the night of Wade's death, I never left my room without having something sharp and pointy on my person. I refused to be caught surrounded by baddies again, with no way of protecting myself or those I cared about. I'd already paid far too steep of a price for that lesson.

Unsheathing it from the holster, I gripped the handle—not too tight, but hard enough that I felt the comforting and familiar weight in my fingers. My head was still slightly fuzzy from the alcohol, but the fresh air was doing wonders for keeping me alert and aware.

Behind me, a twig snapped, so I whipped my arm up, ready to strike as I spun around.

"Jesus, Bentley, watch where you're swinging that thing," Atlas said as he lifted his palms into the air in case he needed to stop the blade's trajectory into his stomach.

I pulled up short, before the blade pierced his skin. Half in shock, I dropped the dagger into the brush, trying to slow the heavy beating of my heart. "Atlas? What are you doing out here?"

His eyes narrowed slightly, the moon hitting him at just the right angle to make me question how I'd ever been unaware of the wolf living below the surface. It was so obvious, that strange yellow glow. Everything about him was too intense, too ethereal, for him to be nothing more than a protector.

"Same as you, I assume," his words were slow, like he was afraid I would run away and go charging into the distance. "Heard someone scream. I also saw you tearing off through the trees like you were in pursuit of something, so I followed. You shouldn't have come out here by yourself. You keep doing that. It doesn't end well."

How long had he been following me? I clenched my jaw, realizing how oblivious I'd been. I didn't even clock his position until he was an arm's reach away from me. What if he had been someone else—a different monster with more malicious intent?

"I don't know where the screams originated," I said slowly, my lips moving mechanically like they were stuck together. It was so rare, being alone with Atlas, and I wasn't sure how to carry a conversation with him now that I knew the truth. I wasn't afraid of him, not necessarily, but I was acutely aware of the fact that he was much more than the intimidating protector I'd met a couple months ago, that he was a predator now as well.

"We're close to where the sound originated, but I haven't heard anything since. Probably best to go back and find Seamus or Cyrus and get a team out here searching. I don't want to risk going further, only for there to be an ambush out here," he said, his eyes focusing on the path ahead of us.

He didn't say the word 'again,' but I heard it in his tone regardless. Was whatever caused that terrified shriek the same creature responsible for Wade's death? Part of me wondered if the only reason he suggested going back was because I was out here too. Atlas didn't really strike me as the type who typically waited for backup. Then again, that night likely changed him as much as it changed me, probably even more so.

"How much farther into the woods can you see?" I asked, overtaken with curiosity.

He took a step back, like he was surprised by the question, and scratched roughly at the scruff lining his jaw. "Farther than you. My senses are considerably sharper than they were before, if that's what you mean."

Before he was a werewolf.

"And you don't see a sign of a struggle?" I squinted into the darkness, as if I could somehow trace the details he could envision so vividly. But all I saw were ambiguous shadows and small bursts of movement from random rodents hunting for their dinner.

The thought of hunting had my anxiety hiking again. I spun back around to Atlas, suddenly no longer worried about my safety around him, but desperate for his help. "Ralph. He wasn't near the hut. It's why I was out here in the first place. You don't think he's been attacked?"

"Ralph?" he asked, his brows bent in question. "Your hellhound?" An uncharacteristic grin crossed the bottom half of his face, and I hated the way it made my heart rate jump. "Not a chance. You are aware of the fact that that creature finished off a wolf and a vampire on his own, right? And, if given the time, probably could've taken on more than that? Whatever's out here has more reason to be afraid of...Ralph than he of them."

That eased some of my tension, and I rolled my head from side-to-side, loosening up my muscles. "Do you think someone saw him? That they ran into a giant hellhound and screamed? Because no one knows he's out here besides Six and—"

He took a rushed step towards me, wrapping his hand around my mouth and spinning me around so that my back was pressed flush against his chest. My heart beat so quickly, that I was certain he could feel it too. The sound of my blood rushing was broken up by his soft whispers, the breath of each word warming the shell of my ear.

"Don't move. I heard something." He took a few deep, steady breaths, as I tried desperately to hear anything but the sound of silence around us. "And there's blood. There's a lot of blood."

I opened my mouth to respond, only to realize that his hand was still covering it, so I had to settle for a low, whispered grunt.

As if suddenly coming to the same realization, he slowly pulled his fingers away from my lips, centimeter by centimeter.

"We need to get out of here," he said, his words so low I had to strain to hear them.

"Shouldn't we make sure that no one is hurt?" I hated feeling like we were abandoning someone. It seemed like the opposite thing protectors should be doing at a time like this. It was just a few short weeks ago that I was out here, surrounded by monsters, hoping that someone might come to my rescue.

Then again, someone did come to my rescue, and that night ended worse than I thought it could.

"We will, but they'll stand a better chance if we go and get backup."

No longer willing to listen to my arguments, he gripped my hand in his and took off running back towards the main campus at a speed I struggled to keep up with.

Developing heightened powers at nineteen was definitely all legend then, and not at all my lived reality. But I clung to him in desperation and kept up as best as I could, shadowing each of his steps as soon as his foot lifted to take another one.

It seemed like we made it back in a fraction of the time it took me to land on the spot he'd found me in the first place, but when we finally wound through the cabins, my ears were ringing with adrenaline.

Standing outside of Ten's cabin, Atlas fished out a phone from his back pocket and nodded his head towards the door. "You should get inside. I'll take care of this."

Before I had a chance to argue and tell him exactly what I thought of that plan—as if I could just go back to a party after the events of the last ten minutes, or without knowing for certain that Ralph was okay—a blond curtain fell across my face.

"Thank god you're okay," Reza said, her face buried into Atlas's neck. "My mother just called. All recruits are going into lockdown."

He let her slide down his body like a pole, until she took a step back from him and noticed me. The concern in her eyes melted instantly into a hatred that surpassed anything she'd directed at me before.

When I followed her gaze, I realized that Atlas was still holding my hand in his, latched on with a grip that was simultaneously unwavering and gentle. Expecting him to drop my hand at her glare, I started to pull away, only to feel his resistance.

"Do they know what's happened?" Atlas asked, the muscles in his back flexing with tension.

The cabin in front of us was much quieter than when I'd left the party, but somehow much more tense. I couldn't see anyone in the windows, other than Ro's chiseled glare from upstairs in his bedroom. The ice in his eyes told me all that I needed to know—I was going to be in a world of shit for leaving without telling anyone.

I had a feeling that most of the other guests who didn't belong to Ten were back home already, locked in their rooms waiting for further instructions.

With what looked like great effort, Reza pulled her attention from our entwined hands, back to Atlas. "It's Lucy, she's in the infirmary—" she ran a shaky hand through her blond hair, like she was stalling long enough for her nerves to calm.

I waited with bated breath. I didn't know Lucy well, she was a year or two younger than me, but on the few occasions when we'd talked, she seemed warm and kind. Had she run into Ralph?

"Is she okay?" I asked, losing my patience while Reza collected her thoughts. I needed to know if it was Ralph. I needed her to confirm for me that it wasn't.

Her sharp blue eyes narrowed in my direction. "No, she's not alright," she spat out, as if it was my fault.

My gut clenched, hoping with every fiber of my being that it wasn't, that I wasn't responsible for another person having a close call on Guild Headquarters.

"Reza," Atlas said, trying to refocus her attention on him, rather than on her frustration with me.

"She's been bitten. She made it back, but Amus and Savannah—"

My head spun, and I tried once again to pull away from Atlas, my brain trying to siphon through the thoughts whirling through my mind, but he only tightened his grip.

"What happened to Amus and Savannah?" My voice was hollow, and for a moment, I didn't recognize it as my own. "And bitten by what?"

"Amus is dead," Reza bit out, her eyes glazing over with tears. I didn't know him well either, but he was at my party earlier in the night, and I knew that Reza was close with him. "Lucy isn't sure about Savannah. She was down when Lucy got away. She left them to run and get help and medical attention. My mother and Seamus—they're collecting a group to go looking for them now."

My body stilled, and I felt Atlas still along with me. I was suddenly aware of every inch of his skin touching mine. He'd been out there, had shown up at the very spot where I stopped tracing the screams. Instead of going further into the woods to find them, he'd encouraged me to leave, to head back to campus, almost like he knew what awaited us if we walked any further.

I thought back to Michael, the way that Atlas pulled him from me into the alley, the way that he showed up in the middle of town and fought with Jer, the way he was suddenly so quiet and somber now.

"Reza," I said, sure I knew the answer to the question before it even left my lips. "What bit Lucy?"

"What the hell do you think?" she snapped, as she took a step towards me like she wanted to shake me and send me as far away from her as possible. "A fucking werewolf. There was a wolf on campus grounds. Maybe there still is. It's why we're on lockdown."

I felt the blood rush to my head, the sound of my pounding heart and a faint whistle the only things that I could hear. This time, when I pulled my hand away from Atlas, he let me.

Not waiting for another second, I took off towards the main

cluster of buildings, confident I'd find someone on my way—if not Cyrus, then Seamus or Alleva.

Declan was wrong. We were all wrong.

Atlas was dangerous.

And now he'd killed one, maybe two of the students on campus. Whether he meant to or not was another story, but one thing was clear: he was not in control of his wolf and if I didn't do something about it, who knew how many more lives would be lost.

8
DECLAN

"Her phone was in between two couch cushions," Izzy said as she tossed me the device. Her eyes were wide with worry as she paced from one end of the room to the other. "I mean, where the hell would she have gone? It was her own birthday party." She took a deep breath and let out a heavy exhale. "Maybe it overwhelmed her. I shouldn't have invited so many people. I wasn't thinking."

I looked down at the phone, the screen blaring with dozens of missed calls from Izzy, Ro, Me, Cyrus. Why would she have left this behind? Who the hell in this day and age left the house without a phone? Especially when the woods near you were occasionally full of terrifying monsters?

"Do you think she went to see Ralph?" Izzy asked, stopping briefly to look at me, before starting on her path again. "I'm sure that's where she went. Maybe we should go look for her before the rest of Ten gets back. I don't want her to get into trouble, so it would be better for us to find her, rather than Cyrus or Alleva, you know? Unless she's in trouble, in which case, we should go now—"

My stomach dropped at the thought of her out there, potentially grappling with a werewolf. Alone. Again. Why was this girl so fucking difficult to keep track of? A soft cracking noise drew my attention down.

Shit. Her screen had started to fracture from my grip.

Finally still, Izzy looked at me, then closed the distance between us, her hand resting gently on my own. "It's okay, you know. You're allowed to care about her. Contrary to popular belief, giving a shit is not a bad thing, and it's not the end of the world. If anything, it's a reason to live in it."

Her gray, stormcloud eyes were glassy with emotion, but I broke eye contact as soon as I recognized affection. "I care about all of the recruits, Izzy. It's my job."

Her mouth tightened as she let out a sigh, rolling her eyes. "Sure, Dec." Her hand dropped mine when she turned to greet Ro.

He was just as worried as she was, his normally kind face suddenly older and filled with fear. He ran his hands through his hair, his fingers poised over his phone as he made call after call, Max's phone buzzing softly in my hand. "Any word?"

I held up her phone as answer enough, my own stomach dropping at the way his face sank in recognition.

Low voices drew him to the window, and I watched as he visibly exhaled with relief, his forehead pressing against the window as if it would hold him up, would carry his burden for a little while. "Oh thank god. She's down there with Atlas. And Reza."

My head went dizzy with relief, so I set her phone down on Ro's bed and walked downstairs. By the time I closed the door to the cabin though, Max was taking off at a blistering pace, and Atlas was ashen and tight-jawed, with Reza's arm wrapped around his.

"Where does she think she's going?" I asked, doing my best to ignore Reza's simpering.

"Who knows," she responded, letting go of Atlas long

enough to cross her arms in front of her chest. "Apparently, as usual, the princess doesn't think the rules apply to her. Hopefully my mother finds her and rectifies those beliefs real quick. We're all getting tired of her acting like she owns this place."

"Reza," I said, trying to keep my annoyance from bleeding into the word. "I need to talk to Atlas for a minute, so can you wait inside until one of us is ready to walk you back home?"

She opened her mouth to argue, but snapped it shut at one look from Atlas. "Fine, but don't be long."

Generally, that sort of pompous comment from an underling would infuriate me, but the defeated look in Atlas's eyes had me hopping over that emotion and moving right to concerned. As soon as the door shut, I walked a few feet into the woods, Atlas following reluctantly, just in case anyone was lingering nearby and overheard us.

"Where did Max go, and why did you let her go off by herself?"

"She's heading towards the main campus, so she won't run into any real trouble. And she's under the impression that I'm the one picking off kids in the woods. I suspect that she's doing the right thing and telling someone with authority what I am." His tone was flat, and there was a heated self-hatred in his eyes, in the tightness of his jaw.

I clenched my teeth, ready to shake some sense back into him. "It wasn't you, why didn't you stop her? Or at least try to reason with her?"

Max had listened to me once before. She desperately wanted to believe that Atlas wasn't a threat to anyone living here, she just needed some reassurance, someone to help her with the burden. It was a heavy load to carry when you felt like you had to carry it all by yourself.

His only answer was a shrug, which meant he was too far in the hole of self-pity to fight his way back up.

"Damn it Atlas, if I end up losing you too because of this, I'm going to kill you—do you understand me? This whole sacrificing yourself out of some misguided heroism is not brave or helpful. It's selfish. Eli, me—we need you here. And Max does too."

The haze over his expression started to melt a bit, so that the usually stubborn asshole was visible just below the surface.

"Now," I added, taking the rare opportunity to boss him around, "don't wolf out or anything, but get out there, use your senses, and see if you can find the real wolf before it kills anyone else."

Without another word, I took off running, my feet sinking into each step, desperate to reach Max before she did anything reckless like get my friend killed.

Campus was absolute chaos, with every field team out searching for the wolf—or wolves—and ushering the remaining students and recruits to safety. Judging by the number still out and about, Max wasn't the only one who didn't keep track of her phone.

I could feel every breath I took, every achingly fast beat of my heart as I scanned the jumble of bodies trying to find her. It would take less than a minute for her to bring Atlas's freedom and position crumbling down to pieces, and all of us along with it.

Finally, I spotted the infuriatingly familiar head of long dark hair. She was standing outside of the door, waiting for Alleva and Seamus to finish their hurried, tense conversation a few feet away.

I exhaled in relief, hoping like hell that they were discussing the attack and not whatever information Max just divulged.

Gripping her arm, I swung her around, her large eyes round with worry and glazed with unshed tears. My initial plan to tell her off for betraying Atlas and her word melted immediately. She wasn't very good at hiding her emotions, probably because she'd never really needed to, living in such isolation. The map of her thoughts was clear.

She was afraid, sad, and, more than anything, she was buried under layers of guilt so deep that it made Atlas's pity party look laughable by comparison.

"It wasn't him, Max, okay—" I ran my hands up and down her arms from shoulder to elbow, trying to breathe some sense back into her. "I need you to understand that it wasn't him. Did you—" I took a deep breath, scared to ask the question I was terrified to get an answer to. "Did you tell them the truth? Did you tell them about him?"

"Not yet, but Declan," she said, pulling at her hair like she was a frustrated cartoon character—and damn if it wasn't adorable—and looking from left to right like she was afraid of being overheard. "I was out there; I ran towards the girl when I heard her scream."

My nails dug into my palm as I realized how close she was, once again, to being mauled by one of these characters. Seriously, it was like she was trying to get herself killed. "What the hell were you doing out there and why the fuck would you go running towards danger?"

Her brows bent down defiantly. "I'm a protector. It's literally our job to run into dangerous situations, especially when someone needs help." She sighed, shaking her head as she disregarded whatever argument she wanted to continue with. "But that's not the point. He was out there too."

"Who?"

She let out a frustrated grunt, her eyes widening like they could convey her point without words. "Atlas." She paused, waiting for me to connect the dots, only continuing when my lips parted in surprise. "I turned around, right near where I'd heard the scream stop. And there he was, completely alone. What am I supposed to think?"

I forced air in and out of my lungs for a few moments, trying to collect my thoughts, trying to find another solution for the conclusions Max drew. The thought of Atlas—the kid I grew up with, the kid who saved me over and over again—killing someone just did not compute. I opened my mouth to tell her so, to tell her that there was no way on earth that the attack tonight was Atlas, but the words refused to come.

The corners of her mouth dipped down, her entire face sinking, like she was hoping I'd be able to convince her she was wrong, that I'd be able to come up with a suitable solution or reason for why he was there at the scene of the crime.

She nodded solemnly and took a deep breath like she was steeling herself for what she had to do. When she turned around, I reached out and grabbed her hand, wanting desperately to bring her back, to go find Atlas and clear this whole thing up.

"Please," I whispered, her back to me, as Seamus and Alleva finished their conversation. "There has to be—this can't have been him." The pain in my voice made me cringe, but I couldn't shove it down, couldn't disguise it like I usually did. So I swallowed my pride and begged. Willing, even, to let her see me vulnerable, just this once. "Max, please."

Max stiffened, and turned her head back to me, her eyes filled with so many things I couldn't decipher.

"Max?" Seamus asked, walking over towards us, Alleva keeping a few paces back. "Declan, you shouldn't have let her come over here, all recruits are to be in lockdown, it's too dangerous."

I couldn't speak, I was too terrified to hear Max's confession come spilling out of her mouth; I was too terrified of losing the only family that I had left.

"I just—" Max started, her voice shaky as she looked at Seamus and then back at me. "It wasn't Declan's fault, I came here on my own."

Seamus arched a brow, studying us both. "And why exactly did you come here at all, Max? Orders were to lockdown. A good protector knows to always obey orders."

Her shoulders slumped so heavily that I was tempted to stand in front of her, to shield her from Seamus's disappointed chastisement. She nodded, straightening her spine slightly. "You're right sir, I just—"

Shouts to our left came echoing as a cluster of people surrounded Mavis and Jer, each of them supporting one half of a body. If the dark hair and pale skin were anything to go by, it was Amus.

Bypassing Alleva, and earning a deep scowl for doing so, they made their way over to Seamus, the heavy head shake saying all they couldn't. Lucy was correct, Amus was dead.

"And Savannah?" Max asked, the timidness there just moments before, now nowhere to be seen. "Did you find her, is she—"

Eli came shuffling over, shoving his way through the growing crowd. Eli plopped a wolf head down on the ground, the deep brown fur so close to Atlas's wolf that my stomach plummeted.

Eli met my eyes, shaking his head minutely, as if to assure me that it wasn't. As soon as I realized that the wolf meant that Atlas was innocent, I filled with shame, revulsion spiraling through my gut at the realization that I'd doubted him, even if for only a moment.

"The wolf was dead when I got there," he said, "limbs in pieces. There was a second though."

"And the girl? Get on with it, son," Seamus prodded, his usual patience marled by the night's events.

Eli clenched his jaw, matching his father's stare. It was in these moments that their similarities became almost impossible to ignore—in the set of their jaws, in the way they radiated power.

"She was alive, but badly bitten," Eli shook his head, his eyes narrowing, like he was trying to make sense of what he saw. "But there was another wolf, a larger one. He grabbed her and took off. I tried, but I couldn't match its speed, until eventually I lost track of it altogether. They just, I don't know, disappeared."

Any relief I'd been feeling evaporated instantly. Another

breach of Guild boundaries by an unknown pack and they took another of our own.

Why?

My head was dizzy trying to come up with possibilities as Seamus ordered extra parties to pair up and search the woods before taking Eli to debrief the turn of events.

I looked down, only to realize that Max's hand was still gripped in mine.

9
MAX

Monday's classes were cancelled, so that the teams could meet to discuss the attack. I tried leaving once to find Ralph, but Jer and Mavis stopped me flat before I reached the landing.

Ro made me promise not to disappear again until Alleva and Seamus cleared the grounds. During our time in lockdown, we ran through theories and ultimately determined that Ralph was behind the death of the werewolf. I'd already seen him rip one hellbeast apart, so that wasn't too surprising, but I was still concerned that he'd been injured.

Declan sent me a text late into the evening letting me know that she'd swung by his doghouse, but there was no sign of him. As if she could read my increase in heart rate through the phone, she sent a follow-up clarifying that there was no sign of him having an injury either and that he definitely wasn't recaptured.

Still, when Tuesday morning came, I woke up extra early and went looking for him myself on the way to our sparring session.

Like Declan had said, there was no sign of him at the cabin and no evidence he'd been hunting at any of his usual spots. I wasn't really sure how or where to start looking for a hellhound who was already in a different realm than he was supposed to be.

And part of me was selfishly terrified that he'd up and left altogether, ready to return home for good after yet another evening of chaos.

I met Izzy and Ro outside of the gym, my body caked in sweat from running from site to site in hurried desperation. Usually Ro came with me on my runs, whether I wanted him to or not, but this morning he was fully preoccupied with Arnell.

For the fifth morning in a row.

My shoulder nudged into Ro's side. "Have a good morning?"

We both knew the answer. Arnell and Ro had been casually dating for a few weeks now and I was ecstatic about it. Ro hadn't been this happy in longer than I could remember, even if he tried to hide it from me out of some misguided sympathy for my own misery these days.

"Better than yours, anyway," Izzy added, flicking my ponytail. "You have raccoon bags under your eyes again."

My mouth tightened into a scowly grin, "Raccoons are adorable though, right?"

My dreams were steadily getting worse, and this morning I gave up on getting anymore shuteye around three in the morning. Instead, I reorganized my room and binged half a season of some trashy reality TV show.

It also didn't help that I was feeling extremely guilty for blaming the attacks the other night on Atlas. Even though I didn't let Seamus or Alleva in on his secret, the close call left me at a bitter edge all night. Not to mention the fact that while I wasn't close with Amus, his death hung heavy on my mind. This was the second time a protector had been picked off right on our own grounds.

It didn't escape my attention how close I'd been to the action both times. But Ro and Izzy made me promise to focus on more positive things, like hunting down the assholes who kept attacking us, so that was exactly what I intended to do.

At least externally, anyway. I wasn't great at editing my own thoughts or nightmares, as the last month had made abundantly clear. The fact of the matter was that watching Mavis and Jer carry Amus back, pushed Wade's death to the front of my mind—the images, sounds, and smells, even more inescapable than they usually were. I also couldn't help but feel angry that Amus would be mourned properly, returned to his people, while Wade was just—gone.

I wiped some sweat from my brow and pushed open the doors to the gym. We walked down the hall and I breathed a sigh of relief. These days, the gym was where I let myself forget the images that filtered through my mind from that night.

Here, I didn't see Wade or the vampires, or Atlas's werewolf form. It was just me, whoever I was sparring with, and enough exertion to run my muscles into spasms and fatigue.

It was bliss, in its own weird way. Probably wasn't the healthiest coping mechanism, but I wasn't going to question it.

And The Guild knew how to set the place up right. There were mats all over the place, high ceilings, and private rooms if you didn't want to spar with the larger groups. The basement held tons of workout equipment and more weapons than I knew how to use. They didn't spare expenses. I wasn't exactly sure how The Guild had so much money, since it wasn't like we charged humans for saving them, but it was clear that they had a ton of it, all the same.

Generally, people were already here, getting an early workout in or practicing some new maneuvers. But after the long and chaotic weekend, I expected people to take this week easy, maybe sleep in a bit. Especially since the teams were running around like mad, trying to secure the perimeter and identify any weak spots that allowed these breaches to keep happening. Losing protectors who worked in the field wasn't all that surprising or uncommon, but everyone was rattled by the fact that now, we were losing recruits. Teenagers.

As usual, I was wrong. There was a large crowd circling the center mat, which was significantly larger than any of the other sparring areas. A quick glance around the audience confirmed that nearly every member of my cohort, plus most of the team members I was familiar with, were present for our training session today.

"What's going on?" I asked, glancing first at Ro and then at Izzy.

Izzy's expression mirrored my own confusion, making it obvious she had no idea how to answer my question, but Ro was significantly taller than us so he could see over most of the crowd. His brows flattened into a scowl, so I pushed my way forward, weaving between bodies—which wasn't too difficult, most of the people were pushing back a little, like they didn't want to be too near the action.

Within thirty seconds, I was in the front row, my sweaty body pushed up against other equally sweaty bodies—a gross factor I tried not to think about too much. Being a protector was almost never glamorous, that much was for sure.

Atlas was standing in the center, a stern expression coloring his already stern features. He was dressed in his usual uniform of black sweatpants and a tight-fitting black t-shirt that didn't leave much to the imagination. His dark eyes that sometimes held a yellowish hue landed on me, but his expression didn't change. If anything, it hardened even more.

We hadn't spoken since the attack the other night, my accusations settling like concrete blocks between us.

"You have been fighting each other for months—in fact, most of you have been fighting each other for years," he said. His voice was soft, but everyone was so terrifyingly silent that I knew it carried throughout the gym. Atlas was a bit of an asshat, but he could command a presence like no one I'd met before. I couldn't look away from him right now if I tried using every ounce of my willpower.

Apparently now that Six was settled in again, he was picking right back up at being in charge of training.

Great. Here I was, getting used to Alleva's predictable intensity. Atlas only ever gave me whiplash.

He started pacing slightly, locking eyes with several of the protectors, none of whom I knew very well. I caught sight of Reza, watching her as she studied him like a hawk, clocking every movement he made with absolute precision. She might as well just pee on him and get it over with. Her territorial vibes were enough to bowl me over and I wasn't even the object of her scrutiny.

She could have him; I wasn't joining in on that pissing contest.

"But when you are out in the field, you won't be fighting other protectors," Atlas continued, stopping suddenly. His eyes landed on me again, this time lingering for longer than I was comfortable with. "You'll be facing the very things we train you to hunt. Vampires, werewolves...these creatures move differently than we do, fight differently."

My jaw clenched at that. We both knew that Atlas moved and fought *exactly* like one of those creatures. I felt a slight pressure against my fingers and turned to my right. Jer was standing next to me, his posture rigid.

I hadn't seen much of him since our kiss, but something seemed a bit off. His normally open expression was guarded, his jaw tightened into a harsh angle.

He was worried about something, concerned. I let him wrap his fingers around mine, no sweat off my back. I was happy to provide support to a friend if I could, especially when it was as simple as a small gesture.

I turned back to Atlas and saw a muscle in his temple pulsing slightly, his dark eyes glaring daggers at Jer. Those two had some serious baggage, but I was sure as hell staying out of it. I had enough issues in my life without devoting energy to worrying about all of the weird bro rivalries riddling the walls of The Guild. Because, damn, there were a lot.

"It's tradition, those of you entering your apprenticeship year, to give you the opportunity to face the very creatures you will be expected to hunt," Atlas said, his words crisp, emotionless. "Recent events have demonstrated that this tradition is more important than ever before."

I saw bodies part behind Atlas as Eli and Declan made their ways through, ushering a couple of tied-up people with them.

Declan shoved her prisoner into the center of the ring, a few feet from Atlas. It was a girl—at least she looked like a girl—with long red, ratty hair, and deep emerald eyes; eyes just a shade lighter than her captor's. The color flashed yellow briefly—a breath of familiarity skating down my spine. I knew instantly what she was.

A wolf.

Her small, heart-shaped face was stretched in fear, as her eyes darted around the room, like she was desperate for a helping hand she knew wouldn't come.

I didn't pay her much attention though, because when I glanced towards Eli, I found him shoving a man with white-blond hair. He dropped the creature to his knees, and a pair of familiar eyes locked onto mine. His left eye was a dark brown, so dark it almost looked black, like it swallowed the pupil whole. His right was a golden color, mottled with streaks of yellow and brown.

Darius.

The left side of his mouth quirked up a touch, and my own lips burned as I remembered the last time I'd spoken to him. He'd stolen a kiss before running off into the forest with Ralph, only to be captured again by Atlas and the rest of his team. It was the night that Wade died.

I hadn't allowed myself to think of him much since that night, but he was like an impossible force, pushing back through my thoughts whenever I thought I'd blocked him off completely.

"Hello little protector," he said, voice taunting as he tilted his head sideways, studying me from head to toe, like I was the one usually found behind glass. "Long time no see."

My heart was beating so hard at the sight of him, that I was sure others could hear it. I could feel multiple sets of eyes on me, as the crowd tried to decipher what Darius meant and who he was talking to.

My body was drawn to him in a way that I hadn't let myself think about since that night. I had to physically tighten my muscles to keep from going to him, to unravel his restraints and send him back to wherever he'd come from down in the lab. Out of sight out of mind, though I doubted it would be that simple.

I was certain though that whatever he was doing here—it wasn't good.

I looked back up at Atlas and found him studying me as I watched Darius. His face darkened as he watched, unable to hide his disgust. Atlas had witnessed the kiss, though he never confronted me about it—something I was deeply thankful for. I didn't kiss Darius back exactly, but I also didn't shove him away.

If anyone else found out, I'd be in deep shit. That wasn't the sort of reputation a protector could come back from.

Cyrus and Seamus were already beyond pissed at me for letting him out in the first place. If I had been anyone else, I would've been imprisoned or kicked out of The Guild. But they were all covering for me—a realization that sent shame coursing like molten lava down my body.

I turned to Jer and found him studying Darius with a look of recognition and concern. Jer's father was high up in the research labs, so it wasn't surprising that Jer was familiar with most of the occupants down there.

Concern though? That was unexpected.

"These are two of the creatures from the research labs," Eli said, his voice echoing louder than Atlas's and filled with a bored amusement—a contradiction only Eli seemed able to pull off. "You'll be fighting them today."

Blood hummed through my veins, and I tried desperately not to think about fighting Darius. I wasn't ready to confront whatever weird thrall he held me under.

"You'll be fighting two protectors to one creature," Declan said, eyeing Darius and the girl with disgust. "If you make it through three minutes working together, without a broken limb or our intervention, you've passed the test. If you don't do that, you'll be going through another year of training before you can formally join a team. It's not exactly time that we can afford, but we also can't chance having you out in the field if your inexperience will put everyone on your team at risk."

A rush of inhaled breaths filled the gym. The stakes were high. We were all eager to get out there, especially since joining a team meant more freedom and privileges.

But that eagerness was off the charts now, since creatures from the hell realm seemed to be replicating like wildfire, and we were the only ones standing between them and the humans they survived on and murdered.

"If you manage to kill the creature, however," Atlas said, his eyes flashing to me, brow arching in clear challenge, "you and your partner will get to choose the team you join at the end of the year. This is the only time you will be given direct power to choose your future path. You'll be given one weapon, so select wisely and pair up. There are different strengths and weaknesses between vampires and werewolves. You've studied them thoroughly, now choose your fate."

Ominous. If anyone else uttered that phrase, it would sound like a cheesy line from a video game; but Atlas's delivery just drilled in the importance of our decision.

I rolled my neck, trying to distract myself from my traitorous body. I was trained to kill vampires and werewolves. So why did the idea of killing Darius fill me with a prickly dread?

He was evil. I knew that. Except...well, maybe he wasn't? I wasn't entirely sure, not the way that I had been before meeting him. The dude was a clusterfuck of confusion and every time I encountered him, I was left annoyed and wanting to break something. That had to mean evil. Evil. Yeah, I was going with that. I forced my brain to focus on the fact that he killed a protector right in front of me—drained him dry like his life meant nothing. And if he hadn't been recaptured by

Six, there'd probably be a trail of bodies following him by now.

I would focus on that. I would *not* let myself think about how he helped me save Ralph's life. That was just a mutually beneficial trade for both of us.

Jer squeezed my hand, harder than he probably meant to. "Go with the wolf, Max. That vamp—he's stronger than he looks and he's been in captivity so long that he's not totally there, if you get what I mean." Without another word, he walked away, heading for the doors.

I watched as he left the gym, suppressing my desire to go with him. I didn't want to do this. Between Darius and Atlas, my feelings about monsters were impossible to dissect.

But Jer? What was his deal here? Protectors loved this shit, so why wasn't he staying to watch the big show? Glancing around at the crowd, it seemed like the room was practically vibrating with anticipation. Jer's expression had been filled with a solemn dread.

"You're my partner," Ro said, walking towards me looking all stern and bossy in that way only older brothers knew how to pull off. There was no ask in his tone, and I found myself scanning the room for Izzy. "Izzy is going to partner with someone else, I already told her I'm with you."

I nodded, too nervous about the exercise to fight Ro on this. Ever since the first vamp attack a few months ago, he'd been extremely protective. But after that night in the woods? His brotherly instincts had become downright suffocating.

I couldn't blame him though, not really. If the situation had been reversed, and he'd been the one experiencing one too many close calls with death, I'd be attached to him like a leech too.

"And I want us to take on the wolf," he said, running a hand through his light blond hair. For someone who was a bossy badass, he looked a lot like the typical guy-next-door trope. The soft edges mixed with hard always gave me pause—there was so much going on in his head. Not for the first time, I wished for the ability to peek inside, to smooth the bubbles of concern that would show up in a forehead crease here, a heavy sigh there.

"We go for the vampire," I said, turning away from him to select my weapons. I was short at five-foot-four, so I never bothered with the swords. They were too bulky and cumbersome. And as much as I admired the people who used them, all dance and grace and precision, I knew they would never suit me.

I was one hundred percent all about the daggers. Grabbing two, I strapped them into a thigh holster and walked back towards the main ring, writing our names underneath the list of recruits signing up for the vampire.

I breathed out a sigh of relief, when I saw that most people opted to go for the werewolf. I wasn't sure if it was because she was smaller and female, or the fact that Darius had a bit of a feral gleam in his eyes, like he was actually looking forward to fighting us all.

Whatever it was, I scolded myself for being pleased that she would have to fight off more protectors than Darius. It looked like he mostly had the bigger guys and the ones who felt they had something to prove. I was unsurprised to find Reza on his list—she wanted free reign to pick Team Six, so I knew she'd be going for a kill shot. And with the dynamic between her and Alleva, I knew that she wanted to make a splash, prove her value in a big way. Killing a vampire was her ticket in.

I watched as the first two boys took on Darius. One of them was Theo, Izzy's older brother who she barely tolerated, and the other was a guy I hadn't officially met yet.

My head started to get fuzzy until I realized I was holding my breath. I unclenched my fists, and glanced at Atlas, unsurprised to see him studying me as he leaned casually against the wall, like this was nothing but a lazy, typical afternoon and not a blood-hungry battle.

Theo opted for a sword, which meant he was aiming to decapitate. Generally speaking, swords were too bulky for protectors to do fieldwork with, so this was pure hubris on his part. His partner had a set of daggers, like me, and his footwork was a lot more impressive. I made a mental note to tap him for a sparring match later on.

They danced around Darius, so that one of them was on either side of him at all times. Darius watched, his eyes shining with amusement, like a lion waiting to spring on a couple of mice. In a flash, too fast for any of Six to prevent, he moved briefly to the side, grabbing Theo and wrapping his hands around either side of his neck.

"No!" I screamed, unable to keep it in. Theo was a douche, no doubt about it, but he was Izzy's brother and if he died, she'd be devastated.

Shockingly, Darius stilled, shoving Theo away instead of snapping his neck. I let go of my breath, relief trickling through my body.

Atlas and Declan glanced at each other, communicating in silence, their faces expressionless.

Atlas took a step forward, and looked down with disgust at Theo. "One minute, you're done. The vamp could have broken your neck."

"You've got to be fucking kidding me," Theo yelled, face burning red with anger and shame. "I had him, I was just spreading out the fun."

"You're done," Eli said, nodding his head for Theo to get off the mat, the threat in his eyes clear as day. "Greg, if you want you can find another partner and go again later today. I recommend choosing based on competence, not friendship."

Theo stormed out, slamming the door closed as he disappeared.

"He's going to be insufferable to be around now," Izzy said, sliding up next to us. "Serves him right for being so cocky though. Maybe another few months of training will knock some humility into him." She caught my questioning stare and shook her head. "They say that you have to go through another year before joining a team formally, but they almost never make you do more than six months. Especially now, with the rush order on all of us as it is. They don't have the womanpower to wait that long for us to get out into the field. I'm taking on the werewolf with Will."

I'd met Will a few times, and he seemed nice enough. A bit shy, but he kept to himself and got his work done, which was a win in my book. He was also stacked with muscle, and surprisingly quick on his feet, so I knew he'd be a good partner for Izzy.

"Just between us girls," Izzy said, winking at me and Ro, "I think he has a bit of a crush." She shrugged, a grin creeping up her face. "Which speaks to his impeccable taste, of course."

"Max, Rowan, you're next," Eli called, avoiding eye contact as he gestured for us to come forward.

"Good luck," Izzy said, her hand closing around my wrist until she had my full attention. "Don't let your guard down, no matter what. There's something off about that one."

"Let's just make this quick. I'm going to go for a decapitation and hopefully we'll be done within the minute. Then, we can angle ourselves for joining Ten officially," Ro said, whispering in my ear.

My body broke out in chills as we walked across the platform. I met Darius's teasing eyes and swallowed thickly as we took our starting positions.

"Always a delight to see you again, little protector."

10
MAX

I pulled a dagger from my holster, my fingers suddenly feeling like rubber as I stared Darius down. He was easily a foot taller than me and looked a little worse for wear since the last time I'd seen him. My stomach dipped as I considered what they must be doing to him down there. The research unit ran a ridiculous number of tests on Ralph when he was locked up. And I imagined they were doubling down on Darius now that he'd escaped once already. It was probably a twisted form of punishment.

Ro looked in my direction, taking in my stiff posture, and the sweat breaking out on my forehead. The concern on his face was palpable, and he was probably afraid I was freezing up again. And, I was, just not for the reasons that he probably thought that I was.

I'd always meant to fill Ro and Izzy in on what happened that night with Darius, but every time I tried, the words dried up and died on my tongue. I didn't know how to explain to them why I trusted Darius in the first place, because I still didn't understand it myself.

Before Ro could initiate his attack, I went running towards Darius, swiping the edge of my blade against his cheek. A slim line of blood emerged, and I felt sick to my stomach that I was the cause. And even more disgusted because I knew that I wasn't supposed to feel guilt for this; that killing vampires would be part of my daily job soon enough.

Darius grinned, recentering his focus on me, not concerned at all by the small slice. If anything, he seemed excited by it. He licked his lip and stalked closer.

I wasn't afraid of him though, which scared me more than anything else. He was a vampire, a stone-cold killer. It was my job, my whole purpose, to hate him.

So why didn't I?

My feet dug into the soft mat as Darius pounced. Suddenly, in a single blink, he was pinning me down to the ground beneath him. I squirmed as his unusual eyes came to meet my own. He was so close, and I was suddenly aware of all of the points of our bodies that were touching. A blush heated my skin as Darius chuckled, his breath blowing against the shell of my ear. My entire body shivered at the sensation, and I forced myself to concentrate on the task at hand.

My body wasn't supposed to react like this when a monster had me in such a vulnerable position. I should be afraid, should be using my adrenaline to get out of this very precarious position and turn the fight to my favor.

In my peripheral, I saw Ro lifting his axe, trying to assess how he could strike at Darius without hurting me. At the same time, I saw Eli, Declan, and Atlas all tensed and ready to interfere.

It was now or never. I released the daggers in my hand, dropping them at my side. Then I stared deeply into Darius's eyes. "Please," I whispered, so quietly almost no sound left my lips, "you have to work with me."

Curiosity flashed in his eyes and I used the moment to twist my hips, flipping us over so that I was on top now. The maneuver would never have worked if Darius hadn't allowed it to, hadn't helped it along.

He was trusting me. Positioning both of my hands on either side of his head, I used all of my strength to snap his spine, watching as the whisper of a grin left Darius's face, until all that was left was an alarmingly blank stare—different only in color from the blank stare that haunted me in so many of my nightmares.

Cheers broke out through the room, and I heard Izzy chanting about how her best friend was a badass as I climbed off Darius, doing my best to swallow any concern that might have leaked through my walls.

I could feel Ro's questioning look eating through my skin, but I avoided looking back at him. The smart thing would be to decapitate Darius now, while he's down for the count unable to react. But I couldn't do it, and I couldn't let Ro do it either. I just had to hope that no one else would take the opportunity.

Ro was the one person I couldn't lie to, and I didn't think he was ready to hear the truth.

Hell, I wasn't ready to hear the truth, wasn't ready to admit that I wasn't okay with Darius dying. Losing Wade had changed everything, and I wasn't ready to lose anyone else, even if it included a snarky, infuriating vampire. And I was far too uncomfortable with that realization to examine it any further, let alone speak it out loud.

"She didn't kill him though," Reza said, her arms crossed over her chest as she curled her lip. "So it's not a true win."

She was right. Vampires couldn't be killed by a broken neck. Darius would be knocked unconscious for a few hours, but he'd survive, waking up in his reinforced cell with a gnarly headache, nothing more. But it was better than if Ro got a solid hit on him. I couldn't risk the chance of Ro killing him.

And I also wasn't willing to trust Ro's life in Darius's hands. I didn't think Darius would kill me—probably not, anyway—but I wasn't so sure about how he'd handle Ro if he came swinging in with his axe.

"A big part of our job is bringing monsters back to Headquarters," I said, desperately trying to quell the shake in my voice as I turned towards Reza. "Alive. A lot of times, that's the more difficult thing to accomplish."

My fists clenched as I desperately hoped that the room would buy that line. It was the one chance I had; the one chance Darius had.

"It's a pass," Atlas said, stepping up and nudging Darius with his foot. "Not a win. The rest of you will take on the wolf. The vampire is going to be incapacitated for the rest of the session today." He turned in my direction, coldly examining me as I looked away from Darius's lifeless body.

I let out the breath I didn't realize I was holding, squirming under Atlas's scrutiny. Without another word, I left the mat, walking over to Izzy. I limply let her hug me congratulations and listened halfheartedly to her play-by-play descriptions as everyone fought the female wolf.

Ro walked over and stood behind me. I could feel all of his silent questions lapping at the back of my neck, but I focused all of my attention on ignoring him. Instead, I cheered lazily when Izzy cheered, booed when she booed, and otherwise stood in silence, my thoughts swimming through my head as the room spun around me.

What the hell was I doing? And why was I so fucking confused all of the time? It was one thing to protect Atlas. He was a protector, at least partially anyway. He'd been raised with our morals, at any rate. So I could vaguely convince myself that even though he occasionally turned into a werewolf, he wasn't a completely awful dude.

But Darius? He was one hundred percent vampire. And more than that, I witnessed him murder a protector. The only reason he even helped me rescue Ralph in the first place was because I unlocked his cell and helped him escape right along with my hellhound. It was a temporary, risky, thoughtless alliance. An alliance that was supposed to be broken as soon as the terms were met.

And now what? Would Atlas, Eli, and Declan know that I snapped his neck as a way to save him from Ro? Did Ro know? My breathing started to feel erratic, like my lungs couldn't fill enough or couldn't fill quickly enough. What would Cyrus say? I was already in some serious shit with Seamus and Cyrus because of the breakout to begin with. And now I was throwing spars and fucking up real missions.

Izzy's hand gripped my wrist, jarring me back to the moment. I was silently thankful for her fingernails as they dug into my skin, it helped ground me, give me something other than my thoughts to focus on. I breathed in slowly, the scent of plastic mats and sweaty bodies filling my nostrils. I heard...nothing.

And then the room broke out in a loud wave of cheers.

"Shit," Izzy said next to me, her head shaking back and forth. "She's going to be insufferable after this. More insufferable anyway."

Confused, I glanced up at the mats. Reza was standing triumphantly, her smooth skin sticky with sweat as she swept stray pieces of hair against her scalp. Her perfectly white teeth were stretched into a wide smile filled with pride. My eyes traveled lower, until I saw the reason for all of the excitement.

In her left hand, Reza was gripping the werewolf girl's head by the hair, her fingers entangled in the red locks. The body lay forgotten several feet away.

She won.

Reza's bright blue eyes scoured the crowd until they landed on Atlas. If possible, her smile grew even bigger. We all knew which team she would be claiming as her reward.

"I'm sorry, Max," Izzy said as she sifted through her pile of workout clothes. She held up a pair of black leggings, examining them for holes, before she tossed them into her bag.

"Seriously, it's absolute shit, and if I could sneak you in with me, I would."

"Don't even think about it," Ro said, his tone drier than usual. He walked into Izzy's bedroom without either of us knowing. Turbulent blue eyes met mine and I broke contact first. "She shouldn't be going. Cyrus is right, a few more weeks will be good for her before she gets back out on the field. That last mission was too much, too soon. You'll be back out there in no time, just not yet."

I clenched my jaw so tightly that I half expected to crack a tooth. Izzy and Ro were getting ready to leave for another mission with Ten. They'd be gone for a few days.

But I wasn't going with them. I was more or less on protector timeout, all thanks to Ro.

"What did you say to him?" I stood up, my fists balled at my sides. It wasn't often that Ro and I didn't see eye-to-eye on something. And more than staying behind, it killed me that he'd gone behind my back. That he was the reason I would be left alone in this cabin for who knew how long.

Was this just about the mission? Or was this about how I handled the fight with Darius?

Ro let out a frustrated sigh before settling some of his weight on Izzy's desk. "The truth, Max. You almost got yourself killed during the last mission. I don't know where you were, but you weren't there with us. And then the other day? With that vampire? You went off book and jumped him without even working with me." He ran a hand through his blond hair, mussing it up in multiple directions. I watched as it all fell back down, perfectly in place. "I couldn't find an in—couldn't swipe at the vamp without risking your neck too."

I exhaled, relieved that his issue was my lack of teamwork and not that I left Darius alive. It helped soothe some of the ache of his betrayal, if not all of it.

I shrugged, narrowing my eyes at him. "And your suggestion

for me to get better is to keep me here, indefinitely? How exactly am I supposed to get any practice that way, Ro?"

He shook his head, and I watched as he and Izzy shared a private glance with each other.

I narrowed my eyes at her and pushed away a few feet until I felt the cool glass of the window against my back. "You agree with him on this? On my staying behind? Are you kidding me?"

A look of horror crossed her face as she stepped towards me, but the venom in my eyes had her stopping short.

"No, Max! Jesus, I mean not exactly. But you have to admit that you've been so withdrawn ever since things went down with Wade. And your dreams? Every night—it's like your brain won't give you a single moment of peace, of rest. I mean, we're just worried about you." She nibbled on her bottom lip as she looked at Ro for some help.

"We're worried about you, Max," Ro echoed, stepping over to the door and shutting it softly. "We're ride or die, you know that. But you've had too many close calls the last few months. Too many times that you almost d—" he cut off, and sat back on Izzy's bed, like he could no longer bear his own weight. "This, keeping you here—right now, it's how we have your back."

"We want you to be safe," Izzy said, and this time when she reached for my hand, I let her. "Do we want you out there with us? Hell yeah." A wry grin crossed her face. "But we have a lifetime for that. We need you to be safe before you get back out there. And that means you need some time. You need to process things before you jump back in. They always prepare us for the physical aspects of being a protector, but it comes with a lot of mental trauma too. And that's just as important to work through. In a lot of ways, probably even more important."

I knew that they were right, that I completely fucked up on our last mission.

But Atlas, Declan, and Eli were there that night Wade died, and they were out doing field work like nothing happened. Hell,

Wade was Atlas's brother, so I knew he was going through way more emotional and mental distress than I was.

And then there was Ro. He was there for part of the night too, had been there when we were surrounded. It was because of him that I was even alive—he was responsible for finding the other guys and bringing them to me. Why did that experience make Ro stronger when all it did for me was open up a gulf of guilt, anger, and a whirlwind of nightmares?

"Cyrus isn't mad, Max," Ro said, "he knows why you did what you did. Now, he just wants you to focus on healing properly, rather than rushing you out there before you're ready and getting yourself killed."

I let out a breath and felt relief sliding into my belly. Cy and I hadn't spoken too much since my birthday—while the anger and distrust from the days that led up to Wade's death were slowly slipping away, it wasn't completely gone. We were both too stubborn, both too sure that the other was wrong. But hearing that Cyrus wasn't angry with me, that the damage to our relationship since moving here wasn't irreparable filled me with warmth. My fingers toyed with the locket at my throat; it had become a source of comfort over the last few days, a reminder of what mattered most.

I nodded once before squeezing Izzy's hand and collapsing onto Ro for one of his rare but impossibly soothing hugs.

"You promise?" I whispered, so softly I wasn't sure he'd heard.

"I do."

I turned back to look at Izzy. "And you promise you'll both be safe and watch each other's backs? And that you'll bring me back a really cool souvenir?"

A giant smile split her face. "Abso-fucking-lutely, girl."

With a running start, she jumped onto her bed, collapsing onto us both. And we all laughed, an impossible tangle of limbs.

After helping Izzy finish packing, the three of us cuddled up on the couch, watching Buffy reruns until we couldn't keep our eyes open for another moment longer.

※

WHEN I WOKE UP, MY BACK WAS LYING ON WHAT FELT LIKE A harsh slab of concrete. I shivered, inching closer to the source of heat on my right. My eyes peeled open, and I stared at a stone wall that seemed to go on forever. Letting out a short breath, I closed my eyes again.

I knew where I was. I'd dreamt of this place most nights. I knew that if I turned around, I'd find Wade next to me, body contorted in pain as a filmy sheen covered his usually smooth, brown skin. It was the image that haunted me through most of my days—Wade in pain, isolated and alone in some creepy gothic cell.

Except, I normally viewed the scene from above, like an awkward voyeur. I swept my finger along the smooth bumps of the cold wall, temporarily transfixed by how real this place suddenly felt.

Was it normal to feel in dreams? A soft breath skated across my neck and my eyes popped open again. I could feel my heart hammering, like it was desperately trying to escape my ribcage.

Wade.

I turned around, slowly, expecting to be confronted by the image of him I saw in my sleep—torn and bloody, body contorted and thrashing in pain, lost in an eternal, terrible slumber.

Instead, I saw what I didn't think I'd ever see again for as long as I lived.

Piercing blue eyes, somehow simultaneously warm and filled with ice.

An involuntary gasp left my lips and I watched, perfectly still, as Wade's gaze dropped to my mouth. His skin was still clammy, the sheets below him cloaked in sweat, but he was...awake.

"Wade?" I whispered, unsure of where we were or who might hear. A ridiculous thought really, since this was a dream.

Dark brows furrowed and he lifted himself up slightly, bending at the elbow. "Max?" He scanned the room. It was nothing more than a circular holding cell, with no windows in sight. Other than the small cot we were both lying on, the room was empty. "Where are we? What happened?" His voice was jagged from lack of use, and he looked around the room searching. "Do you have any water?"

I shook my head, my lips trembling at the sight of him. In all of my dreams, Wade was never alive. I never got this version of him. Instead, my brain played reruns of his death, of his neck snapping over and over, or of his tormented agony in this room.

Never alive, never aware of me here with him.

"You—you're al-alive," I said, choking on a sob. I threw my arms around him, burying my face against the warm skin of his neck, breathing him in like he was air, like I'd been suffocating for weeks.

I knew it was a dream, but I was so grateful to be with him here, like this.

Strong arms wrapped around me, squeezing hard enough to bruise. Soft lips pressed into the curve of my neck and my stomach fluttered at his closeness. Close as he was, he was still somehow not close enough.

"Where are we?" he asked, pulling back just enough to study my face, his hand moving to my cheek. "Are you hurt? Are you okay?"

I nodded, eyes filling up with tears at the warmth in his eyes. He was here, in my arms.

But something was different. There was an edge to his features that wasn't there before, a darkness that seemed to shadow him. An unusual energy crawled up my limbs, pulsating under my skin.

"What's wrong?" His lips bent down in concern and his hands fell down along my sides, like he was looking for breaks or scrapes, assessing me for injuries with a hurried precision.

My heartbeat picked up at his touch and I was suddenly aware that I was dressed in nothing but one of Ro's long T-shirts, baggy with wear. Chills broke out along my legs, as his fingers trailed lower and lower, reaching my bare skin.

I sucked in a sharp breath as his pale blue eyes suddenly darkened to indigo.

"Max," he said, gripping my hips with his strong fingers. His hold was hard enough to bruise. "Where are we? Something doesn't feel right, what's—"

I shook my head again, buying time for my lips and voice to find a way to work again.

"I, I don't know," I finally stuttered out. "You're always here, it's always this room."

He looked confused and for the first time since waking up, he turned away from me, studying the dark cell.

"Always here? I've never been here before." He sat up abruptly, and when his touch left me, I felt the grief of his death all over again. I felt...drained. "The vampire. What happened? Did they take us?"

How did you tell someone they were dead? That you were dreaming them up and that while it felt so real and so *right*, the moment would fade like a memory at dawn? Would it be bad to just linger here, with him, for a few long moments? To pretend that he was alive and just a boy, and I was just a girl having a fun and flirty dream?

But this didn't feel like a regular dream, this didn't feel like a fantasy.

"Wade," I sucked in a steadying breath, placing my hand over his. "That night, the night with the vampire and werewolves. Y-you died." I blurted the sentence out so quickly that I knew it would take him a second to unravel the words.

His lips pulled up in a smirk, but they slowly pulled down

again, his eyes clouding over with confusion. "I don't feel very dead, Max."

He didn't feel very dead to me either. I studied our hands, fingers intertwined, so that if my hand wasn't completely dwarfed by his, I'd find it hard to tell where his hand ended and mine began. But the longer that I stared, it seemed like his skin was getting brighter somehow, like he was almost glowing. And mine—my skin seemed so dim in comparison, so dull and lifeless.

"You don't feel very dead to me, either," I whispered, blinking back the tears threatening to bubble over my lash line. "But this is a dream. Almost every night since you died, I dream of you here, in this room, tangled up in these sheets, thrashing about in the wildest pain."

He pulled my hand up to his chest, pressing it against his heartbeat. It was hard, strong. Alive.

"I've had lucid dreams before, but they don't feel like this, Max. Is it just me? Do you not feel the heat of my skin?" He moved his palm against my cheek. "The cool air?" He swept my tangled hair to the side, exposing my neck. His breath prickled against my skin and I sucked in a breath. "And I'm not tangled up in sheets right now, thrashing about in pain. I feel—" he furrowed his brows, like he was trying to parse something out. "Hungry? Weak?" He shook his head. "But I don't feel dead. And neither do you."

"I—" I cut off my words and fell into his stare. The color was so much more chaotic than it had ever been when he was alive—a whirling mass of blues, light and dark, married together, at war with each other.

"I can feel you," he said, his face inching towards mine, his lips a breath away from my own. "I can—" he pulled back abruptly, his face marled with uncertainty and a crippling fear. "You should go."

"I—what? Go? Why?"

He pushed off the bed and stood, dressed in nothing but a

pair of black sweatpants. He turned away from me and I noticed a tattoo spiraling over his shoulder and across the side of chest. I didn't recall him having one when he was alive. His hands rushed through his dark hair, now a mess with curls, like the dream Wade's hair had gone months without a cut.

"You need to leave, Max. Now."

I opened my mouth as he turned back to face me, his eyes almost glowing now, so intense I had to close my eyes.

When I opened them again, I felt a soft mattress against my side, a fluffy pillow below my neck. I sat up in bed—my bed—and looked around the room. I was awake, my body caked in so much sweat that Ro's old shirt was sticking to me like glue. My hands were shaking and I could feel my pulse racing as I turned to my bedside table, switching on the lamp. I cringed in pain as a soft, warm glow filled my room.

Kicking off my blankets, I pushed up from my bed and walked to my mirror. Slowly, I peeled my shirt away from my skin, lifting it up.

My chest squeezed when I looked down at my hips, at the outline of an emerging bruise.

The outline was subtle, but it was there: four long, perfectly shaped fingers.

11

ELI

I drained the bottom of my glass, relishing the burn as it slid down my throat. Four in the morning and I was still up—and not for a fun reason either. Insomnia was a bitch, and mine had been going haywire over the last few months.

I got off the couch and turned the porn on the television off. I wasn't really watching, but part of me hoped that Reza would walk downstairs for a glass of water, see it, and flip her shit. Maybe it'd be her last straw and she'd move out.

Declan and I were still fighting the idea of her joining our team permanently, and I half hated Atlas for not finding a loophole in the rule. A lot of the fight seemed to leave him when Wade died though, like it didn't matter one way or another whether Reza occupied a room or not. He wouldn't give a shit about anything either way.

And the worst part was, I couldn't completely blame Reza either. It wasn't surprising that someone would choose to join our team.

We kicked ass. I'd want to be with us, if I wasn't already.

But I don't think any of us really expected anyone to kill one of the beasts, and we sure as hell didn't expect Reza to. It was made even more frustrating when her win came minutes after Max had the opportunity to kill the vampire.

But no, she had to fucking stun him for a bit instead. It was infuriating, and I hated how conflicted the moment made me feel. On the one hand, she would've had the opportunity to pick our team; on the other, I'd have to pretend not to give a shit when she chose Ten instead.

I'd have to get used to it though. Odds were that she would wind up with Ten eventually, and Reza would be bound to Atlas by the end of the year.

Which left me having to make some serious decisions. I needed to figure out whether it was better to stick around on the team or go find my own. Chances were that if I stuck with Atlas and Dec, my dad wouldn't let me push off bonding with Reza much longer. I'd be out of excuses.

I bought some time when I handed over a few strands of Max's hair, and my saliva mixed with hers—a bargain that still made my skin feel slimy.

Not least of all, because I couldn't stop thinking about the way her lips felt against mine. That was definitely not what I was expecting when I took that particular approach to getting close to her. Whatever weird attraction I had to her amplified like wildfire that night.

Even more concerning was the fact that I felt bad about the whole thing. My father was my superior—he gave me an order, I followed it. No guilt, no question—just orders. But now, guilt was the only thing I could focus on. I was so ashamed about the whole thing that I couldn't even bring myself to mention it to Atlas or Dec—and the three of us never kept secrets from one another. But I knew that when I told them I couldn't brush the whole thing aside and forget about it—telling them meant owning my role in the consequences, whatever they may be. And their judgment—I just didn't want to add that to my plate right now.

Any time I asked for the results—desperate to get some

answers about the girl, like her fucking DNA could resolve whatever ache was left in the pit of my stomach—he shrugged me off and told me to mind my damn business and get back to my job. Like I was just some petulant child, and not the son he confided in in the middle of the night when he was acting like a man on a bridge.

Still, if he found anything worth worrying about, he didn't seem to be acting on it. He was still protecting her and hiding her role in the way things went down the night Wade died. If he'd found something truly alarming, something told me he'd have handed her over already.

I shuddered. If he did give her up, it would be because of me. I'd deal with that guilt later on, no use worrying about it now.

Most of his time now was spent locked in the cabin with Cyrus, planning and sending teams off to try and stem the flow of beasts pouring into our world.

Of course, when I was around, he was damn vocal about how much he hated the fact that Max broke the vampire out. Hell, we all did, but I think he was secretly impressed with how ballsy she was.

Nobody stood up to Cyrus or Seamus. Like, ever. But she did. That might be ignorance, since she didn't know much about either of their reputations, but I doubted she'd ever acted demurely around Cyrus, no matter what.

Every time I thought about having to bind to someone else, my stomach turned sour and I couldn't stop thinking about that night at the pond. I'd been meeting up with Sharla as often as possible lately, desperate to scratch the invisible itch, but it was like the itch was too far down, below the skin.

I walked to the kitchen, readjusting myself. It was annoying that one thought of Max could affect me as much as watching girl-on-girl on the big screen. Ridiculous, really. Part of me wanted Atlas to sweep us all up again on a series of missions, just to get away from Headquarters. Away from her. Maybe if I left her behind again, this time it'd stick.

I set my empty glass in the sink and stretched my neck, first to one side and then the other. I was exhausted, but I doubted I'd have much luck actually getting any solid sleep tonight. My foot came down on the first step of the stairs when a desperate pounding echoed around the room. I gripped the dagger at my hip, blinking back my buzz, and rushed to the door.

What the fuck did we have to deal with now? Was two seconds of fucking quiet too much to ask for?

"This better be damn important," I said, opening the door. "It's the middle of the fucking ni—"

"I think he's alive." Max was standing in front me, the dark circles under her eyes even heavier than they'd been all week. Her normally vibrant skin was clammy and pale, her body shaking with tremors. She was wearing what looked like a wet rag, the material cutting off at the top of her thighs, even though it was freezing out.

I curled my lip, annoyed with myself for finding her attractive even when she looked like she'd just gotten back from a month-long bender. "What?"

She rolled her eyes, and pushed inside, her small hand pressing into my chest hard enough for me to make some room for her to pass.

I followed her to the living room, stupefied. "Are you not even wearing shoes? Jesus, Max, I don't know what's going on with you lately, but you're starting to unravel. You need to get some help."

I'd intended for that to sound teasing, but I couldn't keep the concern from my voice.

"Eli, pay attention," she snapped, stopping short and turning around to face me. Her eyes were angry, and maybe even a little bit afraid.

I had to physically restrain myself from closing the distance between us and smoothing the worry lines between her eyes. The need to comfort her was suffocating.

I needed a drink.

I held my hands up in surrender, trying to usher her towards the couch. "Okay, okay, sit down. What's wrong, Max?"

"Wade," she said, her dark eyes looking down now, hiding behind long, unruly lashes. The individual strands were clumped together like she'd been crying, a thought that made me want to scoop her up and tuck her into my chest. Fucking annoying. "Wade's alive."

A dark laugh escaped me before I could stop it. My father told me she was having trouble processing what happened. That Cyrus had been concerned about her for weeks. She was taking the events of that night harder than we thought. And I could tell from the second I laid eyes on her that she wasn't sleeping.

But this? This was next level avoidance.

I sucked in a long breath, praying for patience as I sat down next to her. I studied her briefly, patting her awkwardly on the shoulder. "Max, I know that what you went through was difficult. But Wade is dead. And you need to accept that. This isn't healthy. Have you thought about talking to someone, professionally? The medical unit has some people on hand who do trauma work. You might benef—" I cut off when I caught sight of her face.

Fierce anger glared at me through her eyes, and I sat back as her nostrils flared. It was clear what was written on her face—she was not a timid animal to be tamed. She took a deep breath, like she was praying for the patience to deal with me.

"I'm not dense, Eli. I know what I saw when he died. I know how ridiculous this sounds. But you have to believe me. I think that Wade is alive. At least in some capacity. I know that doesn't make sense, that you probably think I'm losing it." Her eyes locked on mine, the anger slipping into a fierce determination. She was exhausted, drained as hell, but in that moment, I could see in her the same thing everyone saw in Cyrus—a fucking force not to be trifled with. "But I'm not."

I sat for a second, studying her, trying to figure out how best to handle this, whatever it was. Just as I was debating whether or not to wake up Declan or Atlas, two pairs of feet came rushing down the stairs in a stormcloud of steps.

"Eli what the hell," Declan said, her voice lilting more than usual with the dregs of sleep. It was the sort of accent that could have girls tossing their panties at her, and she didn't even use it to her advantage. Such a waste. "Thought we agreed you keep your girls in your room where things are soundpro—" she cut off as her eyes moved from me to the small figure next to me. She took a step closer but then stopped, like she was trying to restrain herself from something. "Max? What the hell are you doing here?"

"What's she doing here, Eli?" Atlas echoed, his glare moving to me, not even acknowledging her with a hello. I bit back a smirk, thinking how hard it must be for him to pretend like she didn't exist when she kept getting shoved under his nose all the time. I'd feel bad for the guy if I wasn't dealing with the same damn thing myself. "It's the middle of the fucking night."

Max sank back into the couch cushions, her steely determination faltering slightly as she played with her fingers in her lap. Her eyelids were so heavy that I was amazed she was able to keep her eyes open at all.

Part of me wondered if this was some sick prank. And I half hoped she'd keep her mouth shut, go back to her cabin, and fall asleep. Atlas had been through enough after Wade's death. He didn't need to rehash it all through whatever breakdown Max was in the middle of right now. He was on the edge as it was. We all were.

I watched as she sucked in a breath, straightened her posture, and locked her eyes on Atlas. "I think that Wade is alive."

Well, shit.

12
MAX

Declan and Atlas looked at me, varying expressions of annoyance and confusion on their faces. And then there was Eli. His eyes screamed pity and I half expected him to walk me straight over to the lab for a psych evaluation before the sun had a chance to rise. Honestly, maybe I needed one.

"Come again?" Declan asked, clearing her throat as her eyes danced between Eli and Atlas. They were all locked in some silent conversation, trying to decide how out of it I was.

And I might very well be, but that didn't mean that Wade wasn't also alive.

"Look, I know it's ridiculous, but I think he's alive." I stood between the three of them, redirecting their focus to me. And then I lifted up my shirt.

"What the hell, Max—"

"Jesus, put your clothes on—"

"Pink lace? Huh, lost that bet—"

Their reactions layered over each other until they all shut up. As if of one mind and body, they all took a step closer to me, eyes locked on the bruise that was more prominent now. Protectors didn't bruise easily. And I was thrown as hell by the whole thing already, since bruises took hours or days to appear in the first place. But this one? It was there the second I woke up.

I swallowed, suddenly aware that I had three people, one of whom I'd made out with, staring at me in my underwear. If this wasn't so important, I'd cut my losses, run home, and pretend this whole thing never happened. No boy had ever seen me in my underwear. Except for Ro, maybe, and that didn't count.

"Who did that?" Atlas asked, his voice so hushed and deep that it was almost a growl. He took a step closer to me, but then stepped back, like he changed his mind and needed more distance, not less. The yellow glow that crept up every once in a while was back in his brown eyes, flashing bright and alerting me to what lingered below the surface.

I sucked in a sharp breath as Eli swept a long finger along the markings, his skin touching mine in a decadent test, Declan and Atlas both grumbling in protest. I tried desperately to ignore the chills creeping along my flesh, hoping like hell that Eli didn't see the effect his touch had on me, as visible as it was.

"Someone has quite a grip," Eli said. "Either you're not as vanilla as the unrefined eye might guess, or we need to bash some heads in." His brow was arched in jest, but there was an anger in his eyes that I hadn't seen before, a small tremor as his finger pulled back from my body.

He was so close that I could feel his breath wash over me. Whiskey. I licked my lips and stepped away, heart hammering.

Declan was studying me, and I tried to ignore the fact that she was wearing nothing but a tight tank top and a pair of black underwear. "What does this have to do with Wade, Max?"

I took a breath, thankful for her question. My thoughts were starting to swim, and I needed to stay on track. I was too tired and my senses and reactions were blurring in a confusing muddle.

"I've been having dreams about Wade," I burst out. "Literally almost every single night since the night that he died."

Eli's hand dropped on my shoulder in what I guess was

supposed to be a comforting gesture. "That's normal, Max. You experienced a trauma. It's pretty common for your unconscious to—"

"Yeah, Max," Declan continued, shoving Eli's hand off of me, her eyes bugging out as if to tell him to back off. "Dreaming about someone doesn't mean that they're al—"

"Continue," Atlas said, one word shutting them both up. His features were hard, his eyes angry, but there was almost...hope there too, like he desperately wanted to believe me, but needed help getting there. "But upstairs, in the office. That room is soundproof, and I don't want to wake Reza." He turned and walked soundlessly up the stairs, Declan following.

"After you, beautiful," Eli said, his lips tilting in an echo of his usual grin, though it didn't reach his eyes.

I followed Declan and Atlas, trying not to bristle too much at the idea of Reza sleeping in my room as I passed it.

Well, not *my* room exactly. But the room that I stayed in.

Then again, maybe she was staying in Atlas's room? How was I to know? My stomach tightened at the thought of her wrapped up in his sheets, a feeling that frustrated me even more. I shook my head, shuffling the thoughts away. Reza wasn't important. Neither was hers or anyone else's love life.

Maybe I should've waited until morning to talk to them all. Barging into their cabin in the middle of the night felt intrusive and impulsive on a whole other level, and I wasn't exactly sure what I expected them to do about Wade being lodged somewhere in my dream world.

Now that I was wandering the halls of Six's cabin, the whole dream with Wade felt like a million miles away, like it wasn't real. I half expected to walk into this old room and find him there, just as he was the last time I was here. His presence lingered in the air, suffocating me every time I tried to take a breath.

Maybe I really was losing my grasp on reality.

Before I had a chance to chicken out, run back home, and lock myself in Ten's empty cabin, I was standing in the office. As far as offices went, it was pretty big. There were two wall-length desks and four chairs. But when Atlas, Eli, and Declan were hovering above me, tall and muscled and imposing...well, it felt more like a closet.

Moonlight bathed the room in a soft glow, and I latched onto it through the window, almost disappointed when Declan flipped the light switch.

"Alright Max," she said, her shoulder leaning against the locked door. "We're here. You have our ears. Speak."

Was it too late to run home? Something told me that it was. But standing here, under the scrutiny of three of the scariest protectors The Guild had to offer...I was half ready to cut my losses and try making a run for it anyway.

Whoever thought Cy was scary had never been under the combined scrutiny of the three standing before me.

I closed my eyes, my mind filling with the image of Wade, the fear and confusion wrapping around his features. The dream was starting to slip away, as dreams tended to do, and I couldn't remember every detail with as much precision as I would have hoped. My fingers pressed softly into my hip and I grinned at the pulse of pain.

It was real. Wade was alive...or something.

Clearing my throat, I opened my eyes and stared at Eli. Of the three of them, he was the least intimidating. There was always a glint of flirtation and mystery in his warm brown eyes, his dark hair always perfectly messy in that annoying way that only Hollywood actors seemed capable of achieving.

"Like I said," I started, lightly gripping my hip, holding onto the pain like a damn security blanket. I wasn't imagining things. I wasn't imagining things. I wasn't imagining things. "I've been having dreams about Wade." When Declan opened her mouth to interrupt, I held up a hand, not breaking my eye contact with Eli. "I know that dreaming about him after—after what happened is normal. This dream tonight though, was not.

"Every time that I dream about him, I either see the image

of the vampire snapping his neck over and over and over—" I paused, swallowing thickly. Eli tilted his head, expression soft, silently urging me to continue. "Or else he's in this weird cell. Like a medieval castle dungeon or something. And he's always been unconscious, just writhing in pain. Always in this constant agony." The sound of wood splintering filled the room and I turned to Atlas, catching the muscles in his arms as he squeezed the desk. He wasn't looking at me, but had his head bent over, dark hair tilted over his face, as he thought whatever thoughts he was thinking.

"And tonight was different?" Declan asked, moving to sit on the desk, just a few inches from where I was leaning. I tried to ignore the amount of her skin on display; tried not to trace the tattoo that crawled over her thigh and hip, disappearing under the hem of her shirt.

"No." I shook my head, annoyed with my distracted and disoriented thoughts, "I mean yes. Not different in that the room was the same. He was there. But different because I was there with him, not just watching over him as some amorphous dream camera. I was there." I paused, praying like hell that my cheeks weren't blushing with the heat that I felt. I'd been in bed with Wade. Woke up next to him, like we'd spent the night together, tangled limbs enshrined in the sheets. "And Wade was awake," I finished, leaving out the part about how I was wrapped in his blankets with him.

Atlas was still a certified statue, but Eli broke the silence. "Not to be indelicate," he said, head tilting as he studied me, "but so what?" He shrugged, swiping a lock of hair from his forehead. "You dreamt he was awake, that's still pretty normal, Max."

He wasn't wrong. And the details of the dream were slipping the longer I was awake.

"It wasn't normal," I said, shocked by the loud determination in my voice. "It wasn't. None of this has been normal." I lifted my shirt up a few inches again, no longer bothered by the embarrassment of being seen in my underwear. "These prints were left by

Wade. Everything in that dream felt real, present, in a way that dreams never do. The way he looked at me, he was terrified. Of himself. And told me to leave. I woke up, drenched in sweat, more exhausted than if I hadn't slept for days, and with a replica of his handprint etched out in blue and yellow bruises. That. Is. Not. Normal." I was seething and I closed my eyes, counting to ten as slowly as I could manage. Anger wasn't really my thing, and I wasn't used to this flood of emotion. I was just so fucking exhausted.

And so very confused. I wanted desperately for them to believe that Wade was alive, because then it would mean that I could give myself over to that reality—that I wouldn't be alone with these twisted thoughts and hopes. I wanted them to smile and laugh and celebrate, to tell me that this was a normal protector thing to go through that I just hadn't learned about yet —that yes, yes, this meant that Wade was alive and well and he would be back here with us all soon.

My back pressed against the desk and Declan slid over a chair, encouraging me to collapse into it. I obliged, the energy draining from my body not giving me another option. I stared at my feet, pressing my toes into the soft shag rug, a mixture of grays and black yarn burying my feet. My bed sounded so nice right now and my story sounded ridiculous even to me. And I was the one who'd experienced it. I didn't know how to make them believe it if I hardly did.

"Okay, not a normal dream," Eli said, the words calm and slow like he was speaking to a dangerous zoo animal. And, honestly, he wasn't far off. "But there's got to be an explanation. People don't just come back from the dead. Not even in our world."

A low chuckle pulled from my lips and I slowly drew my head up to stare at them. "Yeah, no shit, Sherlock."

Atlas peeled his head up and closed the distance between us. Dark brows bent in concern as he swept his thumb underneath my left eye. The contact of his skin against mine pulled my breath away. "You wake up more tired every time you dream of him."

It wasn't a question, but I nodded my head anyway, annoyingly aware of the way his rough skin pressed against my face. It would be bad to push my cheek into his palm, right? Still, it was tempting.

"Tonight, worse than other nights?"

I nodded again, transfixed by the thin golden swirls in his irises. They were almost invisible, if you didn't know to look for them. But I'd encountered his turbulence enough that recognizing the subtle hues was almost like a sixth sense now. It was the wolf, peering out at me, but in this moment, for once, I wasn't scared of him.

"Atlas, you don't really think," Declan said, slamming her mouth closed as she pinned her bright green eyes to my face. She shoved Atlas away without a word, grabbing my face in her hands, her skin much smoother than his. It wasn't a caress, exactly, but damn did it feel good to feel the weight of my head supported for just a moment.

Were face hugs a thing? They needed to be a thing.

"Um hello," Eli called from his spot near the door, waving his hands around in exasperation. "We aren't seriously entertaining this are we? Atlas, I know you want your brother back. We all do. But he's not a fucking dream zombie. This is ridiculous. We saw him die. Watched the life literally leave his body. With our own eyes. Protectors don't come back from neck breaks. It's not a thing we do. It would be cool if it was. Fucking awesome, really. But it's not."

Eli was right. I knew that. I'd watched that vampire snap Wade's neck like a twig. There was no doubt about it—a protector could not have survived that. But maybe Wade wasn't just a protector.

My shoulders straightened as I glanced at Atlas. "Was he like you? Is it possible that Wade was also turned into a wolf? Eli's right. But maybe Wade wasn't just a protector. Maybe he was —more."

"Him being a werewolf wouldn't explain the dreams, Max," Declan said, hands still on my face as she studied me, her eyes narrowed and shrewd. "But I do believe you. These are not normal dreams. You look like hell."

I let out a sigh, ignoring the last comment, my chest decompressing like one of those boxed mattresses. "You believe me," I echoed, feeling my lips pull up slightly in a grin. "Thank you."

Declan nodded, dropping her hands and taking a step back, like she suddenly realized how close she was standing.

"What happened after he died?" I asked, scrunching my face up as I tried to think back to that night. It wasn't something I generally allowed myself to do. The last thing I remembered was Wade dying, and then I was in a hospital bed. Maybe I'd missed something, a clue as to what was going on.

The three of them looked at each other, tension evident on all of their faces.

"You don't remember?" Declan's brow arched.

I shook my head.

"He was taken," Atlas said. Which I knew already, I just didn't know by who. Or why. Or how. It wasn't exactly standard demon practice to take dead bodies. "By a man."

"Vampire?" I ran my hand over the soft leather of the chair's arm, feeling lighter and happier, now that I knew I wasn't imagining things. They didn't know what was going on with me, but they at least as good as acknowledged that *something* was going on with me. For now, that was enough. It was everything.

"No," Atlas answered while the others just shook their heads. "Not a wolf either."

"He flashed," Eli said, running a hand roughly over the stubble on his cheek. He was usually freshly shaven, but this look fit well with his devil-may-care persona. I could hear the soft scratching sound from here. "One minute he was there. Then he was gone. I've never seen anything like it."

Flashed? Like full on teleported? Was that even a thing? Quickly, I tried cycling my thoughts through every book on the supernatural I'd read—through all of my classes since arriving at Guild Headquarters. Nothing. "What kind of creatures have that power?"

"We don't know," Eli said. "My father thinks we half imagined it. But that man, he called the other creatures off. We were outnumbered. Would have all died. There were so many—more than I've ever seen, more even than any single team has encountered on a mission. And they had us, if they wanted to take us all out, they could have. Instead, they scattered, and the man disappeared with Wade."

"Where would he have taken him?" My memory sparked as I mulled over their explanation of the night. I vaguely recalled a man: tall, dark hair, eyes so brown they were almost black. He reeked of power. Like I could almost smell it. There was something almost, I don't know, familiar about it?

"Hell," Atlas answered, the word sounding empty on his lips, hollow. I could see him trying to control the wolf, his eyes flashing gold every few moments. Would he change right here? In the middle of the office? Was he in control at all when he shifted?

"Then if he's alive, if there's even a chance, we need to get Wade back." I stood, ignoring my lightheadedness as blood rushed to my head.

"Easier said than done. No protector has ever found a way into hell," Eli said. He looked from Atlas to Declan, all jesting gone from his face. "And trust me, hundreds have tried. For as far back into history as we can remember. No one has done it."

"It's true," Declan added. "Protectors have done everything they can, tortured countless captive creatures, to try and find a way in. No one's succeeded in getting any information."

"I might know someone who can help," I said, a timid grin stretching across my face.

13

MAX

I woke up burritoed in a tangle of dark green sheets, a bright ray of sun bouncing off my face. The bed was comfortable, and it was the first time in ages that I'd slept without nightmares. The room was relatively neat, and very familiar. After Declan and the guys spent half an hour debating the very loose plan I suggested, I fell asleep slouching in the chair. Exhaustion hit me like a wave of bricks and I didn't even remember waking up and moving to a bed.

Breathing in, my cheeks warmed. I pressed my face into the pillow, trying to place the scent. I wasn't one of those girls who could pick out different competing layers of notes. All I could say was that it reminded me of a dark and cozy winter night and felt distinctly masculine. Sitting up, I stared around the room, surprised by how neat it was. Other than Wade's room, Eli's was the only one that I'd seen, and I was fairly certain that's where I was now. The dresser and small desk were made of a dark wood, and there were surprisingly few personal items.

Cyrus wasn't exactly a warm and fuzzy person; we never had many sentimental knick knacks or decorations filling our old place. So I guess I shouldn't be surprised that Seamus was the same, nor that he'd probably raised his son in the same vein.

Still, Eli was mischievous and fun enough that something about the place just felt off for him. Like it wasn't really *home*.

Where had he slept last night? I wasn't a light sleeper, but I definitely would have noticed if someone else slept next to me the whole night.

When I stood, a rush of cool air chilled my legs, reminding me that I was still wearing nothing but a baggy T-shirt. Last night, under the weird haze between waking and sleeping, it hadn't been a big deal, and clothing wasn't the first thing on my mind. But now, in the light of day, when I'd spent the night huddled up in Eli's bed, I was distinctly aware of the fact that I was uncomfortably close to naked. What were the odds that I could sneak down the stairs, out the door, and back into my cabin without the guys or anyone else seeing me?

Probably not great.

I briefly weighed the options and decided that while I was generally anti-snooping, in this case, I would go through a few drawers until I found a pair of sweatpants or shorts that I could borrow.

On the top of the dresser was a new toothbrush, still wrapped in plastic. I couldn't suppress the eye roll. Why was I not surprised that Eli would have a steady supply of fresh toiletries for his guests? Honestly, I was kind of shocked there wasn't a girl in his bed when I showed up last night.

Instantly, my mind filled with an image of Sharla—had she been curled up in these very blankets with Eli before she left for Ten's new mission? My breath hitched, so I refocused my energy on finding myself a new wardrobe before I had time to follow my thoughts down that very dangerous and annoying hole of feelings.

My hands gingerly slid down the wood of the dresser, a weird mixture of guilt and excitement creeping up my spine at the idea of familiarizing myself with Eli's room. It didn't exactly count in the way that mattered, but this was still my first time spending a night in a guy's bedroom. With just a moment of hesitation, I pulled open the first drawer.

And I immediately regretted it.

I wasn't standing in front of a mirror, but there was no doubt in my mind that my skin was bright red with embarrassment. While I didn't know what all of the silicone, metal, and rope items in the drawer were for, I was absolutely certain they had to do with Eli's more discreet...pursuits. My eyelids slammed closed as I shut the door, willing my brain to stop sending me heated images of Eli making use of this drawer, that coy grin on his face as he rifled through his toys.

Focus.

I moved to the next drawer, spotting neatly folded boxers and socks, and eventually made my way to a pile of fresh sweats. I grabbed the pair on top and slid them on, rolling the waist and leg bottoms several times so I could walk without tripping.

Chances that I looked absolutely ridiculous? Super fucking high. But whatever, I'd rather look like a plump blob of fabric than chance running into anyone with my underwear exposed. Again.

From my very brief stint as a Team Six resident, I knew where the bathroom was, so I made quick work of freshening up, excessively grateful to Eli for leaving a new toothbrush for me to use. My eyes traveled around the pale blue room, tastefully decorated, and landed on the mirror. My toothbrush nearly fell from my mouth when I saw the girl staring back at me. The dark circles that had taken up permanent residence on my face were still there, even though I finally had a restful few hours of sleep. But my skin looked so dull, my eyes practically lifeless, like there was a strange film dimming the usually vibrant brown. What the hell was happening to me? I hadn't even looked this bad when Reza beat the shit out of me.

Still, as terrible as I looked, my body felt buoyed, suddenly lighter. Wade was alive, and I wasn't the only person to believe it.

And we were going to find him, bring him home where he belonged.

I lifted my shirt up, studying my hips in the mirror. The markings that were there in the middle of the night were starting to disappear, thankfully, but there was just enough discoloration left to convince me I hadn't thought up the whole thing in the mystery of the night—when it was always somehow so much easier to be afraid, to believe unbelievable things.

A loud gurgle interrupted my thoughts, and I pressed a hand to my stomach. I was starving. Like next-level, eat-an-entire-cow kind of starving.

I wasn't sure what time it was, but hopefully the cafeteria was still serving breakfast. Or lunch? How long was I out? I didn't see a clock in Eli's room and I hadn't bothered grabbing my phone when I came scrambling into their cabin last night. I had a bad habit of forgetting that thing everywhere. I blamed the fact that I grew up without one.

I swung the door open, ready to check in with the guys and then scarf down some food, but instantly swallowed the smile creeping up my face.

"What the hell are you doing here?" Reza was standing in the hallway, dressed in a bright pink sports bra and leggings. She was coated in a sheen that made her look like a supermodel, so she must have just gotten back from a workout. I lowkey hated that she was one of those girls who somehow looked even more perfect after strenuous exercise.

When I was done working out, I looked like a swamp-monster-alien hybrid. The world just wasn't always fair.

"I er," I looked around the hallway, like the beige walls could somehow help me come up with a believable answer. It wasn't like I could announce to Reza that I had weird freaky dreams with Wade and that I was completely convinced he was somehow still alive in the hell realm after an unknown demon spirited him away with magical, invisible, fairy dust. We were trained to fight monsters at The Guild, sure, but we still had limits when it came to believability.

"Whose shirt is that?" She was studying me with a mask of disgust, and I noticed that I'd dripped toothpaste all down my front. Gross.

But also, if I was being honest with myself, totally on brand for me.

"Mine," I said, drawing the word out for a while, like she might get distracted by my awkwardness and stop asking questions.

"And those pants?" Her general attitude was haughty, but I'd gotten to know Reza enough to know that it covered a hefty dose of insecurity. She glanced briefly down the hall before meeting my stare again. There was a vulnerability and fear on her face that I hadn't seen before. "Did you sleep here? Who were you staying with last night?"

Right. She was afraid I was hooking up with Atlas, her basically bond-betrothed. Honestly, the level of anxiety eking out of her was starting to make me uncomfortable. Those two needed to have a discussion, and soon. I had enough drama in my life without adding theirs into the mix.

"I had to talk to Declan and the guys about something and ended up crashing in Eli's room." I shrugged, trying unsuccessfully to remove the toothpaste stain from my shirt. "Alone. It was late and I didn't want to go back to the cabin. My whole team is on a mission without me, so they took pity and let me crash here."

All in a second, the vulnerability slipped from her features, and she was back to being the Reza I was more comfortable with. Her dark blue eyes studied me, a small grin turning up her lips. "Right. Forgot they ditched you. Maybe next mission you won't completely choke."

Her mother was the headmistress of the academy portion of The Guild, so I wasn't shocked she had that intel. I doubted Ro,

Izzy, or Cyrus had ratted on me. But still, what a low fucking blow.

I shrugged, letting the insult roll off of me. Better the enemy you know. This Reza was easier for me to blow off, and I had way more important things to worry about today.

"Yup, maybe," I said, brushing past her and moving towards the stairs. "Only time will tell."

I took the stairs at a light jog and made my way to the front door. I heard Reza's door slam and cringed, hoping I wouldn't have to deal with her again today. The girl's moods were a damn pendulum. My fingers started to turn the knob when Declan's loud voice stopped me in my tracks.

"Breakfast is ready if you want some, Max." She walked out from behind the counter, dressed in a pair of dark jeans and a long-sleeved green shirt that almost perfectly matched her eyes. Her black wavy hair was mussed up like she'd just gotten back from a beach vacation, luxuriously spilling over her shoulder. And I instantly felt like a slob in comparison.

"Uh," I looked down at my toothpaste stain and overly baggy pants. "What time is it?"

Declan grinned and her teeth slid over her bottom lip. I tried to look away, but my eyes were glued to her mouth like a damn magnet. She didn't even look real sometimes, it was like she just walked right out of a movie or something.

"Almost three in the afternoon. Cafeteria stopped serving lunch, but I figured you'd need sustenance. And breakfast is about the only meal I know how to make taste...not terrible."

Wow. I must've slept for ages. Apparently my body was trying to tell me something. The scent of bacon and sausage filled the room as I moved closer to her, not even trying to pretend that the grease wasn't singing to me from the door. "Breakfast is perfect."

Her eyes narrowed as they scanned me from head to toe, humor dancing in her expression when she caught sight of the stain and my outfit. "I see you borrowed a pair of Eli's sweats."

Right, last time she'd seen me, I was wandering around in my underwear like a sleepwalker.

Then again, so was she.

"Yeah. Think he'll mind if I borrow them for a bit?"

A low chuckle filled the room. Declan laughed—hell, smiled—so rarely that I was legitimately shocked it came from her. "Unlikely. They look better on you anyway."

"Yeah," Eli added, coming up behind me and making me jump. "You're like an adorable elf drowning in fabric. Just my type," he added with a wink.

Declan grabbed a plate and piled it with pancakes, sausage, bacon, and eggs. And then she did a beautiful thing: she set it down in front of me.

Without any further encouragement, I went to town, stuffing my face with more ferocity than I devoted to my sparring matches. "This—this is incredible," I mumbled, not even ashamed to be talking with my mouth full.

I looked up, finding Declan and Eli completely focused on me.

"Damn," Eli said, shaking his head with mirth. "You sure know how to eat. Pretty sure that was a platter we were all supposed to share."

I swallowed the lump of syrupy goodness, embarrassment coloring my features. "Er, my bad."

Declan chuckled—again, what a sound—before turning back to the fridge. "Don't worry, we have enough for me to make another batch. From the way you attacked that plate, I have a feeling you need the energy surge more than we do right now."

"Speaking of which," Eli said, eyes still focused on me as I continued stuffing my face. "Our plan is going to be a bit more complicated than we thought. Because the creep already managed to escape once—thanks to you, of course—and because only Seamus and Cyrus know the real reason he did, the vamp has been locked up with extra protocols."

Oops, my bad. In all of the chaos, I almost forgot that I

helped Darius escape not that long ago. Breaking him out was going to be an even bigger pain in the ass now.

Declan's face darkened, like a stormcloud was suddenly on top of her. She turned back to the stove, frying in silence for a moment.

"I still don't see why we have to break him out," she suddenly snapped. "It's not like he's actually going to be helpful. Protectors have been trying to get information out of these creatures for ages. And even if we had to use one of them, I don't see why it has to be that specific one. Any of them would do."

Eli stared at Declan's back, her body so tense I could see every muscle stiffen beneath her shirt. A look of pity flashed across Eli's face before he shook his head, grabbed a fork, and stabbed at the one piece of sausage left on my plate.

I tried not to growl. Tried.

"Darius will help," I said, ignoring Eli's taunting grin as I turned back towards Declan. And I knew he would too. Darius enjoyed being in control and playing games far too much to not take us up on the offer—freedom in exchange for sneaking us into the hell realm. He would do it, I was sure of it. It was our only chance.

"How can you be so sure?" Eli asked.

"And why do you know his name?" Declan didn't even try to disguise the disgust lacing her question.

"He told me his name." I shrugged, guilt lining my stomach. It was weird being on a first name basis with a vampire. And even weirder knowing that the vampire would help me if I asked. "And he'll help us because the alternative is staying in a cage dying a slow death. And no one wants that, monster or not."

"True," Eli said, wagging his fork at me. "Ever since he escaped, they've been amping up the torture, trying to discover how." His brows scrunched together. "And, weirdly, he hasn't ratted you out. He mostly just laughs as he writhes in pain. He's got a screw loose, that one, if you ask me. Most vampires down there do, but that one more than most. Still, if he'll take us to

Wade, I guess for the first time all week, I'm actually glad you didn't decapitate him when you had the chance."

More guilt. But the fact that he hadn't sold me out just confirmed my point. Darius wouldn't betray us. Or if he did, he'd at least wait until he upheld his side of the bargain. He might not share our moral code, but he'd made it abundantly clear that he had some type of moral compass of his own.

"Whatever, I just can't believe Atlas is even considering this sick fuck as an option," Declan mumbled. Her grip on the spatula was so tight that her knuckles were turning white. "But I guess whatever boss man wants, boss man gets."

"It's his brother, Dec. There's nothing he wouldn't do." Eli swiped a piece of sizzling bacon from the pan, sliding it onto my plate. With a grateful grin, I took a bite, not even bothering to let it cool off to a normal temperature. When it came to fresh bacon, the pain was always worth it.

"We don't even know that Wade is really alive." Declan looked at me briefly, tilting her lips in apology. "I mean, no offense, Max. I totally get that those dreams are fucked up. And something uncanny is definitely going on. But we're just trusting some random vampire to take us into the hell realm, on the off chance that that's where Wade is, even if he is miraculously alive? And," Declan added, sliding some scrambled eggs in front of Eli, "even if he *is* alive, we don't know why or how or what the hell that even means."

I studied Declan, the way her jaw was clenched, the fear shading her eyes, and it all fell into place. "You think he might be evil. That if we find him, we might have to kill him."

Emerald eyes met mine and though she didn't answer, that was answer enough.

"I don't think Atlas would survive that," Eli said, his voice soft. Reza's footprints could be heard above our heads, and we all seemed to remember at once that she was still here. Hopefully she hadn't heard anything. "But now that he knows there's a chance that Wade is alive, and that he's being kept prisoner somewhere, I don't think we have a choice. If we don't go with him, Atlas will go on his own. And that will be a disaster."

Declan nodded, and I could see the resignation falling over her. She hated this plan, hated that we'd have to work with a creature from hell, that we'd potentially find ourselves in the hell realm itself, and that we might do all of this for nothing. Wade might not really be alive. And if he was, he might not be the Wade we all knew. But even with all these doubts, her connection to Atlas was too strong. She wouldn't let him do this alone.

None of us would.

THAT NIGHT, DECLAN AND THE BOYS WAITED UNTIL REZA WAS sound asleep and met me at my cabin. I would've stayed with them, but after breakfast, Reza came down and made it abundantly clear that so long as I stayed there, she wasn't letting me out of her sight. And judging by the way they all stiffened up when she was around, I could tell that they all absolutely hated her presence in the cabin, something that filled me with a weird sense of relief that I didn't want to dissect.

I spent all day waiting, trying desperately to think about anything other than our plan or the fact that Wade was suffering in hell, all alone. But the more I tried not to think about it, the more impossible it became to think about anything else. By the time three sharp knocks finally ricocheted on my door, I felt like I'd lived through four years in the space of a single day.

I swung the heavy wood door open to find all three of them outside, dressed in black and deadly serious expressions. I noticed that they each had a bag packed and tossed over their shoulders. I grabbed my own, filled with a few outfit changes—who knew how long it took to go to hell and back—and some toiletries. And my knives, both my new set and the one I'd had for years.

A girl couldn't leave home without her personal arsenal.

"We're going to leave our bags outside of the research center, hidden behind some of the trees," Atlas said, voice devoid of emotion. "The less we have to worry about while breaking this asshole out, the better."

Eli glanced down at me, a flash of concern crossing his face. "You sure you're willing to do this? When we're all missing in the morning, there's going to be no way to cover this up. We'll effectively be going rogue and who knows what we'll have to go through when we get back. We might not be welcomed back at all after breaking out a subject. You could just let us handle this, you know? No harm, no foul."

I nodded, zero hesitation. "The only thing I'm worried about is leaving without knowing where Ralph is."

Declan chuckled and bumped her elbow into mine. "Max, this is the same dog that came out of nowhere to rescue you twice, in two very different locations. Also the same dog that took on multiple monsters at once and tore up one of the werewolves just a few nights ago."

"Good point," Eli said, winking at me. "I think he'll be found when and only when he actually wants to be. So let that particular worry, at least, slip your mind for now."

A weight I didn't realize I'd been carrying fell away. They were right. Ralph was the most badass creature I'd ever met. He was fine. And if he wasn't, I had a weird suspicion that I would know.

Before we left, I hid a note vaguely explaining that I was leaving and would be back tucked under the pillows in Ro's room. He'd be absolutely furious with me for not waiting until he was back. Not because he wouldn't believe in what we're doing, but because he'd want to come too. In this case, it seemed better to ask for forgiveness than permission. Hopefully he wouldn't hate me when he returned...and hopefully Cyrus wouldn't disown me. I could handle not being welcomed back by The Guild, but I could most definitely not take Cy shutting me out forever.

We crept quietly towards the medical building, careful to stay in the shadows. It was well past midnight, so no one was out and the odds of us making it there unseen were in our favor.

"How exactly did you break out the vamp in the first place?" Declan asked, her voice a hushed whisper that still somehow felt too loud in the isolated halls of the building.

"After Atlas attacked us in town that night," I grinned when Atlas snorted, "I wiped Jer's blood onto a cloth and used it to unlock Darius's cell."

Jer's father worked high up in the research center, and since Jer was a direct descendant, his protector blood worked just fine. It was a risk, and I felt guilty for taking advantage of Jer like that, but it paid off in the end. At least that part of the plan did anyway.

An evil grin slid across Eli's face. "Brilliant. Explains why his father has been placed on administrative leave. They must've thought he was the one who left the cell open since the lock was coded to his entry."

Guilt rushed through me. I didn't know Jer's father particularly well, and from what I knew about him, he didn't seem like a great guy. But I didn't love being the reason his career was sidelined either. It wasn't his fault Darius escaped and I was surprised Cyrus and Seamus were okay with him being the scapegoat.

Atlas elbowed me softly in the side. "Don't go feeling guilty, Bentley. Jer's father is an asshole."

"Not unlike his son," Declan muttered.

I wasn't sure why they all seemed to dislike Jer so much. I mean, he could come on kind of strong, but he mostly seemed to be a tolerable dude. While I didn't want to date the guy, I still considered him a friend. He'd been there for me a lot since Wade died. He picked up a lot of my slack.

We scattered our bags behind some leaves and bushes and stood outside the building. Dark shadows were cast across most of the windows and, from where we stood, it looked like very few rooms had lights on.

"Maybe you should stay back by the stuff, Max. Act as a lookout," Eli suggested, scratching the back of his neck while he stared at the door.

Fat chance. I was not getting cast aside like a child. This was my suggestion in the first place. And if it weren't for my fucked-up dreams, there would be no rescue mission at all. "Not happening."

"Eli's right," Declan added. "It'll be better if we have someone waiting out here. And we have more experience. Plus none of us are still in training, so people won't bat an eye if they see us wandering around in the labs. You though," she shrugged, "you might raise some alarms."

"Fine, if we need a lookout, one of you can stay behind for the role," I said with a smug grin, crossing my arms over my chest. "I broke Darius out before, so I'm not completely inept. Plus you guys all used him as bait the other day, basically offering his death up on a silver platter. I'm the only one of us that he even remotely trusts. You guys go storming in there, and he'll try to kill you the second he's let out. With me, we stand at least a modicum of a chance."

Eli chuckled, but there wasn't much humor to it. "She has a point there."

Declan looked like she wanted to deck Eli in the chin. She opened her mouth to argue, but Atlas pressed a firm hand to her shoulder.

"Enough." Atlas's tone was final, brokering no argument. "We're all going together, we don't have time for this childish shit." He looked down at me, shooting me with an icy glare. "But Declan is right. We have more authority here and more experience. You'll do as we say and follow our lead. No arguing. If you can't agree to that, then just stay behind."

This was an argument I knew I wasn't going to win. And since we had a long, unpredictable mission on our hands, I had a feeling I was going to need to pick my battles. If they wanted to deal with all of the security protocols rolling through this place, they'd get no further argument from me. I nodded, opened the side door, and walked into the building.

"Jesus, Bentley," Atlas grumbled, "that means you don't go barging into doors first without making sure no one is there. What the fuck is wrong with you? We're going to get busted before we even get started with the first step of the plan."

Oops, fair point. I shrugged, scrunching my nose in apology. I swept my arms in front of me. "After you then, princess."

He shook his head, clearly annoyed, before shoving forward with Declan behind him. Maybe taunting him wasn't the smartest way to get him to take me seriously. I needed to remember that for future use.

"You know," Eli whispered, "calling someone princess like it's a bad thing or an insult is kind of sexist." He winked and then nodded for me to go in front of him so that he could bring up the rear. We went through several halls, not meeting anyone. I still had the keycard I'd taken from Greta, the nurse in the infirmary, but I had a feeling that we wouldn't need it. Declan and the boys were pretty high up on the food chain here, even if they didn't spend too much time in the lab portion of The Guild. They were the second-highest ranking team with permanent residence on campus, after all.

"What part of the dungeon is Darius being kept in?" I whispered to Eli, but Declan was the one who responded.

"It's not a dungeon, Max. It's a secure area for researchers to study and learn from the creatures that kill both us and humans. But to answer your question, he's below the level he was in before. Access is a lot more restricted and no one wanted to risk him escaping again. Especially since they couldn't figure out how he pulled it off in the first place."

"So how exactly are we going to get him out then?" There didn't seem to be anyone around right now, so once we actually broke him out, I didn't think it would be difficult to get off campus unseen. If it came to fighting other protectors who might try to stop us, I wasn't sure how far my new colleagues were willing to go.

Eli cocked an eyebrow and winked at me. "Did you forget about the part where we had the vamp in question out for class this week? We were granted special privileges to use him, since everyone is convinced he's not going to break and spill any information at this point—they've kind of exhausted their strategies already. He's a liability and they're all but ready to decapitate him themselves. To tell you the truth, I'm honestly stunned that they've bothered keeping him alive this long in the first place."

A bitter taste swept over my tongue at that, but I swallowed my disgust and carried on walking. It seemed I would be saving yet another creature from death row and, for the moment, I didn't want to think about how many others down there were awaiting similar fates.

14
ATLAS

We made it to the vampire's cell without meeting more than a handful of guards. A few passed us with confused expressions, but when I mumbled something about wanting to prep the beast for tomorrow's combat sessions, they let me pass without another thought. I didn't miss the suspicion in their eyes when they spotted Max, though. Nor did I miss the way Eli gripped her by the waist and pressed his lips to her cheek.

He was clearly trying to pass her presence off as some twisted date he was taking to see the vamp, but the wolf living under my skin wasn't amused. Max turned fifty shades of red, and I wasn't sure whether it was embarrassment or fury coating her skin.

Eli and I stepped up to a large metal door, both staring at the security print box. This cell required two protectors with clearance to deposit fresh blood within ten seconds of the other. The protocol wasn't necessary for most of the creatures, just the ones The Guild deemed too dangerous and too much of a liability. And this one, Darius, as Max called him, was currently the biggest liability we had in lockdown. I wasn't even sure when the last time was that a prisoner escaped the entire compound before, so it wasn't surprising how seriously they were taking the breach down here.

"Ready?" Eli whispered, his eyes not leaving the spot that hid a small needle.

This was our last chance to change our minds—to go back home, pretend that Max's dreams were the manifestations of trauma and nothing more. And, truth be told, there was a hell of a chance that's all they were. None of this made any sense. But if there was a chance that Wade was still alive, even a small one, I wouldn't be able to ignore it.

Even if it meant that we would essentially be disowned from the entire organization after this. Unless we could come up with one hell of an excuse when we returned; that, or return with Wade in tow, to prove that we acted for a good reason.

Personally, I was okay letting go of this life, of my duties to my father and The Guild. I was already living on borrowed time as it was. While Dec, Eli—and now Max and Rowan—did everything they could to protect my secret, I couldn't expect them to live with it forever. It was only a matter of time before someone found out, someone who didn't owe me any loyalty. Hell, I was damn shocked that Max hadn't said anything to anyone yet. From what I could tell, she seemed to think even her brother was in the dark. Which meant that the two of them weren't just keeping my secret, but they were unknowingly keeping my secret from each other.

That night, Rowan saw me shift, watched me go tearing off after Wade and Max. But he hadn't said a word to anyone, hadn't even approached me about it afterwards. It was like all of his focus was bound up in keeping Max safe—he didn't have time or energy to deal with anything else.

Eli though, he had a lot more to lose on this new mission. He loved and respected his father, in a way that I never did my own. He had a promising career and future ahead of him.

"You don't have to do this Eli," I whispered to him as we

both studied the needle that would change our paths indefinitely. Once our blood was recorded, there was no going back.

His lips turned up in a smirk before he shoved me out of the way and pressed his finger down on the pad, wincing briefly as he started to bleed.

I nodded, unable to verbalize my appreciation, before I followed suit. The door swung open and we had less than ten seconds to shuffle through into the airlock before we had to repeat the process. The space was cramped and I was all too aware of the fact that Max was pressed up against my back, her breath dancing along my arm and sending chills down my spine. Before I could get too lost in the scent or feel of her, I opened the next door, shuttling us through the vampire's cage.

He was locked up in a system of chains that kept his arms and head in place. It was a miserable existence, and he'd been living in isolation, unable to move for more than a month now. Would I be able to survive if I were in his place? Would Seamus or Alleva throw me in a dark, sterile pit like this if they learned the truth of what I'd become? Or would they have mercy and just end my suffering, ignoring the fact that I didn't admit to the truth after my first transformation?

"Back to play again then, are we?" The vampire grinned, his fangs descending against his bottom lip. "Let's keep it fair this time and give me just a taste." His nostrils flared and I watched as the creature's mismatched eyes widened with surprise as Max stepped around me and came into his view.

"He's left like this at all times? Starved?" She nervously swept some of the hair behind her ear, glancing between all of us. "Th-this is inhumane, fucking sick." She made to walk beyond me, but I gripped her small wrist in mine, keeping her in place. I didn't miss the way the vampire growled as I made contact with her skin.

His obsession with her grated my nerves. If we didn't need to find Wade, the look on his face as he studied her would have been enough for me to rip his skull from his spine right here and now. Hell, the memory of his lips against hers was already more than enough to make the wolf rise to the surface.

"Little Protector," he said, a genuine smile now making an appearance on his ethereally pale face. What was his fascination with her? In all my time with The Guild, I had never seen a vampire fixate on a protector like this. "Miss me, did you? I must say, I rather enjoyed our last tumble. Well, until you tried to kill me and end all of our fun, that is."

Declan positioned her body so that she covered Max from the vampire's view. I wasn't surprised to find cold hatred in my friend's eyes, but I was surprised by how Max's soft grip on her hand seemed to walk her down from the ledge. Declan didn't do well with vampires, and she'd wanted this one dead since she learned of the creature's role in Wade's death. We all did, if I was being honest. For weeks I'd pictured being the one to carry out the deathblow that would end him for good.

Max gently stepped to the side a bit, positioning herself between me and Declan, but in a way that gave the vampire a clear view of her face. She cleared her throat and stood taller, as if she was beginning a business meeting. "We have a proposition for you, Darius."

Amusement colored the vampire's features as every muscle in his body tensed. His eyes seemed to dance back and forth between Max's face and the spot where she touched Declan's hand. "I do love your propositions, little protector. Though I will say that the last deal we made wound up with me in a significantly worse spot than I started in. So you'll have to excuse me in advance for driving a harder bargain this time."

Cool determination crossed Max's features and I watched as she steadied herself, hyper aware of every breath that she took, every tremor of her muscles. "And I am sorry for that."

There was honesty to her statement that shocked us all, including the vampire. She had a bad habit of empathizing with monsters, myself included. One I'd need to break her of as soon as I could bear to see her study me with nothing but cool, professional disdain.

"Truly," she continued. "This is inhumane, and no one deserves to be kept in conditions like this, no matter what atrocities they've committed. You can't help the fact that you're a vampire. I understand that. But what you can help is how you treat people."

"What is it that you want?" the vampire asked, narrowing his eyes slightly and tilting his head as much as his restraints would allow. As far as he was concerned, she seemed to be the only thing that existed in this room—the rest of us nothing more than air to him.

I saw now that she was right to insist on coming with us. We didn't stand a chance without her.

"We will free you," Max said, taking a long breath in. Her dark eyes sparkled with conviction as she stared the vampire down, unblinking. "But you must promise something in return."

"Am I to believe that the members of one of The Guild's most elite teams are willing to let me walk out of here a free man? The very team that recaptured me and shoved me down here? And then brought me out as a plaything for baby protectors to try and destroy? Do you take me for a mindless drone?"

"Free vampire," Declan said, voice crisp and low. "You are not a man. You are a vampire."

I glanced at her, encouraging her to back down before her latent hatred destroyed the mission before it even started.

The vampire completely ignored Declan, his unusual eyes focused only on Max. "What is it that you want from me, then?"

Even though he was the one imprisoned, it felt like the four of us had wandered into a spider's trap. I wasn't sure how long we'd be able to maintain control of the situation once he was free. If it weren't for Wade, I wouldn't even consider putting Dec, Eli, and Max at risk. At the very least though, I was certain he wouldn't kill her. Almost certain anyway. Obsessions were tricky things to predict.

"We need your help," Max started, her eyes glancing nervously around the cell. It was as if she was avoiding eye contact with the vampire at all costs. "Our friend—" she let out a long breath, trying to thread together her thoughts into a coherent and persuasive argument. "The night you were recaptured, some supernatural creature took our friend."

"And," the vampire drew the word out slowly, savoring his part in the story, "you want me to help you locate this friend?"

Max nodded, finally making eye contact with the vampire. His smile didn't grow, but his eyes seemed to devour her completely. The pair of them were like a moth and a flame—until I could be certain, I just had to hope like hell that Max was the flame.

"What makes you think I could locate your friend? Not that I'm arguing for my continued detainment, but I was already recaptured, as you put it, before the protectors ran into trouble that night. I wasn't there to see who captured him."

"This is pointless," Declan muttered. Her body was rigid, and I could tell, even with just a brief glance, that every muscle in her body was tensed, like she was using all of her focus to restrain herself from ending the vampire right now.

"The creature who took him," Eli said, voice loud and clear, as unconcerned as always, "he disappeared. Like straight up teleported like he was a goddamn magician. What kind of creature can do that?"

The vampire seemed to almost freeze, interest coating his expression as his eyes traveled from Max to Eli. It was the first time he'd looked anywhere but in her direction since he noticed her presence.

"Well, that's an interesting bit of information." He straightened up a bit, which was pretty comical considering the chains didn't allow him much movement.

"Please, Darius," Max said, her words dripping with concern. "If you know who took him, please tell us."

He frowned slightly at her. "Sorry little protector, but this is out of my pay grade. I can't be of assistance to you, unfortunately. I recommend that you forget about your friend. Chances are he's dead."

"He's draining her," I said, the words rushing out in a hushed hurry. I wasn't sure why the vampire was enthralled by Max, but maybe relying on that fascination was our best chance. "My brother was taken by some creature, and he's been meeting Max in her dreams."

The vampire's features hardened, the restraints straining a bit as he leaned into them.

"He's draining her," I said again. I could feel my fingernails leaving small, half-moon imprints in the soft flesh of my palms. I wasn't used to negotiating with the creatures I was trained to hunt. And I was even more uncomfortable with how the vampire watched Max, as if she was his favorite dessert. It was purely clinical, his fascination with her.

"You do seem to surround yourself with an unusual band of creatures, Max," the vampire said, using her name for the first time since we'd entered. The words were steely in his mouth, like something I said finally snapped him awake. "Well, this is certainly a predicament. Very few creatures are able to teleport like that, and even fewer are powerful enough to do it outside of the hell realm."

"What does that mean?" Max asked as she rolled her hands back in her sleeves like there was a sudden chill in the air she couldn't quite escape. "Do you know who took Wade?"

The vampire tried to shake his head, but when the restraints didn't budge, he just growled in frustration. "No, I can't be sure who. But I do know it must be one of the ancients."

"A vampire?" Declan's hatred was temporarily clouded by intrigue as she took a step closer to the beast.

"No, not a vampire. But yes, if it's as you described, and your friend is indeed alive, he will be in the hell realm. The ancients lose their powers quickly on this plane so their visits are never extended."

"Can you tell us how to get there?" I asked, trying to keep the frustration from my voice. I was partially convinced he just wanted to string us along for as long as it amused him, but that he had no real information for us to make use of—no real answer to help us save Wade. The lingering, annoying hope that he might was the only thing holding me back from ending this now.

"Please, Darius. If he's alive we need to find him." Max took a step towards the vampire, ignoring Declan's attempt to pull her back. "Is there a way for us to gain access?"

The vampire studied her, and judging from what looked like concern in his expression, I guessed he was clocking the dark shadows under her eyes, and her sunken-in cheekbones. The creature growled so low that I felt it more than heard it, my own beast responding in kind.

"I can't tell you how to get there," he finally said. "There is magic in place that keeps us from speaking of it, but I can maybe take you there, to one of the portals."

Max's face cracked into a large smile as she looked back at us encouragingly and then took another step towards the vampire. "Thank you."

"I said I could take you there, little protector, not that I would. I have conditions of my own."

I narrowed my eyes and took a few steps forward so that I was next to Max. "And what exactly are those conditions, vamp? Is your freedom and survival not enough? If you stay here, you'll be put down within the week."

He rolled his eyes. If I weren't so frustrated, I'd find the gesture almost humorous—it was so human coming from a creature bent on killing us, so strange coming from a creature physically restrained against a wall. "I'm not dense. What's to stop you from decapitating me once I get you through to the hell realm? Protectors aren't exactly known for keeping their end of the bargain." He glanced back down to Max. "Except for her. She's the only one I've known who has at least attempted to keep her promise to me."

I shrugged. He wasn't entirely wrong. If I didn't kill him after he directed us to the other realm, I was confident that Declan would take care of it the second she had a chance. Her hatred was palpable and I doubted the vampire was unaware of it.

Max turned, looking each of us in the eyes, her expression stern and confident. It was strange to see her confront us all like that, like an equal. She couldn't be taller than five-foot-five, but she didn't seem to fear us in the way most people at The Guild did. If anything, I think in some ways, we feared her.

"They won't kill you, Darius," she finally said before turning back to him. "But what else is it that you want?"

A sadistic grin crawled across his face. "If by some miracle we aren't too late, and we rescue your friend and survive the encounter—you do not return to this place, not right away."

"No fucking way—"

"Are you out of your mind?"

"You can't be fucking serious," I said, my protest layering with my team's. "You expect us to just leave her in a place filled with creatures who will try to kill her?"

The vampire tensed, his jaw pumping against the restraints around his chin. "I didn't say she'd stay in the hell realm. That's no place for her, if alive is something she enjoys being. I just said she wouldn't return to this place. You protectors are so preoccupied with hunting monsters that you fail to realize how many of you have become them. She will be safer almost anywhere else. This place will destroy her. And she doesn't belong here."

I opened my mouth to protest again, his accusation cutting deeper than I would've liked, but Max beat me to it.

"Deal."

"You can't seriously be thinking about this?" Eli said, an unusual release of anger clouding his typical smirk and cocky composure.

"I didn't say she could never return. But there are things she needs to learn. If this is the life Max chooses to lead," the vampire said, though his tone made it clear he hoped it wasn't, "then she needs to make the choice fully informed. In order for that to occur, she needs the opportunity to learn without censorship. She won't get that here in this cesspool."

"I already said deal," Max said, but she raised a thin finger in front of him when his grin grew larger with victory. "But there's more. You aren't to hurt anyone."

The vamp's lip curled.

"Yeah, good luck with that, Max," Declan said, huffing out a sarcastic sigh.

"Do you expect me to just continue to starve forever?" the vampire asked.

She shook her head slowly. "No, but we'll figure something out that doesn't result in people dying unnecessarily. No more... repeats of the last time I freed you."

The vampire breathed out dramatically before finally saying, "deal," his tone that of a petulant child.

Not wanting to second guess what we were doing, I unlocked the restraints from the wall, half expecting the beast to try and attack the second he was released. Our deal was verbal, I had no illusions that he would stick to his end of the bargain, even if Max intended on sticking to hers.

He glanced over at me before rolling his eyes again. "I said, deal, I'm not going to attack you. And if I were, I'm certainly not obtuse enough to do it on enemy territory." He shook his hands in front of me expectantly. I arched my brow and shrugged. "You've got to be kidding me. You're actually going to leave me all bound up in this shit?"

Declan's lip curled as she stepped between Max and the vampire. "You didn't honestly expect us to release all of your restraints, did you? We're letting you out of here, and you've got our word we won't take your head off when we're done, but that doesn't mean you have free rein of your limbs. We won't have you attacking us or escaping during our travels."

Max shook her head, clearly frustrated with the whole thing. "We don't have time to bicker." She turned to Darius and grabbed the restraints connecting his hands, pulling him along as she walked towards the entrance, like he was a stubborn dog and not a dangerous monster. "Come on, we need to get out of here before those guards show up again. Atlas convinced them we were checking on you, but I doubt he could get them to ignore us taking you out of here in the middle of the night."

As if she was leading him by a leash, she moved in front of the door, expectantly waiting for me and Eli to release the locks once more.

"Max, you're between Eli and Atlas," Declan said, carefully removing her fingers from the restraints. She wasn't nearly as gentle with the vampire, once she took over pulling him through the maze of hallways.

And with that, we were officially doing this. The second we left this building, we would be past the point of no return.

15

MAX

I was overly conscious of the fact that a vampire was walking just a few feet away from me as we made our way out of the building. I was fairly certain Dairus wouldn't kill me. And it sort of helped that he was still bound up, even if I cringed every time the metal restraints made noise, echoing along the halls. It was like trying to sneak out with our own drumline.

Eli stopped by the control room on the way out to wipe the cameras. None of us were under the impression people wouldn't put together that we were all behind this escape plan, especially when we all turned up missing tomorrow morning, but it couldn't hurt if we slowed Cyrus and the others down a bit. Last thing we needed was to get caught and reprimanded before we had a chance to even leave campus.

Apparently, Cyrus was the one who wiped the tapes last time I helped Darius escape. The thought warmed me to my toes, making me feel even more guilty about lying to him and holding grudges. If it weren't for him, I'd be kicked out of this place already. Maybe even worse. I wasn't exactly sure how they handled protectors who broke the law; and I hoped like hell that I would never find out.

Of course, now thanks to Darius, I wouldn't be able to come

right back after we rescued Wade anyway. That was the sort of promise that would land me in a world of trouble—not necessarily with The Guild, but with Cy and Ro.

Hopefully Declan and the guys could help me find a loophole to get out of that promise. Although I guess the only thing binding me to it was my word. I'd broken worse things in my life.

When we left the building, I exhaled a long breath of relief. My head felt light and dizzy with the anxiety and adrenaline of our escape. Declan shoved Darius out into the fresh air and I bit back a grin as the vampire fell to his knees from the force and broke out into a weird, melodic laughter. He found the strangest things amusing and I was beginning to think that everyone was right about him. Something was just sort of...off.

"Knock it off," Atlas said, knocking his shoulder lightly into Declan. "We don't have time for this shit. The longer it takes for us to get on the road, the bigger the chance that we're caught."

"What the hell are you doing with him?" A heavy voice bit out from a few feet in front of me, startling the smile right off my face in an instant.

"Errr—" I said, watching as Eli and Atlas exchanged a quick look with each other.

"Sorry about this, Rick," Eli said with a shrug, "wrong place, wrong time. Happens to the best of us."

"Sorry about wh—" the man, Rick I guess, went down with a soft thump as Atlas held him in a chokehold until he was out.

Holy shit. If the guys weren't at the point of no return when we unlocked Darius's cage, they sure as hell were now.

"Nicely done, boys. You sure I can't just take a quick sip?" Darius asked, running his tongue along his bottom lip. "It's been weeks since I've had a drop and it seems like such a waste. I don't even need a straw."

Repulsion racked through me at the thought of Darius descending upon the guy—Rick apparently. But underneath that repulsion, there was an inkling of pity that I couldn't quite shake. The protectors had been starving Darius for weeks. And I was pretty certain at least part of the reason had to do with the fact that he killed one of the researchers during his last escape. But still. My stomach went nuts if I didn't get my full three meals a day—hell, it usually even demanded a fourth.

"Shut it, vamp," Declan said, her cheeks reddening as she studied Darius with an impenetrable glare.

The other guys clearly disliked Darius, that was a given. But there was a hatred in Declan's expression that seemed more personal somehow.

"We need to get out of here, now," Eli said, running a hand through his mussed hair. "I don't like the idea of attacking any more of our own tonight, and who knows how long we have before the compound realizes that the vamp is gone...and that we are as well. If anyone sounds an alarm before we get the chance to knock them out, we're done. We can't take on the full cavalry."

Eli's eyes were wild as he scanned the perimeter of the woods. And though he didn't say it, I knew he was concerned about running into his dad. I didn't know Eli particularly well, and while he seemed to be a lot more carefree and mischievous than Seamus, it was clear he respected his father and his position at The Guild.

And honestly, I could relate. It was taking everything in me not to think about the disappointment I'd seen on Cyrus's face the night after the attack. The way he looked at me now, with a lingering layer of worry and distrust, broke something essential in me—a crack I couldn't fully repair or explain. The thought of Cyrus catching us now, with a newly-released Darius in tow—again—sent a shiver down my spine.

"We'll need a car of sorts, some form of transportation. We can't exactly walk to the other realm from here," Darius said, his voice lilting in a sing-song way. He was clearly excited to be free, but there was an amusement in his voice as he studied the guys that I didn't quite understand. He almost seemed to be enjoying every aspect of his escape, even the things that didn't go smoothly for him.

"Jesus, didn't think of that," Eli said, his brow furrowing. "I guess we could steal one of the SUV's. We're already in it this far, why not add grand theft auto. We'll have to ditch it almost immediately though, but it could do for a bit of a head start."

Atlas nodded to Eli before glancing briefly at me. "Take her to the car, I'll meet you there in a minute."

Adrenaline rushed through me at the thought of us leaving tonight. I wasn't sure how long it would take for Darius to guide us to Wade, but I could feel it in my bones that we would find our way to him eventually. We just had to.

There wasn't another option.

When we got to the car, Declan opened the passenger door for me. Probably wanting to keep me as far from Darius as possible.

"I'm not going to hurt her, you brooding buffoon, I always keep my word," Darius said, as he ducked into the back of the car to sit between her and Eli.

When I turned in my seat to see them, they looked ridiculous. Eli and Darius were both over six feet tall and had lean, muscular builds—and even though Declan was considerably more petite than them, the venom in her eyes made sure that Darius didn't scooch so much as an inch into her space. I rolled my eyes at the way she and Eli squished their bodies into the car doors like they were trying to avoid touching Darius at all costs.

"Vampirism isn't contagious you guys," I said with a shake of my head.

Declan scowled in response, but I didn't miss the way her shoulders dropped half an inch, like she was at least trying to release some of the tension in her body.

Atlas pulled the door open and threw something into the backseat. He didn't say anything, but I caught the way his eyes latched onto my neck briefly, like he was checking for bites.

I found myself weirdly wanting to stick up for Darius, but bit the retort back. They were right not to trust Darius and it didn't hurt being cautious. Even though he didn't attack me the night I freed him, that didn't make him a nun. And he'd been starving for weeks. Vampires were volatile creatures, and I had a feeling this one was especially so.

I craned my neck, trying to see what Atlas threw and choked down a disgusted squeal. Darius's face was covered in blood as he pressed the carcass of what looked like a rabbit to his mouth. He caught me staring and winked, mocking my repulsion.

"Rabbit isn't my top choice, but unless you're willing to open up one of your veins, little protector, this will have to do for now. I'm far beyond hoping for a five-star meal at this point."

Without another word, he continued devouring Bugs while Declan and Eli tried like hell to look away. But even with the four of us desperate to look anywhere but at Darius while he sucked the poor animal dry, we couldn't escape the slurping noises quite as easily.

My stomach tightened and I turned the radio on, but that only added a pop soundtrack to the suckfest.

Atlas drove for a few minutes and the second we passed Guild grounds, we all let out a collective breath of relief. We were far from out of the woods with this ridiculous plan, but we had made it beyond the first hurdle. This morning, even succeeding this far seemed almost impossible.

"Alright vamp, where am I going?" Atlas watched Darius in the rearview mirror, and I realized that the whole vampire-reflection thing was apparently a complete Hollywood fabrication. That would explain why our instructors never brought up that particular superpower in class—it didn't exist.

When I looked up, Darius was grinning into his reflection, his face filled with grotesque red splotches. I shivered when he licked his lips, his eyes meeting mine. Declan threw the remains of the carcass out the window and wiped her hands furiously against her pants.

"Drive towards Seattle," Darius answered as he rolled his

neck from shoulder-to-shoulder, no doubt enjoying his new freedom from most of his restraints, if not all of them.

He stared out at the passing trees as we wound down the hilly path, devouring the sights. It was dark as hell, but the starlight provided some illumination of our surroundings; and I had no doubt that his heightened senses provided the rest.

How long had he been locked away in The Guild labs? His first escape was short-lived, but I wasn't exactly sure how long the subjects were kept alive down there. Were they usually just disposed of when researchers couldn't get more information or data from them? Or were they kept there forever, like they were serving out life in prison?

Whatever the case, he was soaking in his newfound freedom with relish, his eyes opened nice and wide, taking in everything he could see, first out one window, then another. It felt oddly like taking a road trip with a young child, the excitement was almost contagious.

"Seattle?" Eli asked. "That's where the mouth of hell is? Really?"

"No," Darius answered, pulling against his restraints slightly. "Is it really necessary that I remain tied up in all of this nonsense?" When Declan glared at him, he continued. "There are several gates into the hell realm. But the simultaneously closest and easiest for me to get us through is there. And so that is where we should drive."

I had to beat back the rush of excitement brewing in my gut. I'd always wanted to visit Seattle. Hell, I'd always wanted to visit any city. The town outside of Guild Headquarters was the most populous place I'd ever been.

"It's going to take me a few days to find my contacts," Darius added, closing his eyes as he sunk his head against the backseat like he was settling in for a nap. He looked so absurd, his body tangled up in coils and restraints.

Atlas slammed the breaks down and my fingers bit into the dashboard. "Days?"

Darius opened his golden eye, his full lips pulling into a small smirk. "What? You didn't think we could just walk right on into hell, did you? There's a reason protectors haven't located it. It's not exactly easy for us hell beasts to find it either. And once we leave, returning is a complicated process. I've been gone for years, thanks to your sort." His voice was dripping with sarcasm.

"Seems like enough of you make it here to keep us plenty busy," Eli said, matching Darius's tone.

"Yeah, well, that's not always by choice," Darius answered, his eyes glazing over slightly as he watched the trees skate past the window.

Protectors knew almost nothing about the politics of hell—nor did we understand much about why creatures chose to traverse into our world. Whatever the gossip was, Darius didn't seem in the mood to spill. At least not yet.

The tension in the car was tangible and I could hear Declan grumbling in the back, though her voice was too low for me to discern any individual words. Judging by the side glances she kept shooting Darius though, I was pretty sure she was visualizing some graphic ways to make the vampire's life hell over the next few days. Getting lost in the fantasies of destroying him limb-by-limb was probably the only thing that would get her through the slow stretch of time.

We drove in silence, until I eventually dozed off, my face pressed against the chilly window, the sound of the radio piercing through the heavy silence.

"You're back," Wade said, standing up from the concrete slab that masqueraded as a bed. If the creature who took him was so hellbent on keeping him, I wasn't sure why he didn't make the living arrangements a bit more comfortable. It was freezing down here. Which was, of course, not what I was expecting in hell. "You shouldn't be here, Max."

I pushed off the bed and jumped onto him, wrapping my arms around his neck. I was so excited to see him that tears pricked my eyes. Even though I'd convinced the guys to literally chase my dreams, I was half convinced that I was imagining everything, that Wade wasn't really meeting me here. But I breathed in deep, taking in his scent, the feel of his warm skin. He was too real for this to be a mirage, for this to be any regular dream.

"We're coming for you," I said, choking on my breath. "Atlas, Declan, and Eli—we're going to find you and bring you back home."

He stiffened in my arms, slowly tightening his grip around me. "You shouldn't be here, Max." He took a long, steady breath in as he pushed his face into my hair. Chills exploded along my arms as his breath lingered against the shell of my ear. "Do not, under any circumstances, come for me."

My heartbeat started racing and I pushed away from him so that I could give myself a second to adjust to the overwhelming sensation of being near him after all of this time. The walls were just as dark and damp as I remembered, and I glanced around, trying to see if there was any way out, any clue as to where exactly we even were.

"Wade, where are you? What is this place?" I asked, noticing that the room was still completely empty, except for the bed. It felt like ages since the last time I saw him, even if it was only one day. "Are they feeding you?"

He shook his head, his icy blue eyes hardening in an expression I wasn't used to from him. "I don't know, Max. I haven't seen anyone but you. I-I'm not really sure what's going on with me or how you're even here at all. I had almost convinced myself you were a hallucination last time. But now that you're here, I know you're not a figment of my imagination—this, it's too real. None of this makes any sense." He let out a steady breath, running his hands over his face. "Something isn't right though, I don't feel the same. I don't feel like myself."

"Wade, it's been about twenty-four hours since I last saw you. Are you saying that you've just been in this room by yourself the whole time?"

He nodded, his eyes narrowing slightly, like he was having trouble unraveling his thoughts. "I think so, only it doesn't feel like it's been that long since you were here. I think I've mostly been asleep since you last visited."

"Aren't you starving?" I ran my hands down my sides, patting my pockets, like I would somehow find food or water packed away in the pockets of my dream self.

He nodded, his eyelids going heavy as he took a step closer to me. He swept his right hand up the side of my arm, until his fingers were tangled in the hair at my scalp.

I swallowed, unable to look away from his eyes, the deep indigo now overpowering the pale sky, scared that if I so much as blinked, I'd break this moment. He was here, he was alive. My skin buzzed like it was dancing on a live wire.

His other hand came up to my face, his thumb gently brushing along my bottom lip. My entire body shivered as my tongue unconsciously swept over the spot he touched. His eyes hungrily stared at my mouth as he took a step closer to me.

We had so much to do. We should be trying to figure out where we were—figure out why I, of everyone, was here with him now—but like a fog, the thoughts drifted away and I was left only with the blue pools of his eyes, mesmerized by the weaving of colors.

Wade dipped his head lower, until I could feel his warm breath brush against my lips. The whisper of air on my skin sent chills down my entire body.

He bit his plush bottom lip as he stared at mine. "Can I kiss you, Max?"

His voice was so soft that I almost didn't hear the question. As if afraid to shatter the moment, I answered by closing the distance between us. My lips pressed against his, and I swallowed back a moan when he returned the pressure. For a long stretch, we were completely still—frozen, just taking in the moment, afraid it would break and dissolve around us.

Until, all at once, he deepened the kiss, his tongue swiping against the seam of my mouth, begging for permission to enter. My tongue met his and the slow, tentative dance grew hungry. With a groan, he pulled me closer to him until he gave up and lifted me off the ground, moving us towards the wall.

Feverishly, I wrapped my legs around his waist, swallowing a whimper when I realized just how affected he was. Pressure built up as he pressed my back into the cool, stone wall, and I slowly started to move against him, desperate for more friction between us.

"Max," he said, voice a breathless growl, "I've wanted this for as long as I can remember."

"Mhm," I mumbled, my brain far too fuzzy to say anything more coherent as he pressed his large erection between my legs.

I dug my nails into his shoulders, desperate to be closer, to draw him in. For now, I was here, touching him, but who knew when I would be pulled from his grasp again. He tasted like a cool, summer day at the beach, fresh and intoxicating, completely at odds with the room we were occupying.

Wade's hand untangled from my hair and slowly drew a soft line down my neck and chest. The pressure was like a whisper, a tease, and I wanted more. His fingers found the bottom of my sweater and he pulled it off in one smooth move. I hissed when my skin met the cool stone of the wall.

He pulled back a moment, breath coming out in heaves. "God, you're beautiful." His hand pressed reverently along my stomach until his fingers began tracing the edge of my bra.

I sucked in a breath as he found the clasps at my back and made quick work of detaching them. He moved us over to the bed, dropping my head on the thin, practically nonexistent pillow. My nipples pebbled beneath his touch, and I bucked my hips, already missing the pressure of having him there, between my legs.

With a wicked grin, he brought his lips to my chest, nipping playfully at each peak. The pressure was becoming too much, I needed more.

"Wade," I cried, eyes closed so that I could focus on the sensations pulsing through my body, "please."

I could feel his smile press wickedly into the skin between my breasts and I whimpered as his tongue drew lazy circles down my stomach. He dipped his fingers in the gap between my pants and skin. My brain buzzed with excitement as he peeled off the layer of fabric, the cool air of the room heightening each sensation against my skin. He pressed his lips to my inner left thigh, nipping the skin gently as he moved up, closer to my core.

My heartbeat pounded inside my ears as I reached for his shoulders, desperate to bring his mouth back to mine.

His hands clasped on my wrists as he studied me like a predator scoping out its next meal. "I want to taste you, Max."

My eyes landed on his, and I sucked in a breath. His normally light eyes were swirling with shades of blue so deep they almost looked black, glowing in a way that made him seem both beautiful and feral. Unable to find the capacity for words, I nodded, mesmerized by the image of him poised over me.

The second I relinquished control and granted him permission, a spark of energy pulsed around us. With a quick move of his wrist, he ripped the lace of my underwear, flinging the material across the room. For a moment, we froze in silent anticipation as he looked at me, completely bare beneath him. His chest moved in heavy, languid breaths as he studied me. With a dark grin, he met my eyes, not breaking contact as he lowered down to meet me.

I almost came undone when his lips finally touched the skin at the top of my inner thigh. In one slow, long motion, his tongue swept along one of my vaginal lips before circling my clit. He went slow, excruciatingly slow, until he finally reached the spot, inserting a finger into me just as his lips closed around me.

"Oh my god," I said, bucking my hips up, needing more.

More, more, more.

"Holy shit, Wade." I gripped my fingers into his shoulders, trying to ground myself for fear I'd float away.

He slowly inserted a second finger, speeding up the thrusts as he sucked. His other hand gripped my hip, pulling me closer to him, his nails digging into my flesh in a perfect mix of pleasure and pain. "Jesus, Max," his whisper a growl that danced against my skin. "I want to watch you come." He looked up at me, his breathing nearly as fevered as mine as I writhed against him, both of us desperate for more. "Now."

The second his lips fell back on me, I came undone, the pressure that was building finally too much. My cries echoed around the room, my ears ringing as he drew out the orgasm with slow, steady thrusts.

When I finally couldn't take it anymore, I opened my eyes.

Wade was gone.

16

MAX

"Max, wake up."

I peeled my eyelids open slowly, they felt like they weighed ten pounds each, and waited a second while my eyes adjusted to the bright lights. Declan was standing above me, the passenger door open to let her in. "Max? Oh, thank god."

I was slouched over slightly and turned my head a bit from side to side, trying to wake up a bit. "Where are we?"

"In Western Washington," Atlas said, his words terse.

I sat up a bit and looked over at him, while Declan tried flashing the light of her phone between each of my eyes. Atlas was staring straight ahead, his fingers gripping the steering wheel so hard that his knuckles were white. I followed his line of sight and realized we were on the side of a road. It was still a little dark out, but looked like the sunrise was slowly catching up to us. "What happened?"

As if in a rush, I remembered the events of last night. Quickly, I spun around, and noticed Darius and Eli in the backseat, both of them with uncharacteristically serious expressions on their faces—Darius made all the more ridiculous by the fact that he was still wrapped up in his heavy restraints. The binding at his neck and wrists looked a bit janky though, like he'd spent a good portion of the trip trying to slowly wear it down. I wondered, briefly, if the guys had noticed.

"You were dreaming," Declan bit out, her breath washing over the back of my neck, sending chills down my spine.

My cheeks burned as I instantly recalled the exact nature of that dream. What had they heard? I spun around to meet Declan's emerald eyes as she gently cupped my face with her soft hand, studying me.

"Was I screaming?"

Dear god, let this have been like every other nightmare I'd had with Wade, where I woke the house up screaming and crying in pain. The thought of them listening in on my sex dream had my face heating like I was the devil himself.

I touched my fingers lightly to my cheeks, but they were dry. No tears then.

"You could say that," Darius said with a low chuckle from behind me. "Definitely some screaming involved, though I wouldn't say it sounded altogether unpleasant."

The leather of the steering wheel creaked a bit as Atlas tightened his grip and shot a nasty look at Darius through the rearview mirror.

"You need to tell us what happened," Declan said, stepping back slightly so that she was standing in a ditch at the side of the road. She crouched down a bit so that we were at eye level.

Had we just randomly pulled over because of my dream? Horror washed over me at the kinds of sounds I must've been making. Was it possible to die of shame? Like, was that an actual thing? Because if so, I was in real fucking trouble.

Steadying my hammering pulse, I took a few breaths and closed my eyes. I did not want to look at any one of them while I recalibrated my brain to the real world. My entire body still felt light and tingly from my dream meeting with Wade, from the feel of his skin against mine.

And, speaking of which, what the hell was that about? If I

really did have some weird dream portal into his prison, there were way more important things for me to be focused on than jumping his bones. It was like we had been possessed—all concerns slipped away until we were just focused on each other. Another fresh wave of embarrassment and guilt washed over me. I was royally botching this mission.

"Max," Declan barked, her hand lightly gripping my shoulder as she tried to bring me back to them. "Look, you need to tell us what the hell happened. Something's wrong."

My brows narrowed as I looked up at her. It was easier to focus on her for some reason, to ignore the three-male presence at my back while I tried to articulate what happened. "Wrong?"

"Yes, little protector," Darius said, his voice unusually solemn. "Your heartbeat picked up like a jackhammer, but then all of a sudden, it just—slowed down."

"Like way down," Eli added, his hand reaching up the center console to squeeze my arm. "That's what the vamp said anyway, he's the one with a knack for hearing that sort of thing. Maybe he was lying?"

I saw Atlas shake his head out of the corner of my eye. "No, I could hear the change too. It was like the life was draining out of you."

"She can't fall asleep anymore," Darius said, an edge of finality ringing through the car. "Not until we reach Wade anyway, or figure out a way to stop him."

I spun around, trying to swallow the urge to throat punch him. "What? You expect me to just stay awake indefinitely? You've got to be kidding me. That's not even possible."

A giant grin stretched across his face, making him look even more wild with his restraints framing him. "I'm sure we can find some fun ways to keep you up."

I closed my eyes, gripping my hands around the seatbelt, thankful suddenly that I had my own restraint. The guys started bickering and Eli threatened to straight up stake Darius right here and now until Atlas reluctantly reminded him that we needed him alive to get to Wade.

"I'm the only connection that we have to him right now," I said, my voice was quiet, but they all hushed to listen. I could feel four pairs of eyes homed in on me like I was a damn beacon. "We can't just ignore the fact that I'm our best lead right now. Look, I don't know why I'm the one who's having these dreams about Wade, but I am. And he's alone and scared, and we need to find him. So no," I said, opening my eyes and glaring at Darius, "I won't be just indefinitely avoiding sleep. I'm not a human, I'm a protector. I can survive some weird dreams."

"What. Happened?" Atlas asked, he was back to staring out the windshield, like looking at me right now was painful for him.

"I was back there, with Wade." How much could I say without falling into the very intimate details I absolutely did not want to share? "He's in the same place, a prison of sorts. Archaic looking, almost like a dungeon. He has no idea where he is and no one has been by to see or feed him since he's woken up. No one except me." I racked my brain, trying to remember the details of our meeting, but they were slipping away like sand in my hands. "He mentioned that he hasn't felt quite right, and that he has been asleep for most of the time since I was last there."

Darius chuckled again, a low ominous sound that bounced around the car. "Is that all, little protector? Sounded to me like your dream was a bit more exciting than a simple conversation. Then again, it's been so long since I've had a proper...conversation. It's possible they've changed in style and form during my interment."

I flushed, glancing from one guy to the next, until I looked up at Declan; all of them were avoiding eye contact with me, except for Darius. He looked straight at me, like he could read my mind, and whatever he saw there filled him both with amusement and anger.

"Things...got...weird." It was the best explanation I could

settle on. They all knew what happened. And they knew *I* knew that they knew what happened.

"Well," Darius said, a humorless smile on his face, "can't say this isn't what I expected. But it seems like your lost protector is actually an incubus. Partially anyway. You protectors have always had a knack for hiding your dirty secrets."

Without a word, Atlas opened the door, exited the car, and slammed it shut. We all watched as he walked towards the woods, every limb filled with tension, until he disappeared behind some trees.

Declan turned away from me, like she was going to go after Atlas but thought better of it. She stretched both of her hands up, resting them on the back of her neck like a hammock. "Well, this makes things a hell of a lot more complicated."

Were they taking Darius seriously right now? "Er—" I started, unsure how to proceed, but positive I needed to knock some sense into them all. "Protectors can't be turned into an incubus. Incubi are born. So—"

Eli popped open a bottle of water and drained it in one go. "Is it possible his mother was a succubus?"

Declan shrugged and pressed her arms into the door frame so that she could lean slightly into the car. "I don't know man, no one knows anything about her. Tarren always told them she was a human. As far as I know, everyone, including Atlas and Wade, assumed that to be true. He's never shown any signs of being an incubus for as long as I've known him, anyway."

I cleared my throat, trying desperately not to think about the fact that Declan was leaning just a few inches above me. "Has a protector ever—er—mated with a succubus before? I mean, is that a thing that happens on the reg?"

"Not that I've ever heard," Eli said behind me as a grunt from Darius confirmed the same. "Succubi are also pretty rare. We don't even have one in the lab. And Tarren—he would absolutely never willingly have relations with a supernatural creature.

There's a very good reason why he doesn't know about Atlas yet. It would not go well."

I bristled at the way he said that, like the lab was nothing more than a menagerie of creatures for us to study.

"Should somebody go after Atlas?" I asked. The faint rustling through the trees stopped, so I had no idea where he was. "Or is it normal for him to just take off and leave us stranded on the side of the road?"

"Poor Atlas," Eli said as he leaned his head back on a sigh. "Real lousy luck. First he goes and gets turned into a wolf, and now he learns his brother feeds off sex. Daddy Dearest is going to be wrecked."

The way they talked about Atlas and Wade's father was odd. If the man sent Wade to the States out of shame for his human connection, what would he do if he found out that both of his boys were the same monsters he was sworn to kill? Was he the kind of man who would take out his own children? Ice coursed through my veins at the thought.

Declan looked over at Eli before nodding towards Darius. "Keep an eye on the vamp, I'm going to go see if I can locate him and calm him down a bit. We should get off the road and try to find some shelter soon. Sun's up and we have a lot of moving pieces to consider now."

As she walked away, I turned in my seat, studying the odd picture of Eli sitting next to a vampire. "Did Atlas shift?"

Eli's eyes slid towards Darius, like he wasn't sure how much he wanted to say in front of him. But honestly, if Darius hadn't spilled the truth yet, I doubted he would any time soon. He learned the truth about what Atlas was during the night of his first escape, yet he never told anyone in the lab. Why? Plus, we were all already screwed for letting him out in the first place. Unless we came back with Wade and a solid plan, we were all in a tight spot with The Guild going forward, whether Darius spilled our secrets or not.

As if coming to the same realization, Eli shrugged. "It's possible. When he gets tightly wound, he has a more difficult time keeping the beast in check. Usually he just needs some fresh air and a quick run."

"That's because he's resisting the wolf instead of embracing the truth," Darius muttered, pulling his arms as far apart as the restraints would let him before they bounced back in place. It was like he was playing an odd, painful game with himself, flirting with the limits of his freedom.

"What's the truth?" I asked, my lip turning down at the sight of blood on his arms.

"He isn't a protector with a beast lingering inside of him. He is the wolf now, that is a piece of who—and what—he is. Until he can come to terms with it, he's going to struggle with maintaining control." Darius looked up at me, his expression suddenly serious. "You have a habit of surrounding yourself with dangerous creatures, Max Bentley. It'll get you killed one of these days." As if bored with the path of the current conversation, he turned towards Eli. "You buffoons aren't going to seriously keep me in these restraints the entire time are you? My contacts aren't going to be particularly amenable to helping us find the gate if I show up looking like a damn bondage hostage."

Eli bit his bottom lip, his warm brown eyes meeting mine as he considered Darius's point. We both knew the truth: that the odds of Declan or Atlas agreeing to letting Darius loose were almost impossible. But we also knew that Darius was right. If we wanted this to work, if we wanted a chance of saving Wade, our only option was to eventually trust that Darius wouldn't screw us over. Or, you know, gobble us down like a last meal.

17

DARIUS

After the werewolf finished his temper tantrum and made his way back to the car, we found a hotel suite. I didn't miss the fact that they chose one on the outskirts of the city. Nor that the place seemed to be completely vacant except for us and the sparse staff.

Truthfully, I didn't blame them. The second I had a chance, I was going to have a five course meal. There was no way we stood a chance at entering the hell realm unscathed if I was going to be living off of rodents. We were not living in a goddamn Twilight novel. And, sooner or later, the starvation was going to take a toll.

I wasn't lying about the canine and his beast. Just as the wolf was a part of his nature now, so too was the thirst a part of mine. If I tried to resist for much longer, sooner or later I would snap. And the girl smelled too damn mouth-watering for her own good. She'd be the first one my beast would go for. And for as long as he was intrigued by her, I couldn't guarantee her survival. I wasn't sure why I was so hellbent on her life continuing, but I was. Strange.

They all seemed to have a weird fascination with her, so maybe she would be my in for getting a proper dinner. If I threatened to split open her veins, maybe they'd let me settle for the pool boy as a consolation prize?

The wolf paid for a suite with three bedrooms before departing almost immediately.

"Where's he going?" Max asked, her face contorting in a yawn. I'd been monitoring her pulse obsessively since she woke up from her encounter with the incubus. Sitting by helplessly, strapped up with painful restraints, had been its own kind of torture. I wasn't sure why, entirely, but watching the life slowly drain from her was excruciating. I told myself it was because she was too entertaining to die. If she had expired there in the car, I have no doubt that the brooding Irish woman would've disemboweled me just for fun. Protectors were a gruesome lot.

Except for her. There was a draw there, something not quite expected. I didn't want to linger on it for too long, but I did know one thing—I wouldn't let her die. Not yet anyway.

So it was tantamount that I gained access to the pool boy. And soon. These restraints were effective, but I could feel them weakening. They wouldn't hold me back forever. And starving a vampire was a dangerous game to play, one even I couldn't control the results of.

"He's going to drop the car a bit out of town," the one called Eli said. "And probably pick us up a different one to use while we're here. We'll want to do all that we can to make sure The Guild can't track us down too easily before we cross over."

I hadn't been following their conversation too well, my entire body poised instead to track each of Max's movements: the way her pulse beat against the soft curve of her neck; the way she leaned gently on the furniture when she grew too fatigued; the glazed look in her eyes. I could tell that she was trying to disguise the toll her dream had taken on her body. And I couldn't quell the annoying feeling that she wanted to go back there, to that boy, the first chance she got. I knew that incubi held a particular allure. Hell, I'd bedded my fair share of them and their sisters over the years. But the thought of her in their clutches—

it didn't sit well with me. The sooner we found the boy and severed whatever ties he had to her, the better. Then the real fun could begin.

"Darius?" Max was standing before me, her dark eyes boring into my face like she was trying to unravel my thoughts.

"Yes, little protector?" I grinned, satisfied at the way she trembled whenever she came near. She was so fun to toy with.

"I-I've been trying to get your attention. What's the first step?" She bit her bottom lip gently. I was beginning to see that it was an unconscious habit of hers, but endearing all the same.

"Mmm?" I stared at the soft indent her teeth made, wanting to mimic the gesture with my own.

"We're just outside of Seattle," Declan said, throwing a bag into the far room. She studied me with barely-disguised disgust. When I got my chance, she'd be the first one I'd drain. The girl was beautiful, so it would be a shame. But anger did marvelous things to the taste of blood and that was too good to pass up. "What's the first step? How will we reach your contacts?"

My mood soured at the reminder. The contacts I had in this city weren't exactly cordial. And I'd disappeared for years in that damn dungeon they called a lab. I had no idea who the important players were these days. Vampire hierarchy was an impossible thing to predict long term. And bringing the enemy into my former territory? It was a risky move that would take some serious planning. One that would eventually see me dead if I wasn't careful. What were the odds of me just breaking away now and cutting my losses?

"Darius, please." Those damn brown eyes again. She stepped closer and suddenly all I could see was her. Why did she have this power over me? It couldn't just be idle entertainment. Was she distantly related to a succubus?

No. I'd encountered many over my years and none of them quite captured my attention the way that she did. It was more than a physical, chemical attraction. When I thought she'd been dying I was...concerned? Maybe years living as a lab rat had broken me.

I exhaled, stretching my limbs as much as the bindings would allow. "There's a bar downtown. It's a popular meeting spot for people when they cross over from the hell realm. The gate itself isn't always consistent. And it's been years since I've spoken to anyone in a position of power on this side." I eyed the two not-Max protectors in the room. "Thanks, in part, to your people for caging me."

"You. Eat. People," Eli bit out, disgust crossing his features. He didn't like me, that much was obvious. But it was a casual, generic disgust. The other one, Declan, was different. For her, my presence was personal. If I wound up decapitated, I was coming back to haunt her ass as the number one suspect. "What are we supposed to do? Throw you a damn party whenever we encounter your kind? Ask you nicely to play well with humans and slap you on the wrist when you don't?"

A party would be nice. Much preferable to the alternative anyway.

"Eli," Max said, walking over to him. She gripped his hand softly, and I watched with annoyance as he turned all of his attention to her like she was a damn homing device. He didn't seem to realize it, the effect that she had on him. But all of them —they tracked her every movement and sound like she was the world's most elusive prey. "Please. We need him."

I bit back a pompous grin. "Yeah, Eli. You need me." Okay fine, so I didn't really disguise my triumph. I was a vampire, we weren't known for subtlety.

"Like I said," I continued, lounging back on the ugly green couch in the middle of the room. While I was going for casual comfort, the restraints made it completely impossible. "There's a bar. I'll need to go there, scope out whoever is in power, and see if I can get an in. It's rare that people want back into the hell realm, so it might take some convincing if we want to remain under the radar."

"You can't honestly think that we'd let you go to a bar?" Declan leaned up against the door, her face in that perpetual model-like pout of hers.

"Can we go instead?" Max asked, her calm glance moving from Declan, to me, and back again. "I mean, it's either we go or we will have to free Darius. It's not like they're going to take kindly to us all showing up with one of their own in restraints."

"Unfortunately, Max is correct," I said, barely bothering to disguise my triumph now. If they wanted me to be of any use, I would require all of my freedom.

"Then we find another way," Declan bit out. "The second he's loose, he's just going to go on a killing spree. It's what they do."

Eli let out a loud sigh and dramatically scrubbed his face with his hands, like a parent fed up with his kids. "You know we don't have time for that, Dec." He glanced briefly at Max and I knew that he, too, was aware of the impact the boy's dream walking was having on her. It was impossible to miss, now that we knew to look for the signs. "Besides, between the three of us and Max, it's not like we can't keep an eye on him. I'm sure we can let him off his leash for a few well-timed moments."

"We won't exactly have the benefit of outnumbering him when we enter some creepy beast bar, will we?" Declan said, frustration burning so fiercely inside of her that I could see every lean muscle in her body tense. It was delightfully entertaining. Aside from watching Max, it was my new favorite hobby. "What're you staring at leech?"

"That weird twitchy thing your left eye does when you're angry." I sank further back into the seat of the couch. After years of having nothing but a cold cot and lab tables to relax on, this tiny suite felt like a damn mansion, even with the restraints.

"We don't have a choice, Declan," Max stated again before turning her face towards me. "Can you please try to be more agreeable, Darius? They aren't going to trust you if all you do is poke at them like that."

I opened my mouth to retort, but Max's knees buckled a bit and she stumbled.

"Shit," Eli said, beating us to her. "You okay?"

She nodded and sat down next to me, her thin fingers a mere breath away from mine. It was strange how aware my body was of her presence. "Yes, it's just been a long day."

"You should rest," Eli said.

Declan stepped closer, no longer leaning against the wall. "No she shouldn't. She's exhausted and drained because every time she falls asleep, she encounters an incubus. Rest won't help her regain energy at this point. Not so long as Wade keeps drawing her to him, unconsciously or not." She looked up to me again, her electric green eyes studying me closely. "When does this bar of yours open? I can scope it out when Atlas gets back and then, later, we will take off your restraints and escort you there. Max is right, we don't have time to waste with bickering."

I sucked in my bottom lip, and moved slightly closer to Max. Her pulse was steadying again as she took long, slow breaths and watched Declan pace.

"We can swing by around seven. The place will be open sooner than that, but no one worth speaking to will arrive until later." My neck strained slightly against the restraints as I wrestled with my next thought. "It might not mean much, but you have my word that I won't attack any unwilling victims. But if I'm going to agree to that, it would be ideal if you can at least steal some blood bags from me. If I'm not fed soon, I can't promise that I'll remain as agreeable as I usually am—"

Declan interrupted me with a scoff and a surly echo of "*agreeable.*"

And I meant it. I wouldn't try to run or split open anyone's veins. No matter how badly I wanted to. I made a deal with Max, and for some godforsaken reason, I wanted to keep it.

What the hell was wrong with me?

18
MAX

"Why do you hate them so much?"

My fingers danced along the edges of the blanket. I was lying down in the room I would be sharing with Declan, trying to rest up without falling asleep. It was an aggravating state of limbo to be in. Why was it always so impossible to stay awake when you wanted to? She was in charge of making sure that I didn't drift off into REM while the guys took turns growling at Darius and planning for this evening.

She looked up at me, her dark lashes dancing along her cheek as she sharpened her knives in a corner chair. "Hate who?"

"Vampires, werewolves, hellhounds—all of them. I mean I know it's our job to despise who they are. I get that, I really do. But your best friend is a werewolf now, and you're still protecting him. So you have to see that this world we are living in isn't completely black and white."

"Are you suggesting that I befriend every homicidal creature that comes barreling into my world, Max?"

"No, but if you're able to trust Atlas as much as you do, and now Wade. He's well, you know, not entirely human anymore. And when you first encountered Ralph, you wanted him put down, but now you secretly visit him in the forest to play fetch. You know he's not evil—"

"Your point?" Her dark brow arched as she stared at me with her entrancing eyes. "You want me to get buddy-buddy with the vampire out there? It's not going to happen. I don't care if you have an ass backwards crush on him, he's a killer. The second he gets a chance, even if he stays true to his word and doesn't attack any of us, he's going to kill. Again and again and again. It's what they do. They literally survive by eating humans. The sooner you come to terms with that, the easier it's going to be for you when this whole episode is behind us."

"I don't have a crush on him," I bit out, temporarily ignoring the rest of her tirade. My cheeks burned when I realized that Atlas must've told the rest of the team about Darius kissing me. Was Darius hot? Absolutely. Had he kissed me? Sure had. But I wasn't obtuse enough to catch feelings for the very creature I was trained to kill.

A cruel grin spread across her face as she studied me. "Vampires are different, Max. They are predators. They are literally designed to pull you in. It's how they hunt. Your hellhound? Yeah, he's grown on me. And it's clear that he doesn't mean anyone harm, least of all you. And Atlas? He's good. He's a bit of an asshole sometimes, but he's fighting that creature inside of him with every breath that he takes. In the time since his bite, he hasn't harmed a single human. Not one. And he's been there for me through some of the darkest moments of my life, so he gets my default trust until he breaks it." She stood up and walked towards me before sitting on the edge of the bed. The ends of her long hair danced along the skin of my arm, sending confusing chills up my body.

"That vampire of yours out there?" she continued, her voice quieter than before, "the second you released him the first time, he drained and killed a protector. Have you forgotten that, in your eagerness to free him from those restraints? He doesn't control the monster within him, they are one and the same. He is everything that Atlas is fighting against."

Her words felt like a harsh slap and I recoiled, struggling to keep my eyes level with hers. I understood her point, and she wasn't wrong. Thinking back to the first encounter I had with Atlas in wolf form—he'd attacked Michael. But would he have killed him if Ro and I weren't there to stop him? It wasn't something we'd ever know. What I did know was that here and now, I didn't think Atlas would willingly hurt me or anyone else on his side. I didn't have the same certainty when it came to Darius.

"Still," I said, studying the anger dancing in her eyes. Did I really want to die on this hill? Maybe. Something about Declan just brought out my stubbornness. "Atlas and Eli clearly dislike Darius. Want to see him dead, most likely. But you—your hatred seems so much...more."

For the first time since the start of conversation, she broke eye contact, lifting herself off my bed with a sigh as she stretched her long arms so that her shirt lifted a few inches, revealing her smooth stomach. I forced my eyes to move up to her face. I'd never really thought about girls in a romantic or sexual way before, other than the occasional girl crush on a tv show. But Declan had a way of making me question absolutely everything about the world, my own sexuality included.

"We didn't all have the privilege of living untouched by this world most of our lives," she snapped. For the first time tonight, the anger she'd been reserving for creatures like Darius was focused on me. "I've encountered enough vampires to know what they're capable of—they are more dangerous than any other hell creature you will encounter. The second you let your guard down, you will get hurt. I don't know how to make you understand that, or why it isn't instinctually automatic for you. Hell, you were attacked by a vampire a few short months ago. Have you completely forgotten that, Max?" She exhaled a harsh breath, a wall forming behind her eyes. "If you plan on surviving in this world, you need to grow up."

Without another glance in my direction, she stormed out of the room, leaving me feeling like I'd just been slapped. I didn't have a babysitter keeping me awake but, after that conversation, the guilt broiling in my belly would be enough to keep me fighting off sleep for hours.

"Honestly, it might be better if you let me in by myself. Showing up with a band of protectors in my arsenal isn't exactly going to warm me up to them." Darius slurped out of his blood bag, the sound alone enough to make me gag. He'd been free of restraints for fifteen minutes now and each movement he made was overly exaggerated. He kept going on and on about how nice it was to be able to stretch his limbs again, but I was half convinced he just loved seeing everyone flinch each time he made too dramatic of a movement.

Declan hadn't spoken to me since our conversation, but I watched as she watched him, and understanding and guilt rolled over me in fresh waves.

It wasn't just hatred. She was afraid. Afraid of Darius and of what he might do to her and to her best friends. I couldn't fault that kind of fear. For some unknowable reason, I trusted Darius. But if he had been any other vampire near people I cared about, I'd probably be just as angry about it as she was. And now Darius was gorging himself on some innocent donor's blood, relishing every single drop that touched his tongue, like a child lapping up sugar.

"It's not going to happen, vamp. Just be grateful you're temporarily off your leash." Eli ran a hand through his dark waves. He was definitely the least tense of us all, but I didn't miss the way he kept positioning himself in front of me, like he was unwilling to let Darius get within two feet of me. Still, of everyone, Eli probably had the best rapport with the vampire, and he was the one who spent half the afternoon hunting down blood banks so that Darius wouldn't throw himself on our necks the second he was off leash.

In a lot of ways, Eli seemed like he'd prefer being alone with Darius to being alone with me. We hadn't spoken much since the night he bared his soul and then kissed me. His clear regret and awkwardness around me made me feel seven shades of uncomfortable. But I wasn't sure how to let him know that it was okay—that I could pretend that night never happened if it would ease his thoughts.

Was I hurt? Yes. Terrified that I was a supremely bad kisser capable of turning his interactions with me from flirty to distant? Abso-fucking-lutely. But we had more important things to consider than my own damaged ego.

"Well," Darius said, tossing his last blood bag into a dumpster. I tried not to gag as his tongue lapped up a drop of red from his bottom lip. "In that case, at least one of you smells like Fido, so I guess there's that. Maybe no one will realize that the other half of our entourage secretly wants to murder them all. Everyone gets lucky eventually, right?"

We were a block or so away from our destination and my nerves were amping up. I'd never willingly thrown myself into a supernatural stronghold before, especially without having full reports and intel first, and I knew that if things went sideways, we were all most likely dead. Atlas, Eli, and Declan were three of the best fighters I'd ever encountered. And I wasn't exactly a slouch myself. But who knew how many creatures would be on the inside of the bar? Outnumbered, we didn't stand a chance. Especially if Darius decided to lure us there under false pretenses and then jump ship to the other side of the fight.

Gentle fingers clasped mine briefly before dropping contact and I looked up into Eli's warm honey eyes. I hated the fact that the sight of him looking at me like that made my stomach flip. "You don't have to go in with us, Max. You can head back to the hotel and we can meet you there later."

I swallowed at the legitimate concern I saw on his face. His usually distant, fuckboy attitude washed away almost completely as he looked from me to the bar ahead. Was he worried about me getting hurt or worried about me holding them back?

In the long run, it probably didn't matter, because either way, I was doing this.

"I'm okay, I want to go," I said, grabbing his hand back and squeezing softly before putting some distance between us. They needed to come to terms with the fact that I wasn't some fragile flower. I'd encountered more vampires and werewolves in the last few months than almost everyone in my age group back at The Guild. And I was still alive and kicking ass. Plus, I managed to develop a secret portal into an incubus's mind, so I wasn't exactly useless.

As we edged towards the door, Darius straightened his posture and hardened the planes of his face. Almost instantly, he went from this slightly aloof vampire to something truly terrifying. There was an edge to his expression I hadn't seen before. He winked his golden eye at me, dissolving the illusion almost instantly, before resituating his powerful mask and taking the lead.

A large man was stationed outside the bar. His hair was a bright, fiery red and his face was covered in freckles. If it weren't for his size, I'd think he was a cuddly teddy bear, but something about him just screamed menacing. Did vampires come in shades of terrifying lumberjack? Because if so, this guy definitely nailed the look he was going for.

As we pulled up the man arched a heavy brow and took in our odd motley crew. "Darius? You've got to be shitting me. Thought you were dead. Granted, you sort of look like you might as well be."

Darius shrugged and cracked his neck from side to side. "I'm hard to kill. My friends and I have someone to see tonight."

The man tensed his jaw as he watched Darius, narrowing his eyes like he was afraid the vampire would spring on him at a moment's notice. Then, slowly, he took in the rest of us. I watched as his eyes lingered on Declan, spending far more time staring at her rack than anywhere else.

A low growl vibrated in her chest, and I stepped closer to her, as if I could offer support or somehow draw his attention away. Men could be total douche-canoes.

"And who are your friends," the man asked, his eyes still pinned on Declan. "I haven't seen them around here before."

My nails dug into the soft flesh of my palms as I tried to pull back on my desire to throat punch this jerk. Judging by Declan's stiff posture, she was experiencing the same difficulty with exercising restraint.

Darius stepped in front of the man's line of sight, blocking him from Declan. "I can vouch for them. They are new in this realm and recently helped me out of a very sticky situation. They're to remain unharmed and untouched, Felix." The last sentence was uttered with enough threat that the hair on the back of my neck was standing up. Maybe Declan was right, Darius was a lot more terrifying than I gave him credit for.

Declan tilted her head slightly, staring at the back of Darius's head with a hint of confusion and surprise—and maybe even a bit of respect. When she caught me staring at her, she rolled her eyes and crossed her hands over her chest, face falling back into its usual pout.

Okay, so she wasn't quite ready to become best friends with Darius. But, for the first time, it also didn't look like she wanted to castrate him. More than once. Friendship had to start somewhere, I guess.

Darius took a step closer towards Felix when the guy didn't open the door. He took a long gulp, his Adam's apple bobbing up and down as he tried not breaking eye contact with Darius. "Doubt boss man is going to want to see you but, fine, you and your lot can go in. Just know that if your friends stir up trouble, it's on you, old friend."

Something about the way he drew out the 'old friend' had my skin crawling, and I didn't want to stick around long enough to figure out what sort of complicated frenemy situation they had going on. Darius wasn't exactly an overly likable guy, if my friends' opinions were anything to go by.

His face broke out in a grin as he pulled the door open, not even waiting for Felix to move out of his way first. "Don't kid yourself. We were never friends, Felix. I'm a creature with a rather discerning taste."

Insulting the doorman seemed like an odd thing to do when we were trying to gain entry into the bar, but Felix broke into such a loud belly laugh that I was willing to eat my own judgment. Apparently, creatures from hell operated on different wavelengths when it came to politeness.

Felix patted Darius on the back, as he entered into the old building, before stepping aside so that the rest of us could filter in. I made sure to keep close to Declan, just in case the asshat got any ideas—a gesture that made him laugh even harder.

"Don't worry, pipsqueak, I won't try and wrestle your girl from you." He clamped a hand down on my shoulder, like we were old pals, and I tried my best not to buckle from the weight. I was strong, sure, but I was also half this guy's size.

Declan choked in surprise and I ducked my head down, trying to hide what was likely a bright red flush.

"But," he added as we made our way into the bar, "if she gets tired of you, let her know my door is always open. I don't discriminate by species."

Did he suspect that she wasn't a vampire? Or was he simply not a vampire and under the assumption that she was one because of Darius? One interaction made it abundantly clear that protectors knew next to nothing about the creatures we hunted, least of all their social patterns.

Declan looped her arm through mine, squeezing me to her side.

"Ignore him, pipsqueak," she whispered, but I caught the slight tinge of embarrassment coloring her cheeks. Her pale skin was a lot worse at disguising a blush than mine was. Was she embarrassed about what he insinuated or just from getting the unwanted attention?

My stomach flipped at the close proximity of her body to mine, every inch that pressed up against me was like a flame licking my skin and I vowed to myself that I'd do whatever it took to squash whatever attraction I was developing towards her. We had enough to worry about. With a clear of my throat, I pulled away, walking towards Darius. The draw I felt to the members of Team Six was throwing me for a loop, and I didn't have the time or energy to go down that rabbit hole right now.

"So," I whispered, low enough for only our group to hear. "Who exactly are we looking for?"

The bar was a lot larger on the inside than it looked, with a fairly big crowd for so early in the night. Everyone looked so... human, laughing with friends, sitting on stools along the bar and at tables scattered haphazardly in the big dining area. There was rock music blaring softly throughout the space and the lights were dimmed low enough to create a cozy atmosphere, but not so low that you had to worry about unwelcome hands reaching for your drink. If Darius wasn't the one that brought us here, I would assume this place was just like any bar I'd find in town or on TV.

The utter humanity of the place clawed at my insides as I tried to reconcile the guys laughing over a beer in one corner with the stone-cold killers we were used to hunting.

"Well I'll be damned," a loud, cheerful woman behind the bar yelled. "Darius? As I live and breathe, I never thought I'd see you stepping foot into my bar again."

She had short, reddish-brown hair and small wrinkles along her eyes and mouth. They were the kind of wrinkles released by a long life of laughter and joy and I found myself instantly taking a liking to her. Her smiling lips were painted a deep ruddy red, almost identical to the shade of her long dress that swept over her curves like waves.

"Marge," Darius said, and for the first time since I'd encountered him, I saw genuine warmth light up his features. The sight of it—pure joy—dancing in his unusual eyes took my breath away. All of a sudden, the creepy Hannibal Lecter vibe I was used to him rocking disappeared before my eyes. He was softer like this, more real somehow. "I had no idea you'd be back in this part of town."

"Yeah well, you're out of the loop, son. I've been back here for two years. Claude gave me my old job back." Her jovial expression dried up a bit as she took in the rest of our group. "Where've you been boy? And who did you bring back with you? Last I heard, you were rotting away in the grasp of those damn protectors. How'd you get out?"

Darius glanced back at us, the corner of his lips curling down slightly. I could see the gears moving in his head as he tried to quickly come up with a logical explanation. Was he expecting to run into so many old friends, or did this compromise our plans?

"This one's a werewolf," He nodded briefly towards Atlas. "He was in captivity with me. We got the drop on one of the guards when we had the chance a few nights ago. And then we came this way as quickly as we could."

Marge narrowed her eyes, studying the rest of us. "What're the rest of 'em? Can't quite get a read, but they don't smell human."

I breathed in long and deep, trying to slow the rapid beat of my heart. Were we screwed over already? None of us really planned for this. Most creatures couldn't sense species like this. What the hell was Marge?

Just when I thought Darius would throw us under the bus and use the moment as his opportunity to get us all killed, he simply shrugged.

"That one there," he pointed towards Eli, "is half incubus, and the one next to him," he nodded towards Declan, "Is his sister. Bit of a dud in terms of power, but he's fond of her so we keep her around."

Declan's jaw tensed, her eyes glaring daggers into the back of

Darius's head. I bit back a grin. Just when I thought they were going to declare a truce with each other, Darius had to go and ruin it. These two were going to be the death of me, if Wade didn't beat them to it.

"And what about the short one?" Marge wiped down a glass with a rag that looked ready to dirty up the cup again. "Something's a bit off about her." She flared her nose slightly, tilting her head in my direction as she crouched over the bar in our direction. "Smells funny."

I resisted the urge to discreetly sniff my underarms, but just barely.

Darius's arm swept across my shoulders, pulling me into him. I grunted with surprise but followed his lead. "She's mine."

Marge broke out into a giant smile, revealing a set of slightly crooked teeth that unexpectedly added to her appeal. "You're shitting me? It's finally happened? Ladies and gentlemen, Darius Dixon went and got himself domesticated. You find her in enemy terrain too? I hope you lot took down a solid number of 'em during your escape. The less of those bastards in the world, the better."

My chest started to tighten, and I looked sideways towards the door, secretly planning our escape if things went south. I wasn't sure if Marge completely bought Darius's story about us, but if she found out that we were protectors, we were as good as dead. This wasn't the kind of place you made it out of alive if the inhabitants didn't want you to.

The bar wasn't entirely full, but there were well over three dozen people wandering around and seated at the bar and tables. Way too many for us to take on and remain unscathed. Especially since I wasn't exactly feeling my best. I could probably only barely take on a large human right now, let alone a creature from hell.

Darius squeezed my shoulder sharply, an action that, surprisingly, grounded me. I wasn't exactly sure what he meant by me being his. Was it typical for vamps to cart around their own human blood bags? Would I be expected to slit my wrist over his pint glass during our visit? My skin crawled at the thought of him consuming my blood.

He started nervously rocking, a movement so slight that I only noticed it because my side was glued to his. "Is he around, Marge? I need to talk to him, and I need to meet with Villette. Both as soon as possible."

Marge's brows bent down towards the middle, and I watched a silent conversation play out between her and Darius. He hadn't told us anything about the people we were meeting tonight, so I had no idea what to expect.

"Lately, he's been showing up around nine if he's turning up at all. You sure he'll be willing to see you? Villette is in the back corner with her newest companion." Marge wrinkled her nose as she threw a dark look towards the other side of the bar. "She's been in a bit of a mood lately, so good luck. Might want to butter her up with a few drinks first."

I wasn't sure who the 'he' was in this scenario, but it looked like we had some time to kill.

"Er," I glanced between Darius and Marge, "so, drinks then I guess? I could use some social lubrication before meeting all of your friends." I threw what I hoped to be a coy grin at Darius before leaning against the bar. "Care to make me something fruity and strong, Marge?"

Marge leaned forward and snorted, her large bust dropping on the counter like it was a shelf. She studied me for a moment, her deep eyes so dark that I could almost see the entire bar reflected in them, before slapping her hand down on the wood and reaching for a clean glass. Or, well, cleaner than the glass she was drying anyway.

"I like this one, Darius. Something tells me you're going to have your work cut out for you. She's not what she seems." While she mixed me up something that looked like it had three different clear liquids and a concoction of juices, she turned to the rest of the group with an expectant look on her face.

Atlas flared his nose slightly, and I knew that he was warring with wanting to stay clear-minded in enemy territory and wanting to fit in. It took a lot to get a protector wasted though and I imagined it was even more for a werewolf. He ordered a round of beers for himself, Eli, and Declan.

"And you, darling?" Marge handed me my drink while nodding to Darius. "Your usual?"

He winked his golden eye at Marge in answer and I held my breath, half expecting his usual to be some sort of liquor mixed with blood or at the very least, a Bloody Mary.

But then she filled a glass up with vodka and orange juice. I casually brushed my fingers along my jaw, half expecting it to be hanging open. A screwdriver? That's what the vampire ordered as his usual?

Without waiting for the rest of us, Darius took a long swig through the short black straw, his body relaxing and a genuine grin splitting his face. "I can't even tell you how good it is to have one of these. It's been ages."

Declan snorted, mumbling something too quiet for me to follow, before draining a few sips of her beer. Like Atlas, she was slowly searching the place, cataloguing each individual and doorway. It wasn't so much in the way they stood or stared, but I could almost feel their discomfort and rapt attention. They were in heavy mission-mode. Which meant they were even more uptight than usual.

And then there was Eli. He just seemed so much more amused with the situation, like he'd found himself in some unexpected, weird museum. I also didn't miss the way he was studying a voluptuous girl standing outside the bathroom. Her dress was so tight it was practically painted on and she kept looking at him with bedroom eyes.

My stomach hardened at the sight of her, and I had to force myself to draw my eyes away from their silent flirtation. If anyone could draw information out of a stranger, it was Eli. So I had no reason to be so uncomfortable with his approach. He'd made it abundantly clear months ago that there was nothing between us—a sentiment I kept replaying over and over in my mind, lest I forget.

"My friends will stay here while I chat with Villy. Drinks are on them," Darius said, before lacing his fingers through mine. "What's she drinking these days?"

"Tequila." Marge reached over the counter and clapped him on the back, like she was trying to offer comfort or encouragement. "But you aren't exactly on her good side, my boy, so I recommend bringing her over a double. In fact, other than me, I'm not sure you've really got many friends at all around these parts."

Darius cringed in response, his already pale skin draining the final vestiges of color. "Double it is."

19
MAX

If I had to describe the personification of sex, I would describe it as Villette. She had dark black hair, waved in a way I didn't think anyone other than a Victoria's Secret model could accomplish, with perfectly symmetrical features—bright blue eyes, impossibly plush, pouty lips, the whole works. I was half-convinced that she wasn't real and was instead just a hologram of sorts or at the very least, wearing some sort of magical glamour. Not that I'd ever heard of such a thing.

And then there was the fact that she was dressed like she was getting ready to star in a pretty scandalous adult film. Her boobs were lifted and separated by a thick leather corset that looked uncomfortable as fuck, even though her posture was so relaxed that she might as well have been wearing a fuzzy robe.

I silently sent a thank you to whichever gods created leggings and t-shirts. Women's fashion could be borderline sadistic sometimes, even if Villette could camouflage the pain somehow.

"Villette," Darius drawled, stepping up to her corner booth, "long time no s—"

She threw her date's beer into Dairus's face before he could get a word in edgewise, her petite nose bunched up in disgust. I heard Declan cackle with laughter from back at the bar, and I tried to hide my own grin, even though a few splatters of the hoppy beverage splashed onto me as well.

"Sorry girl, that wasn't meant for you," Villette said, her voice so silky and sultry that it sounded like it was designed for the bedroom.

Her date stared wistfully at the last few dregs of beer still in his pint glass, his arm perched across Villette's shoulder. While Villette was next-level-gorgeous, her date was no slouch. He had disheveled blond hair and bright blue eyes that most Hollywood actors would kill for.

Darius set the shot of tequila down on the wooden table and slid into the other side of the booth. Before I could protest, he pulled me down to sit next to him, my side pressed right against his.

"Villette, dear," he said, grabbing the guy's napkin to dry up his face, "that's hardly a way to say hello to an old friend."

Without a word, she pounded back the tequila, not breaking eye contact with Darius as the liquid slid down her throat. Her expression remained impassive, but I cringed for her—I couldn't do tequila shots without a chaser of sorts—or, at the very least, a lime—much to Izzy's chagrin.

Darius looked at me, then to Villette, and finally to her friend. "Well, this is cozy. I've always been a fan of double dates. How've you been Villy? How's Mikey?"

Villette scoffed, handing her date the empty glass. "Jay, go get me a refill." She jutted her chin towards Darius, her brows pinched, eyes cold as ice, "put it on his tab."

Without a word, Jay left with his empty glass, no doubt pleased with the opportunity to refill his own drink and escape the tension clouding around us.

"See you have a new toy, you always did grow bored easily, Villette. It's one of the things I liked most about our relationship. Never a dull moment."

I choked on my fruity drink, trying to picture Darius with the girl across from me. It would explain the animosity in her eyes, at the very least. He drove everyone he met absolutely wild; I could only imagine that he accomplished it tenfold with the people he dated.

"Mikey is dead," she whispered, sliding her glass from hand to hand, still not breaking eye contact—the sound of glass on wood making a soft whir. "You'd know that if you ever bothered to check in. I see you've found a new friend as well. What does Clarice think about that?"

So many names, I was having trouble keeping track of what the hell we were talking about here. Not that I was actually part of this conversation in the first place. Villette had barely even given me a passing glance. I was half ready to go join Jay at the bar and leave Darius to get eaten alive by this woman on his own.

I'd communicated with him enough to know that she was probably justified in the extreme derision she was floating his way. And I had no intention of sliding my lot in with his. He was a ticking time bomb, and I did not want to be around when that timer dropped to zero.

Darius cleared his throat, sliding his arm around my waist and drawing me just a touch closer to him. I tried to ignore the way the heat of his body filled me with a sense of peace, the way my body fit against his like a glove. I thought vampires were supposed to be all cold and clammy?

The way the muscles in his shoulders relaxed slightly as I settled against him had me wondering if maybe he was the one seeking heat and peace. I couldn't read Darius very well—his mind didn't seem to work in a particularly linear way—but he seemed unsettled here in this bar, even with the casual and teasing air he tried to assume. If I didn't know any better, I'd think he was afraid of something.

What exactly was he getting all of us into?

"I couldn't exactly check in, Villette. Unfortunately, when they take you prisoner and run experiments on you for years, they don't exactly allot you a telephone call. Next time I'm there though, I'll be sure to point that out in their suggestion box."

"I wouldn't have picked up even if they had," she said, her lip turned up in disgust. "You have a lot of nerve showing up here with nothing more than a fucking shot of tequila, D."

With a soft frown, his eyes dropped to the table. "I am sorry to hear about Mikey though, truly. He was a good man." He arched a single brow, reinfusing his expression with playfulness and the chaotic energy I was more used to from him. "At least I had the sense to make it a double."

I cleared my throat awkwardly, tempted to get up and leave but for the fact that we were here to help Wade. I didn't want to interrupt their awkward trip down memory lane or anything—especially when they could both probably kill me before I had a chance to blink—but I wanted to get the information we needed before Darius killed every last strain of good will this woman had. If Declan's reaction to him was anything to go by, he had a pretty good track record of quickly making beautiful women hate him.

Her electric-blue eyes homed in on me like a missile launcher and she tilted her head, studying me like a cat, her expression unreadable. "Who's your new blood bag then? She's not your usual type. Kind of plain and small, if I'm being honest." She didn't say it like she was trying to be cruel, still it obviously stung. "Now, the other bombshell you walked in with," she craned her neck to watch Declan at the bar, her features lined with lust, "that one I could quite happily get on top of. Is she free? I would make her time worth it."

"I need some information," Darius said, his tone losing some of its earlier humor.

"Go get your information elsewhere, Darius," she spun back around, pinning him with her glare. "I don't do you any favors. Not anymore."

He gripped his glass until I was certain it would explode in his hand, showering us all in another alcoholic beverage, this time with an unwanted layer of glass.

The silence drew out for a long moment, both of them stuck in a silent battle of willpower. Unsure of what else to do, I sipped the rest of my drink through my straw, desperate for the moment to end. Whatever Marge put into this thing, it was tasty. If we survived our conversation with Villette, I was going to ask her what it was called. Maybe even order another.

"I'll owe you one," he said finally, tossing the rest of his screwdriver back, as if it was a shot of whiskey and not the drink of choice for sorority girls at brunch.

That seemed rather nonspecific and not entirely worth the price, but Villette looked unexpectedly pleased with his concession.

Catching the gesture, she grinned, her eyes teasing. "Fucking child, you and your orange juice. You'd think after years of those assholes rattling your brain, they'd have accidentally knocked some taste into that little head of yours." She stretched her arms above her head, arching her back so that her ample cleavage was on full display. Unexpectedly, Darius's eyes stayed on her face. "Alright D, you've got yourself a deal. You'll owe me one. In exchange, I'll answer you one question."

One question? That was it? How seriously were deals between supernaturals taken?

Darius looked like he wanted to reject the offer and I could almost feel him lifting out of the chair, ready to go back to Declan and the guys and call it a day with nothing but a shrug and an "I tried."

I wasn't sure what it was about this woman, but she unsettled Darius. And anyone who unsettled the most unsettling creature I'd ever met fucking terrified me.

He glanced down at me, his mouth turning down in the corner. I couldn't read his expression exactly, but there was concern, maybe even a little trace of fear. With his eyes still staring at me, he slammed his empty glass onto the edge of the table, breaking off a jagged piece.

I jumped at the sound, and glared up at him, confused as he took the sliver and carved it through the soft flesh of his palm before turning back to Villette.

With a wry smile, she did the same to her own perfect skin and grasped his hand in hers. "Well then," she said, sitting back into the booth, crossing her arms in front of her chest. "You've got yourself a deal with a succubus. Name your question."

If I'd been taking a sip of my drink, I would've spit all of it across the table. A succubus? For some reason, I'd assumed that she was a vampire. Until recently, our records had shown that the individual supernatural species didn't tend to work well with each other. Clearly the vamp/wolf team-up wasn't as unusual as we'd assumed. And clearly Darius hadn't been kidding when he mentioned interacting with incubi and succubi, a thought that had my mind wandering off in all sorts of unhelpful, undesirable directions. Thinking about Darius rolling around with a creature as beautiful as Villette was not what I needed to focus on right now.

Looking at Villette now though, I couldn't understand how I'd missed it. The woman straight up oozed sex appeal. Every look she threw Darius, though shadowed with anger, spoke to an unyielding attraction. They had a past, a very intimate one if her extreme reaction to seeing him again was any sign.

For some reason I couldn't quite understand, that realization bothered me more than I wanted to admit. Maybe because seeing monsters as people with relationships and lives outside of murdering humans just didn't fit with The Guild party line. Despite some of her harsh edges, the woman in front of me didn't exactly scream evil. If I were on a Guild-sanctioned mission right now, I would be charged with either killing her or capturing her to bring back to our lab of researchers where she would be poked and prodded and kept in a small cage until she was eventually killed.

"It's about incubi," Darius said, glancing down at me one more time. "Is there a way to keep them from feeding off people? A way to stop the drain if you meet them in a dream?"

My head whipped around so quickly that I wouldn't have been surprised if it straight up detached itself from my neck.

One question. We got one question. And this was what he was wasting it on?

"No," I said, no longer willing to sit by demurely like a sidekick of a blood bag. "That's not our question."

A slow, terrifying smile spread across Villette's face as she turned towards me, studying me with an intensity she hadn't bothered with before.

"I didn't make the deal with you, girl," she said, and for the first time I picked up a slow drawl in her voice, like she spent a lot of time down south. "But now that you mention it D, I can see why that might be your question." She narrowed her eyes, studying me with a careful precision typically reserved for studying a painting in a museum. "The dark circles, the dull skin, the exhaustion is clear. The drain isn't entirely recent." Then, she chuckled softly, glancing back at Darius, clearly enjoying something about the turn in conversation, even if I wasn't sure what it was. "You never did like sharing your toys. Pity. If she's survived this long, she might be more fun than I gave her credit for initially. No wonder she seemed so plain in my initial assessment, she's already used up, half consumed by another."

I clenched my jaw, the muscles so tight I was momentarily concerned I might shatter a tooth. "I'm not a toy," I spat out, disregarding my role as puppet now completely. Villette wasn't going to help us—Darius had wasted our one shot. I should've known better than to trust him. Villette might not have been evil, not in the way The Guild portrayed succubi to be anyway, but she was clearly cruel.

She exhaled softly, snapping her fingers once until Jay came running back with her drink, as if he was only waiting for her permission to join us. "That'll be all for now. I'll summon you again when I request your presence back."

He didn't even look dejected. Didn't even seem to care that she treated him like a piece of meat. Were people nothing more than objects to be consumed up and spit out to these creatures? Was Jay an incubus too? Or was he just an unsuspecting human, lost in a spiral under some sort of supernatural thrall? The realization that he might be human, the very creature I was designed to save, sent an avalanche of rocks into the pit of my stomach. Was she killing him?

"Is he—" I asked, not quite sure how to phrase my contempt, but hearing it infuse my words anyway. Succubi were powerful, more powerful than we really understood. Challenging one so openly might see all of us dead before we so much as had a shot at looking for Wade.

Darius's finger whispered up against my side in a gesture that soothed and shocked in equal parts. "Not to worry, little p— one," he corrected, "Jay is a vampire. A very willing one at that. Villette may be many things, but she never takes from anyone who does not consent to feeding her."

Even though he didn't voice it out loud, I could hear the sentiment of his point ring through—*we aren't all monsters, despite what you might think.*

I thought back to what Darius had said when we'd met. That there was so much about the world of supernaturals that I didn't understand, believing mindlessly what I read in Guild books.

Still, whether Darius was speaking the truth about Villette's pursuits or not, the mere chance that he was smoothed down my hackles, if temporarily.

"Why would anyone agree to such a thing?" I asked, skepticism slipping slowly into curiosity.

Villette arched her perfectly-sculpted eyebrow, taking a long pull of her fresh drink. "Do you really have to ask? Have you not had a taste?"

My skin heated as I thought back to my dream with Wade,

the intensity of feeling that washed over us as the world slipped away and we got lost in the sensations of skin and heat until the places where I ended and he began became muddled.

"I—" I cleared my throat awkwardly, suddenly wishing with every fiber of my being that I could talk to Villette without Darius here to listen in, as ridiculous as that was. He knew very well what I'd been dreaming about, having been there while it happened on one rather memorable occasion. "The, er, good sex, you mean?"

The, er, good sex, you mean?

As soon as the words fell from my lips, I wanted to shove them back in. I sounded like an inexperienced doofus. Probably because I was.

She let out a soft peel of laughter, so delicate it sounded like music. "More than just the sex. For humans, the high can last for weeks. Until, of course, it wears off and they die." She shrugged nonchalantly. "Vampires and werewolves usually linger in the high for a day or two, more powerful creatures less so. Have you really never felt it?"

Her languid facade slipped until, for a moment, she looked just like a normal girl, trying to figure out a new, exciting puzzle displayed out in front of her.

She was less intimidating that way, sure, but something about the fact that she was abandoning her persona raised the hair at the back of my neck.

"What exactly did you say you were, girl?" she asked, leaning towards me so that her face was only a few inches from my own. Now I not only felt like a prized display in a museum, but one that she wanted to steal away and consume for herself until there was nothing left but an empty frame.

"She didn't," Darius said, voice clipped. "My question, if you please, Villette. A deal is a deal."

With a wry smile, she turned back towards him, tracing the rim of her glass with a single, long finger. "You're protective over this one, D. How interesting." At a low growl from Darius, she continued, shrugging him off as if this were nothing more than a casual conversation over appetizers and drinks. "There are a few different options, the easiest of which is to wait it out. Other than myself and a few others, it's rare for my kind to stay in one place for too long. Eventually, the incubus in question will move on to another target, farther away. My kind is used to toys getting used up. We like them fresh."

"By which time, she'll already be dead," Darius bit out, his voice filled with venom. For the first time in a while, I was reminded of how very dangerous he actually was.

Her eyes danced with laughter as a result, and I could tell she was toying with him deliberately now, this had become a game that neither Darius nor I had any control of.

But something didn't make sense. If distance was supposed to help with an incubus's ability to drain, how was Wade taking my energy?

"What if the incubus in question is draining me from the hell realm?" I asked, causing Darius to freeze every muscle in his body.

Villette's blue eyes flashed with shock, and she shifted slightly in her seat, no longer invested in her game with Darius. "That shouldn't be possible. Are you certain?"

Was I? It was possible, perhaps, for Wade to still be in our realm, but for some reason, that didn't feel right. Not least of all because Darius mentioned that the ancients—whoever they were—couldn't stay in the human realm for long. He'd said something about their powers not being entirely consistent while they were here.

"Fairly," I said, as Darius's foot pressed down on mine, as if telling me to stop talking. He was so still now that I couldn't tell if he was even breathing.

"Then something quite unusual is happening," she said, pushing closer to me, willing the table separating us to disappear. "Either your incubus is very, very old, or more powerful than any I've encountered, or," she reached a hand towards me, tilting my chin up with her fingers, "there's something very strange about you. An allure that is able to transcend space in ways I don't quite understand. I've never heard of such a thing."

Her fingers danced up my face until her long nails gently slid along my jawline, causing my heartrate to quicken, not out of lust but out of fear.

In a sudden move, too fast for me to track, Darius flung her arm away, holding her wrist against the table in a hard, vicious grip.

"Enough, Villy," he said, the nickname no longer holding any fondness, "this doesn't matter. Your fascination doesn't matter. You have not fully answered my question. How else can she fight being fed from? Can she avoid the dreams altogether?"

Villette whimpered, sinking into the booth as she tried to shy away from the look in Darius's eyes. She no longer looked like she was in full control; it was like the badass succubus who'd been toying with us since we arrived had completely dissolved before our eyes.

I turned to Darius, trying to decipher the change in the atmosphere, only to find myself wanting to shrink back as well. His jaw was tight, the muscles pulsing slightly; his teeth had descended in a menacing way, his eyes hard and unrelenting. There was a wildness to his features that had me recalling what I'd heard people say about him—about there being something not quite right, not altogether stable in his mind.

If the look on his face was directed at me instead of Villette, I'd be halfway to pulling out my dagger already.

He clamped harder on her slim wrist, until I was certain he'd shatter her bones if he exerted any more pressure.

"It will take time," she said, her voice devoid of all seduction now, the words spilling from her lips in a hurry, "but eventually, if the boy doesn't kill her, it's possible she can gain control of the dreams, or at least of being drained. Until then, she can work on giving him less energy to drain."

"Explain," Darius said, the single word filled with more menace than I'd heard from anyone in my entire lifetime.

"My kind—we aren't able to feed on life energy if there isn't sexual energy for us to pull from first. The seduction acts as a catalyst. It opens a door of sorts that grants us entry, letting us pull from the person on other levels. If the girl is...sated properly," she shot Darius a small look of defiance at that, "then she will be less of a target. Shrink the door down and you will shrink how much of her escapes through it."

"What does that mean?" I asked, my words soft so as not to set him even more on edge. I didn't want to breathe, let alone speak right now. "Sated how?"

Without looking at me, she hardened her jaw, not answering until Darius eventually took the hint and released her wrist. The second that he did, she shook her hand out, trying to get the blood flowing again.

"It means," she said, frustration clear in her voice as she cradled her arm against her chest, "that before you sleep, I recommend having a go at it. Release some of your sexual energy so that when sleep takes you under, you'll be less susceptible to a predator's advances. Incubi and Succubi don't ever have sex with subjects who don't want it. If you're being fed on, it's because there is an underlying attraction there. You are encouraging the advances."

My skin burned at her words, but I couldn't help feeling a bit attacked too. "That sounds an awful lot like blaming the victim. I doubt most people taken advantage of by incubi and succubi are giving full consent."

I thought back to my time with Wade in his dream dungeon—an encounter in which I was very willing and in which he probably had no idea that he was pulling from me. Atlas had no clue that Wade was part incubus, so I doubted very much that Wade realized any different. He didn't seem like the type to deliberately keep secrets from those he loved and trusted.

She shrugged, her features hardening some. "Unfortunately,

you're not wrong. Many of us abide by very strict rules and codes. Some, however, do not. Either way, you have my answer and your solution."

I couldn't look at Darius. I wasn't exactly ashamed of having sexual desires, but it didn't mean I wanted to air them out in front of a virtual stranger, or be given instructions to more or less be less thirsty next time I went to sleep.

"Thank you," I said, glancing up at Villette. "I really appreciate you taking the time to walk us through this."

I felt a little bad for her—there was real fear in her eyes when Darius was forcing her hand. No pun intended.

He was silent, sitting back and staring at his empty glass, lost in thought. The final vestiges of the feral expression in his eyes slipped away with every passing second until they were gone altogether.

"You're welcome. I hope that you don't die. You don't seem half bad." She stood up from her booth, finished her drink, and looked down at Darius. "I'll find you when it's time to settle our debt." She crouched low, leaning over me to get closer to his face. "If you ever treat me like that again, even if it's because of a life bond, I will make you regret it. Even if it means attacking the thing you love most. Do not force me to do something we'll both regret."

With that, she walked over to the bar to pick up Jay. And then, together, they left.

"What did she mean by li—" my words were cut off instantly as I watched the blood drain from Darius's face, until he was pale enough that he resembled the vampires so often depicted in pop culture.

"Who the hell let protectors into my bar?" a deep, angry voice spilled into the room.

20

MAX

My stomach sank to my feet, body filling with ice, as I looked around trying to locate Atlas, Declan, and Eli. Did Marge know that Darius was lying? Had she signaled an alarm of sorts to alert someone that protectors infiltrated the bar?

"Fuck," Darius said, hopping over the table to leave the booth, not bothering to wait for me to stand up. His movement was so lithe and sudden that it was difficult to track.

Darius stood in front of me, blocking my view. "They're with me. I can explain," he said, his voice wavering slightly with fear or some other emotion I couldn't quite pick out.

"You. What the fuck are you doing in my bar?" The man's voice was filled with gravel, but it was slightly familiar at the same time, like a warped version of a voice I'd heard before. "I thought I made it very clear that I never wanted to see you in my city again. And now, not only have you disobeyed that promise, but you showed up with the fucking enemy."

"Claude, calm down, I just need to speak to you for a few moments in private, then we'll be out of your hair. You'll never have to see me again, if that's what you wish."

I stood up, pushing Darius to the side, slightly desperate to find the members of Six. We needed to go. This was not working out as planned. Clearly Darius was delusional if he thought this would be a good way for us to get our questions answered, to find our way into the hell realm. Whoever he was talking to sounded like he would happily peel back Darius's skin one layer at a time.

And now I'd persuaded Declan and the guys to break a vampire out of The Guild and follow him to a random city, all under the delusion that he would help us actually find the hell realm and rescue Wade. Instead, I'd gone and gotten us killed at some hole-in-the-wall demon bar. How the fuck did this keep happening? It was like I was living in a constant replay, responsible for slowly but surely killing off everyone I cared about.

Good intentions meant jack shit if the result was nothing but death.

With one hard elbow to the ribs, Darius finally looked down at me, confusion coloring his features. After a moment's hesitation, he moved aside so that I could push my way towards Atlas and the rest of Six, desperate for us to begin the arduous process of fighting our way out of here.

Only I didn't see a fight in front of my eyes.

Instead, I saw Darius. Or, well, someone who looked almost identical to him anyway.

"Holy shit," I said, studying the man in front of me. Like my vampire, this one was tall and lean with white-blond hair and two mismatched eyes. This man appeared stronger, his athletic build clearly visible through his dark jeans and t-shirt, and his hair was shorter and less mussed. He also didn't have quite the level of chaos swirling behind his striking gaze that I'd grown so used to with Darius.

In a way, this man in front of us was a mirror of what Darius could have been if he hadn't been held captive for so long. Instead, Darius was a broken version, a shadow of the man he called Claude, and my belly filled with an uncomfortable pity and anger that The Guild took so much from him. The man standing before me radiated power and control. He was a fucking force.

"You have a twin," I said, the words slow and drawn out, as if my mouth was waiting for my brain to catch up. "You could have mentioned that was who we were coming to see." I studied Claude, the narrow slant to his eyes that did nothing to hide his very clear desire to rip us all limb from limb. It spoke of great restraint that he could contain that impulse long enough to hear Darius out. "Why the hell does he look like he wants to chop you up into pieces and toss you off a bridge? You annoy him as much as you do me?"

I could have sworn that Claude's lip twitched at that, but instead of responding, he took a few steps towards us so that he stood only two or three feet from Darius, blocking out everyone else in the bar.

There weren't any shouting matches or stools breaking yet—instead, the bar was overcome with a creepy stillness and silence, like everyone was waiting for the pin to drop before erupting into chaos. For now, that meant that Declan and the boys were safe. Or at the very least alive.

I had no delusions that we were walking out of here without some violence. The stark hatred in Claude's eyes made that more than obvious. Hopefully we would end up with nothing more than some bruises and broken bones, healable troubles. Of course, that relied on Darius not saying anything unwise or upsetting.

So, basically, we were doomed.

Up close, the similarities between the men were even more striking, but so were the differences. They may be brothers and they may be identical, but they were nothing alike. That much was obvious, even with nothing more than studying their brooding standoff. While I was fairly certain that Darius wouldn't actively kill me, I was equally certain that his brother would, if given the chance.

"Good to see you too, Claude. You look good. Well, angry

more than good, but I have a feeling you'll take that as a compliment."

Claude ignored his brother's clear attempt at humor, ice glazing over his eyes. Even though the tension was tangible, and I was pretty sure we weren't making it out of here alive, I couldn't help but notice that while they both had mismatched eye shades, they were on opposite sides. Darius's right eye was gold, but Claude's was black. They were like mirror images in all ways, yin and yang. It was a strange thing to be captivated by, but I couldn't help but wonder in what other ways the two creatures standing in front of me were different.

A low, menacing growl reverberated in Claude's chest and I pushed myself against Darius's side, as if searching for warmth and safety. If someone told me two days ago that I'd be relying on a vampire to keep me alive, I would've laughed my ass off. But right now, I had a feeling that Darius was our only chance of not dying right now—which was a disheartening realization to come to.

Claude's sharp focus turned from his brother to me as he took a step closer.

In response, Darius shoved me slightly behind him, so that his brother brushed into his shoulder instead of reaching me.

"Ah, ah, ah, brother dear," Darius sing-songed, a clear threat infusing the tone, despite the playfulness, "mind your brooding and respect a woman's personal space."

"What are you?" He asked, his nostrils flaring slightly. He turned back towards his brother, eyes narrowing slightly.

Could vampires really smell the differences in species? Or was this something specific to Claude?

"She's mine," Darius said, the menace from earlier returning to his voice. Nerves filled my stomach, like an angry hive of bees, as they stared at each other in another silent battle of wills, until Claude's eyes widened in surprise. "She will remain unharmed. Two protectors are with me, that much is true. And I also have a werewolf to round out my menagerie of beasts. That said, they aren't the enemy, to me or to you. At least not right now anyway."

"Why did you return and how did you escape?" Claude asked, not backing down, neither of them paying any attention to the other inhabitants of the bar. It was like they existed in a strange bubble, the rest of the world nothing more than a passing backdrop.

I turned my head to the side, scanning the few patrons of the bar that I could see. Most of them were emphatically looking anywhere but at us, as if desperate to not get caught eavesdropping on family matters. Even so, the absolute lack of chatter made it abundantly obvious that no one was missing out on this conversation.

"They broke me out." Darius squeezed my hand in his, as if trying to pull strength from me or give me some of his own, I wasn't sure which. "I was slated to die and now I am not. So, I owe them. Their friend, the wolf's brother, has been taken to the hell realm. Captured by one of the ancients. We think."

At this, Claude took a step back, turning around to glance back towards the bar, where I assumed the rest of the team was waiting with heavy anticipation. "The ancients don't come to this realm. They can't. That's absurd."

Darius shrugged, chuckling without humor. "Apparently they do. I'm out of the loop, but maybe you are too."

"You still haven't addressed why you're here."

"I want you to take me to the portal, so that I can go and help them retrieve the boy. Then, my debt with them will be paid and you can do with me what you want."

Claude looked as if Darius had struck him, his face reddening with anger.

I clung to Darius's arm, trying desperately to pull him back a few inches, to get us out of harm's way. We needed to go. Now. However he'd hoped this conversation would go, he was wrong. Or severely naive.

Apparently vamps did not have warm, fuzzy relationships

with the members of their families. Well, these vamps didn't, anyway.

The atmosphere of the room changed, no longer simply tense. Now, I could feel dozens of eyes on us, each of them filled with a heated animosity. I felt, more than I saw, Atlas and the others close the distance between us. When Atlas reached us, he pulled me sharply from Darius, shoving me between him and Declan.

"You came here for a favor. And you expect me to reveal the whereabouts of the hell gate while you are working with protectors?" Claude's voice trembled with rage. "Are the rumors true? Have you lost your fucking mind?"

Darius took a step back now, and I saw fear, for the first time, start to cloud his features. "Yeah, it was a long shot. But a promise is a promise. I was hoping that after all of these years, you would have forgi—"

In a flash that was almost too fast for me to see, Claude gripped Darius's face on either side and snapped his neck, his body dropping to the floor in a heavy clunk as my breath froze in my lungs.

My heart beat rapidly against my ribs as I looked down at his crumpled body, a mass of limbs so still that he looked dead. I reached a hand out, as if to go to him, but Declan pulled me sharply back against her chest.

He would survive. I kept saying it over in my head as the long moment stretched.

My gaze drifted up to Claude's, fear clinging to my skin like glue. Darius might not be dead, but he was our best chance of getting out of here alive. If Claude treated his brother like that, what chance did the rest of us stand? Even combined, we weren't strong enough to take on a room filled with angry demons and hellbeasts.

Ignoring Atlas, Declan, and Eli altogether, Claude watched me, his chest heaving with heavy breaths, as if he was trying to contain the rage building up. "You will take him and leave here unharmed. I don't permit death battles in my bar, even if that grace must temporarily be extended to fucking protectors. When he wakes up, make sure he is aware that if I ever see him again, I will do more than break his neck." He glanced down briefly at his brother, disdain filling every feature of his face. "I will sever it."

With nothing more than a brief glance at the members of Six, he turned and walked through a door behind the bar, disappearing from sight.

Marge studied me, concern and fear playing out across her warm face. She clapped her hands twice as if to shatter the spell cast over everyone in the bar. Her eyes filled with pity as they found mine. "You heard the man," she barked loudly, her voice permeating every corner of the room, "everyone back as you were. These nice folks will be leaving now."

No one uttered so much as a sound on our way out the bar, Felix studying each of us with a heavy focus as we left as quickly as possible.

DECLAN SHOVED THE DOOR OPEN, ALLOWING ATLAS AND ELI to cart Darius's unmoving body into the hotel suite. They tossed him on the floor—hard—as soon as they cleared the threshold, then ignored him to go rummaging through the kitchen for a glass of water.

Without another word, Declan walked into the room we were sharing and slammed the door shut behind her, the sound ricocheting so loudly that I felt it in my bones.

"What the hell do we know?" Eli asked, hands shoving back his hair as he stared down at Darius with absolute disgust. "The fucking hell realm hates this guy as much as we do—there's no way that he can actually help us get to Wade."

Atlas vibrated with tension as his hands gripped the counter, face turned away from us all. "Did you learn anything while he was talking to the girl?"

My body warmed at the memory of our conversation, and I scrambled for a way to address it without announcing any of the embarrassing details—like the fact that, from now on, I would have to have a go with myself before I wanted to catch any restful sleep.

"She was a, er, succubus," I said, my heart beating angrily. "Darius was just getting some information from her about how I can keep Wade from accidentally killing me."

Atlas turned towards me, his face unreadable. "And?"

"She gave me some strategies to try until we find Wade and figure out a more long-term approach."

Until we find Wade. How the hell were we supposed to do that now?

Atlas pulled a glass from one of the cabinets, filling it with water and downing the whole thing in one gulp.

Eli sunk down on the couch, throwing desperate and angry glances at Darius.

"How long does it take for a vampire to wake up after being stunned like this?" I asked, wanting to turn the conversation in an informational direction so that we could start planning what our next step was going to be.

"Depends," Eli said, not looking at me as he turned on the TV and started flipping through channels, like a lost boy. "Could be an hour, could be a day or two. No way of knowing for sure. Depends how strong he is and how much of a tolerance he's built up. He's an insufferable prick, so I'm sure he's used to getting killed. He had some sustenance tonight, so that might speed things up a bit."

A crashing sound threw my attention back to Atlas. The glass he'd been drowning himself in was shattered in the sink, blood pooling in his left hand.

"Jesus," I said, closing the distance between us. I grabbed a handful of paper towels and grabbed his hand in mine. I wrapped it up, putting pressure on the wound, even though it would close up quickly. Werewolves healed even faster than we did. "What were you—"

I glanced up, catching his eyes on mine, the black orbs dancing with yellow as a hailstorm of emotions passed unreadable behind them. My heartrate picked up as I realized that I was basically holding his hand now, and so I stepped back, infusing some distance between us.

"We'll wait until he wakes up," Atlas said, his focus still trained on me as he slid his hand under the faucet. "Hopefully he has another connection, one who hates him a little less, to give us the information we need."

"And if not?" Eli asked, not looking away from the television. His shoulders were slumped, and I could feel the dejection in his posture. "The guy seems about as popular as syphilis."

I opened my mouth to point out that while not desirable, syphilis was common enough to be considered 'popular,' but a glance from Atlas had me shutting my mouth and reaching for some water of my own.

"We can't just go back to The Guild empty-handed," Eli said, his tone flat.

Atlas exhaled, leaning against the counter, a mere inch away from where my own hips rested. His eyes were calculating now, and I studied him as he built up a new plan in his thoughts.

"If he doesn't have a second option," Atlas started, his jaw clenching, "then we kill him and wait outside the bar he brought us to tonight. We wait for one of the beasts to leave and torture them until we gain entry to a gate."

"Rinse and repeat until we get what we need?" Eli asked, leaning forward, his elbows perched on his knees, neck craned so that he could focus on us.

"Rinse and repeat," Atlas answered.

I glanced down at Darius. He looked so peaceful in sleep, the chaos that normally plagued his mind invisible now. I thought about how he wasted his one question on helping me—on finding a way to keep Wade from unknowingly draining me dry.

A wave of anxiety washed over me as I hoped desperately that he'd have a Plan B when he came to. If not, I was going to have to come up with one myself.

Because one thing was certain—despite the fact that I *shouldn't* stop Atlas or Eli from killing Darius, I knew with absolute certainty that I would.

21

MAX

After sitting with the boys in silence, all three of us pretending to watch the reality TV show Eli had landed on, while shooting covert glances at Darius to see if he was starting to stir, I decided to call it a night and leave them to their brooding.

When I opened the door into the room I was sharing with Declan, I found her pacing back and forth, her hair wavy and voluminous, like she'd spent the last hour running her hands through it in frustration. It was the sort of angsty tick I had more than enough personal experience with.

Her green eyes were wild and filled with a leveled ferocity when they landed on me. It was more emotion than I'd ever seen in her eyes, which were usually so guarded, and enough to make my breath hitch at the sight.

"Are you okay?" I asked, because while it was clear that she wasn't, I didn't know what else to say.

She walked around the edge of the bed towards me, body stiff and slow like a lioness assessing her prey. "Is the cretin still alive?"

She didn't need to mention Darius's name. No one seemed

capable of getting under her skin the way that he did. Not even Eli.

The moment I nodded, she rushed towards the door, stopping only when I grabbed her by the elbow to prevent her from opening it.

"Atlas is really going to let him live after this?" she asked, pain seeping through the rage in her voice. Her jaw clenched as her eyes landed on the spot my hand held onto her, so I dropped my arm. "He nearly got all of us killed. Not only did he walk us into a room filled to the brim with festering creatures from hell, but he did so recklessly, without telling us that we were meeting with his fucking twin who would rather see him dead in a ditch, by the way, than help him."

She sank back against the door, her head staring up as she tried to contain the anger roiling through her. Her lips were moving slightly, and I watched as they shaped each number she mumbled as she counted to ten, her breaths coming out slow and deep. It was the type of soothing technique I'd seen on TV enough to recognize, but it was wild to watch her shoulders lose some of their tension with each passing moment.

Part of me wanted to reach out to her, to press my palm down on her shoulder to help the process along. But I got the feeling that Declan wouldn't appreciate that; that simply allowing me to witness her experiencing this level of discomfort was already far outside of her comfort zone.

"Atlas decided to wait and see if Darius has a second option or plan when he wakes up. Otherwise, we'll find our way through hell without him," I said as I pulled a loose thread from my shirt, watching it slowly unravel, like a release valve had been turned. "If it makes you feel any better," I added, "I don't think that Darius quite expected that level of animosity from his brother. I don't think he would have started there if he thought it would end like that."

She pinned her gaze on me, nostrils flaring slightly as every muscle in her body tensed. "It doesn't. Why do you keep doing that?"

"Doing what?"

"Standing up for him. Expecting a vampire to make choices that don't wind up with all of us killed. You do understand that tonight this fucking bloodsucker of yours almost got us slaughtered? Almost got us all—Jesus, Max, he almost got you killed too. And still, you're ignoring everything to see some bright shining light in him." She shoved away from the door, taking a step towards me. "How? How are you so naive? Let me be alarmingly clear. Whatever good you are hoping to find in him, it doesn't exist. Simple as that."

I sat back on the bed as she prowled towards me. I stared at my hands in my lap, unable to look her in the eyes. "Because," I started, trying to find the words to convey that deep in my gut, I knew that I could trust him, even if I didn't exactly understand how or why. "He saved me tonight," I landed on eventually.

"Explain."

"When we were talking with that woman, his I don't know, his friend I guess—turns out she is a succubus. And he took on a debt tonight. I don't know much about it, but taking on a debt with her seemed like a big deal. There was blood and this solemn look that passed between them. It was—it was important."

"Max," she said, able to cut through my rambling with just one word.

"Right. Anyway, in exchange for some future debt, he found out how to stop Wade from, you know, basically killing me."

Declan arched her dark brows, studying me with crisp focus until she joined me and sat down on the bed. Her thigh was so close to mine that we were almost touching, a realization that had my heart galloping like a racehorse.

The silence stretched between us, like a balloon filling with too much air—the cusp of anticipation and maybe a little bit of anxiety collecting like a pit in my stomach.

"My parents were killed when I was young," she said, her voice so low that I had to strain to hear the words.

I didn't breathe, waiting for her to continue. In my brief time around her, I'd never heard her offer personal information or insights, not once. Even when it came to Sarah, she kept things cool, objective, like she was offering a report rather than processing the information.

"They were researchers at the European Headquarters, the same campus Atlas's father is at now. Anyway," she said, the word coming out on an exhale, "they'd been working with these vampires a lot. They were always so careful in everything they did, but for some reason they let their guards down. It's possible that they started to trust a few of the creatures they were employed to study. I don't remember too well, I was only four or five when they died, and they were always so guarded about work and avoided talking about it with me at all costs."

Tentatively, I reached my hand out, giving her all the time in the world to reject my offering if she wanted to. But she didn't, so I wrapped my fingers around hers, urging her silently to continue, too afraid to break the moment with my condolences or platitudes.

"I think they wanted me far away from The Guild towards the end," she continued, her eyes staring off into some unseeable distance. "Years later, my aunt told me that they tried to keep most of it from me, but I think that's what made it all so shocking in the end. It was late when I found out, or early I guess—that time deep in the night right before the sun comes up. It was a Sunday, and we were supposed to be going on a vacation later that day. They'd been preparing for it and planning all month." She glanced down at me with a soft, whimsical smile. "You don't know this yet, since you're so new to our world, but it's rare for protectors to go on holiday. Almost unheard of. We were all so excited.

"Anyway, instead of waking up with the excitement that comes before a vacation and long road trip, I was woken by two of their coworkers." Tears glazed her eyes, brimming her waterline, but not one fell. "Their throats were slit, ear to ear, and they were drained completely. Found in a puddle of limbs, by the night staff during a patrol."

We were quiet for a long moment, her story settling over both of us. I squeezed her hand again, desperate to provide comfort but unsure of how. Saying I'm sorry, or I'm here for you just seemed so meaningless right now. It wouldn't bring her parents back, wouldn't make her feel safer or better about trusting the lives of her friends with another Guild lab vamp.

"Is that when you came to live in the States?" I asked, unsure of what else to say.

She shook her head, blinking her eyes closed as if she could will the tears away, prevent them from falling if only she tried hard enough. "I stayed with my mother's brother for a few years, but once I reached adolescence, he started devoting more and more time to his research. He became fixated on my mother's work—I think he was desperate for some sort of explanation, some clue as to where they went wrong, how they were tricked into letting their guards down. I didn't need as much supervision and I was starting at the school, so he could focus most of his attention on the lab." She let out a dull, humorless laugh. "He died when I was thirteen.".

"How?" I asked, though I was almost certain I knew the answer, could feel it in her tense muscles, in the way she squeezed my hand, unconsciously asking for strength and support.

"Same way. One of the creatures in the lab got out and killed him." She shook her head, her long waves caging her face like a shroud. "It's like my family is cursed or something. After he died, protectors started petitioning for more protections, more safety protocols. But it was too late for him. Too late for my parents.

"Without any more family in Europe, they packed my bags and sent me to live with my aunt and cousin out here."

Sarah. No wonder they were so close, they spent years living together as sisters—only to eventually end up on the same team.

"That's when I met Atlas," she added, a small, almost invisible smile brightening her face. "He's been like a brother ever since, each of us holding the other up, shielding each other from the shit that comes with this world."

I understood now why she was able to make concessions for him even if he was a werewolf. He was her family, her sense of home.

My stomach dropped, thinking about the yellow room back on campus, the one filled with well-loved records and books.

Declan lost Sarah.

And then Wade.

And now she was forced to trust the last tethers of family she had to another vampire in the lab. Darius wasn't the one who killed her family, but I understood now that, to Declan, that made no difference. He'd never stop being the face of the very thing that took everything from her one-by-one.

We were silent for a long while, both of us, I'm sure, lost in the maze of our thoughts.

Declan walked into the bathroom, ruffling through a bag for a moment or two until I heard the soft whir of the water as she brushed her teeth.

I dug through my bag and changed quickly into pajamas, getting my own toiletries together.

When she came back into the room, her posture was rigid and tense as she shot death glares towards the door leading to the kitchen and living room area. The area Darius was still occupying, even in his unconscious state.

She wouldn't go after him, not tonight. I wasn't sure how I knew that, but I did, could feel it in my bones. Saving Wade mattered more to her than vengeance.

I left her there to get ready for bed, only to find her staring just as intently when I returned, like she hadn't moved so much as an inch, lost in her thoughts.

Hearing about what she'd been through made me feel hollow, like her grief was mine. And suddenly all of her guardedness made sense. She walked through life like she was on the perimeter of the world, never letting herself get close enough to feel anything. Because when she did, she was burned.

Without a word, I climbed back into bed, pulling the covers up to my cheeks.

Eventually, she snapped out of whatever maze she was trying to solve in her mind, and I watched her prowl around the room. Throwing the toiletry bag on her pile of things, she pulled her top off in one fluid movement, so that she was standing in front of me in her pants and a sports bar.

Villette hadn't been wrong earlier—Declan was the sort of stunning that didn't even make sense. She somehow managed to have a body of perfect, lean muscle while still retaining something curvy and soft in the way that she moved.

With a soft thud, her pants fell to the floor next, revealing a pair of silky black cheeky underwear, her skin and tattoos on full display for my perusal.

Fire lapped at my skin as I watched her move, grace and confidence in every step she took. She wasn't putting on a show, simply getting her things together for bed, but even so I couldn't peel my eyes away from her. Unsurprisingly, she pulled a dagger from her holster. She walked towards the bed with it, tossing it with a soft clamor onto the nightstand next to her side.

Her eyes landed on me as she arched a brow, no doubt noticing just how intensely I was noticing her.

"Sorry," I mumbled, clearing my throat and turning around so that my back was to her as she climbed into the bed.

My heart pounded as she slid under the covers, I could feel the heat radiating from her body even though we weren't touching.

The bed let out a soft creak as she fidgeted around, trying to get comfortable, before she clicked the switch on the lamp. I watched as the light disappeared from the room, the blinking screen of the alarm clock somehow so bright in the darkness.

My breathing felt louder somehow, in the dark, and I held my breath, trying desperately to calm it down.

I could feel the moment when she rested her head on the pillow, her long hair spilling over onto my side of the bed, whispering along my neck in a way that sent shivers down my spine.

I'd shared my bed with Izzy before on countless occasions over the last few months. Never once did I feel the way that I felt now, knowing that Declan was inches away from me. Something about being alone together with the lights off sent the flutters in my stomach into overdrive.

The world was so much quieter, so much more intimate when the lights were turned out. Like anything could happen. Like there was no hiding.

Taking deep, slow breaths in and out, I tried to block out the new anxieties convulsing through my body. Ever since I moved to The Guild, my hormones had gone into overdrive. And now, with Declan, they were pushing into a territory that I'd never really allowed myself to explore, not more than passing thoughts and trivial daydreams.

"The woman you met with today," Declan said, breaking the silence, her words soft like she didn't want to wake me even though we both knew I wasn't asleep. "You said that she had a solution to your nightmares with Wade."

Ice filled my blood as I remembered Villette's solution. In the drama of our escape from the club, coupled with Declan's unexpected confessions, I hadn't given myself time to think about and really process her suggestions.

Now, my mind raced as I tried to come up with a way to explain the situation to Declan while we shared a bed. If Izzy were here, she would laugh about it and we would spend the night joking while she searched the internet for the world's strangest porn. She'd give me a running commentary of absurd puns from the outside of my room while I tried to get myself in the mood.

With Declan, I knew it wouldn't be like that.

"Max," she said, and I felt a soft pressure on my shoulder as she tried to turn me towards her, "what did she tell you?"

Closing my eyes, I turned around to face her. I took a heavy breath in and a long, slow, deep exhale out, desperately searching for enough courage and maturity to make it through this conversation without self-combusting.

I opened my eyes and almost all the bravery I deluded myself into acting on fizzled away. Even in the dark, Declan was stunning, her hair cascading onto the white pillow and sheets, her eyes somehow still intoxicating even when hidden in shadow.

But more than that, both of us on our sides, facing each other, I was acutely aware of how close we were, how intimate this moment was. For a long breath, we just stared at each other. I couldn't read the expression on her face, but I had to use all of my willpower to keep from reaching out and touching her, reaching out and closing the distance between us.

Eventually, my strength started to dissipate so that talking about my conversation with Villette would take less energy than resisting this pull, resisting the need inside of me to fold myself against her like a glove. "She mentioned a few things," I said, my voice grumbly as if I'd just woken from a long sleep, "but for now the most effective strategy is to not give him a catalyst to pull my energy from."

Her brows furrowed together in the center as she tried to dissect my words. "I don't understand."

I looked down, unable to stare into her eyes for this next part, focusing instead on the smooth skin of her neck in the places it met the surprisingly fluffy pillow.

"Succubi and incubi use sexual energy as an entryway of sorts, a way to access and drain a person's life energy. I-if there is less sexual desire when I dream, the window shrinks down and I will be harder to pull from."

"Smaller the hole, smaller the leak?"

I nodded, hoping we could leave the conversation there. I was okay with staying awake all night. Hell, I'd even happily fall asleep and let Wade drain me dead tonight if it would get me out of this conversation.

"How did she suggest you do that?" she asked, her voice hitching up a bit at the end, as if she suspected my response.

I cleared my throat, thankful that the darkness wouldn't show the heavy flush creeping up my body. "The way that I understand it, I need to give myself a release before I fall asleep, at least until Wade gets better at controlling his power." Then in a rush, as if my words couldn't exit my lips fast enough, I added, "but don't worry, I'm perfectly okay not sleeping tonight. It's been such a chaotic day that I don't think I could sleep any time soon anyway. But if I get exhausted later, I'll think of something and, like, go to the restroom and have a shower or something. That's where guys usually do that sort of activity, right?"

A soft, musical chuckle fell from her mouth, pulling my eyes to her devastatingly full lips. "Jesus Max, all you had to say was that the solution was you needed to have a good wank. It's nothing to be embarrassed about." She curled the side of her lips up in a coy smirk. "Hell, I have a go at myself all the time."

I think she probably meant that to be comforting, to ease my embarrassment. But instead, my thoughts just filled with images of her sliding her hand down the front of her pants, eyes closed and mouth opened as she brought herself relief.

My stomach tightened as I imagined how it might feel to be the one bringing her to that edge, and then following her over it.

Our eyes met, my heart pulsing so intensely that I could feel it throughout my entire body, hear it, even, in my ears.

"So," she said, a playful challenge in her eyes, "you going to handle your business or what? I can't have you dying on me tonight, Max Bentley."

I froze, trying desperately to process her words, but my mind went numb and all I could focus on was the fact that we were in this room. In this bed. Alone together. With the three guys on the other side of the wall.

Suddenly I missed Izzy and Ro so intensely that I could feel the ache in my bones. They could walk me through this, help me untangle the mess in my brain right now, help me decipher the unrecognizable urges going through my body. Make me feel normal, okay. The thought of being wrapped in one of Ro's large, rare hugs was enough to glaze my eyes over with tears.

"I-I, um," I said, the mush in my brain spilling over into speech.

"Hey, Max, it's okay," Declan's eyes widened in concern, and she reached her soft hand to my shoulder, squeezing gently. Her fingers slid down my arm, causing goosebumps on every inch of skin she touched, until she reached my hand, lacing her fingers in mine. "I shouldn't have teased you. I didn't mean to embarrass you or make you uncomfortable."

There was raw vulnerability in her eyes as she studied my features, concern coloring her expression. It was so rare, Declan in a vulnerable state, and this was the second time tonight. First, when she opened up to me, and now this moment, as she openly showed her concern. For me. The darkness disguised it, but I had a feeling that if the lights were turned on, we'd both be red in the face, the fragile moment shadowing us both in nervous energy.

She scooched closer to me, dropping my hand and slowly, oh so slowly, bringing hers up to my face. Her fingers skated against my cheek as she wove them through my tangled hair, pinky gliding along my ear.

My skin buzzed with the feel of her, her soft, vanilla scent suddenly the only smell I could focus on. She parted her lips softly, revealing her perfectly straight, white teeth slightly. Suddenly all I could think about was what it would feel like to taste her, to have her teeth leave soft indents in my lips, along my body.

Neither of us breathed for a long moment as she inched

closer and closer, giving me all the time in the world to back away, to unravel myself from her grasp if I wanted to.

I didn't. And I wouldn't.

Just as her lips were a hair's breadth away from mine, the scent of her toothpaste lingering with mine, a loud crash sounded in the other room. Declan sprung away from me as if I'd burned her, the moment shattering in a single moment. Loud shouts echoed throughout the hotel suite and we both ran into the other room, neither of us bothering to change or cover up first.

Declan beat me to the door and shoved me gently behind her as if trying to guard me from the sight.

It didn't work. Atlas was fighting against two men while Eli tried desperately to keep the fists pounding against the front door from entering.

His eyes met mine as his strength failed, the door busting in.

The room spilled over with angry bodies, until we were surrounded by almost a dozen creatures—vampires, werewolves, I had no idea which.

Only one thing was clear. They were here with one thing in mind—making sure none of us left this room alive.

22

ELI

Atlas and I sat and stared at the TV while old reruns of Family Guy played. I wasn't sure about him, but I sure as hell wasn't paying attention, my thoughts locked on our encounter tonight. On the fact that we all almost died.

Walking into a den of beasts was probably the most senseless thing I've ever done. Well, almost as senseless as getting a useless crush on a girl I could never have. My obnoxious fixation on Max went beyond my traditional brand of bad decisions.

I was torn between a giddy adrenaline high because we'd survived and absolute shame at how dense we'd been. Trusting a vampire with our safety because Atlas was so fucking desperate to act on the slim possibility that Wade was alive. What the hell were we thinking and why did I go along with it?

Hell, I guess I couldn't really blame him. Wade was like my little brother too, and after losing Sarah, I'd be lying if I didn't admit that our sanity was being plucked away one mission at a time.

But tonight, I almost lost them all. I almost lost her.

I ground my fingers into a fist, resisting the urge to punch something or do something I'd regret, just to keep my fucking feelings from eating me alive all night. I wanted things to go back to normal, back to before Max moved to Guild Headquarters and things went spinning into absolute fucking chaos. Back to before Atlas and Wade got turned into the very creatures we were supposed to be killing. I missed the days of the clear black and white—my job was so much easier back then.

Fuck girls, kill demons. Simple. Fun, even.

I needed to lighten the mood. I opened my mouth to let Atlas know I was going on a beer run when the door burst open, turning my simple statement into an exhausted, angry groan.

Two tall, muscular dudes barged into the room. They were the sort of stacked that you saw in bad wrestling shows, the type who looked almost unnatural in the way their arms and legs bulged. The slightly shorter one, with a shaved head and beady black eyes looked vaguely familiar. I didn't exactly get a great look at everyone in the bar tonight, but this guy was memorable because I'd watched as he downed three pints of beer in under thirty seconds. I was almost impressed.

But they were at the bar. Which meant that we weren't just dealing with some local unruly people hellbent on robbing us. Because that would be almost laughably simple and easy to deal with. These guys were supernatural.

Pounding feet told me that more were climbing the stairs, ready to join their beefy friends. Atlas and I glanced at each other, communicating in that wordless way we always managed to pull off during missions. His eyes were dark and wide, and I stood up as I read his subtle gestures, the brief tick in his glance, the small flex of his forearm. If only he were this easy to read during normal circumstances.

I flew to the door to hold back any more visitors, leaving Atlas to take on these bro-ey douches. He was a hell of a lot stronger than I was, so he had a better chance at taking them out than I did, as infuriating as it was to admit that.

They appeared to be vamps, judging by their speed as they leapt towards Atlas. But I was learning more and more that the culmination of all of my studying over the years barely even nicked the tip of the iceberg when it came to creatures from hell.

This trip made it abundantly clear that what we knew about the other realm and all the creepy crawlies that lived there might as well have been jack shit.

It made this moment almost perfect in its irony, me trying to hold back a flood that none of us were powerful enough to overcome. Protectors didn't stand a fucking chance.

Atlas, however, was a different story. It was ridiculous, really, the way that he could go from his default state of casual brooding to taking on two man-beasts like that, without so much as blinking. If my heart weren't furiously pounding into my ribs, I'd almost be enjoying the show as he attacked and dodged in equal measures.

I dug my feet into the carpet—the sort of carpet with stains you just have to grit your teeth and pretend aren't there—trying to gain traction as I scanned for something to use to help block the rest of them off.

Heavy fists started pounding into my back, with enough strength to push the door open a few centimeters. Thick fingers pressed through the opening, making it impossible for me to shove the door all the way back into the frame to latch.

I opened my mouth to scream for the girls, hoping they weren't already asleep. We needed help. The door to their bedroom flung open before I could yell out. My eyes caught Max's, her eyes wide and doe-like as she tried to process what was going on. And then, all at once, the wall at my back busted open. It flew right off the hinges as a stampede of beasts flooded into the room.

I glanced over at our own vamp prisoner as the room crowded with bodies far more powerful than my own. He was twitching a bit, like he was coming to, but I had a feeling he wouldn't be alert enough to help us fight back these beasts until it was too late. Until the four of us were scattered around the room in pieces and parts.

Hell, for all I knew, he might join them in hacking us all up to bits.

My stomach flooded at the image of him draining Max, of plucking us all one-by-one until he could get to her.

I took a deep breath in, lifting the splintered door from my legs as I pulled out two of my knives.

Most of my weapons were in the bedroom on my nightstand. We weren't exactly expecting an ambush in our hotel suite. Amateur mistake. The trick was to never let your guard down. In this line of work, there was no such thing as a night off or proper downtime. Especially not in unfamiliar, enemy territory.

I swung around, jumping onto the back of the nearest creature. She was a woman, half my height so my weight easily pulled her to the ground. Using her surprise, I lifted my hand and stabbed deep into her chest, not giving her a second to react.

Warm blood pooled over my hands as I ripped my blade out, not waiting a second before charging towards the next one. There were so many. Too many.

Out of the corner of my eyes, I could tell that Atlas was in full wolf form now, leaping through the air to tackle a creature creeping up behind Max. I grinned when he pulled the guy away before he had a chance to reach her.

She and Declan moved back-to-back, both of them still in their underwear and bed clothes, blades in their hands as they double teamed a vamp.

Max wasn't a slouch, and if Declan had her back, she stood a good chance. At least for a little while anyway.

The next guy I reached was tall and thick, so I knew this would be more difficult for me to take on solo.

His fist swung out towards me, but I used his forward momentum to duck and ram into his center, pushing him to the ground. I lifted my arm ready to stab him the same way I took on the girl, but another asswipe ripped me off the dude, and flung me into the wall. Hard.

When I pushed off the ground, my head spinning from the

impact, I was surrounded by three. Judging by their slippery grins that revealed descended fangs, they were all vamps.

Not willing to sit around as a catatonic blood bag, I threw my blade into one while I charged at a second, but I only gained enough of an advantage to keep them back for an extra second or two.

Without a pause, I went after the one with my blade poking out of his shoulder and leapt. We landed in a hard tackle, the leech's teeth scraping the soft skin on my neck.

I shoved my knee into his groin as I tried to wrestle my blade out of his arm and then out of his reach, only for it to escape my own grasp as well.

Thick fingers dug into my wrists, hard enough to fracture and keep me in place. My eyes spun wildly as I tried to scan for backup, but the room was a clusterfuck, my teammates more than occupied with their own tumbles.

Desperate, I kicked out at where I thought his knees might be and missed. I flung my forehead forward, making contact in a blow that hurt me probably as much as it hurt him, but at this point I didn't care. I had no options.

The vamp hissed in my face and pressed his face into my neck. This was it. This was how I was going to die. What a fucking bummer.

The moment the realization melted into my bones, I relaxed some, half accepting my fate.

And then, miraculously, the vamp went limp, body collapsing completely on top of me.

I shoved him off and saw Max in front of me, trying to dodge attacks from the dead vamp's friends, my blade gripped in her hands and fury on her face.

She was so small and naive that half the time I forgot she was a fucking badass.

But here, like this, there was no denying it. Her eyes were narrowed, intelligent, as she studied the room, making use of the landscape we had working for us. In that moment, she reminded me of Cyrus, all quiet contemplation and cool focus. He'd done well training her, that much was for damn sure.

Swiping one of the asshole's legs out from under him, I shoved my fist into his face again and again the second his head reached the floor. More were coming. I stood and looked around, Max and I surrounded by at least four now, with only two weapons between us.

She made like she was going to give me back my blade, but I shook her off, pushing closer to her and gripping my second blade instead. While I was grateful she saved me, I couldn't help but wish that Atlas was in this corner right now instead of me. He had a better chance of keeping her safe than I did.

So now, my only focus was keeping her alive long enough for Declan and Atlas to get her the fuck out of here. If I could do that, I'd lay down my life happily. Some things were worth the sacrifice. And Max—as annoying as it was to admit—she was one of them.

Five creatures surrounded us now, all of them thick with muscles and all of them with anger lacing their features. From what I could tell, they all seemed to be vampires, which was a weird sort of relief. At least we were only dealing with one set of weaknesses and strengths. And we most likely were dealing with a new bunch, not the group of wolves and vamps that we'd been running into over and over again during the last year.

Still, we were screwed. Royally.

Max's shoulder brushed softly against my arm, and I glanced down at her face and swelled with pride. Her expression was so determined, so focused. Even though I could recognize the fear in the way her lips were slightly more pinched than usual, or the slight tilt in her brow, I didn't think the enemy would be able to see it. Only someone like me, who'd spent an absurd amount of time obsessively staring at her, would notice.

She squared her shoulders, her posture crouching like she was getting ready to strike, so I mirrored her motions. When she jumped forward, I jumped too, hoping that the tandem attack would give us better odds, catch the group surrounding us off guard. In a lot of ways, fighting side-by-side with her—ducking when she swung, kicking the knees out of the guy who tried to grab her—felt like fighting with the rest of my team.

Our moves complemented each other, and we seemed naturally able to read each other's body language, even with the heavy atmosphere and small odds.

The vamp in front of me had thick blond hair and an angry scowl on his face. I turned like I was going to strike out at the guy to his left, and used the surprise to punch him in the face. And then, as he recovered, I lodged my knife deep into his chest cavity, tilting my knife up to strike his heart while avoiding as many ribs and pesky cartilage as I could.

The momentum had me crashing to the floor on top of him, but he was dead. One down. With a heavy heave, I yanked my knife out, desperately trying to swallow a breath before lodging myself back up to take on the next one. Using the guy's body as a stabilizer, I steadied myself.

"Eli!" Max's voice radiated around me, like an electric shot. "Watch out, behind you."

My face dropped as a female vamp pulled my arm back, stomach sinking somewhere in the vicinity of my feet as my shoulder ripped out of the socket at best, breaking something at worst. But I didn't feel it. The adrenaline coursing through me was too high. Still, she'd fucked up the arm holding my blade, which wasn't good.

Using my good arm, I elbowed the chick in the face, a triumphant smirk crossing my face as I watched blood spurt across hers. Her nose was most definitely broken—an injury for an injury. Without pausing, I flung myself down, keeping my back to the ground so that I could keep an eye on the girl, her face red with blood like a twisted painting. I grabbed my knife and glanced at Max out of my peripheral. A giant dude was right behind her, but she was too focused on fighting the smaller vamp to her side, beads of sweat dripping down the sides of her face.

Somehow, even through all of the endless exertion and gore, she still looked beautiful.

Just as the bleeding vamp leapt down on top of me, anger rejuvenating her attack, I flung my knife into the guy's eye as his fist came up behind Max ready to pull her down.

The blade landed with satisfying force, right as the girl's fangs dug a wide hole into the side of my neck. One of her friends collapsed down on top of both of us to join in the feeding frenzy.

"Atlas watch out," Declan shouted across the room—too far to get to me in time.

A loud, angry growl that my brain was slowly starting to associate with Atlas's wolf sounded in the distance.

Good, they were okay. At least, for now, they were alive.

I thrashed my limbs wildly as another vampire descended onto the pile of flesh that I, unfortunately, was at the bottom of.

Darius was a few feet away, my eyes landing on his just as they sprang open, the mix of gold and black visible just for a moment as he came to and pulled at his restraints with a loopy desperation.

"Eli," Max shouted, and I felt the panic in her screams as she tried to get to me. "No!"

She drew the word out on a grunt as I heard a body drop a few inches from me, my arms growing exhausted and losing steam.

"Max, go," I screamed, using the last of my energy to warn her away. I wanted her to run, to get as close to Atlas or Declan as she could. Hell, if she could manage it, I wanted her to escape from this room altogether and never look back.

I closed my eyes, my fate sealed as I floated in the sensation of having my blood pulled through my veins and out of my body.

My father. My poor father would lose someone else. Maybe Cyrus would stay longer if I was gone.

A warm shadow filled the backs of my eyelids, painting a beautiful wash of oranges and reds; until the warmth extended from visual to something more tangible, heat lapping against my skin like an old friend.

My lids slammed open and I was surrounded by fire, the flames whipping around me like a terrifying and beautiful whirlwind, but not once touching my skin. Suddenly, all I could hear was the loud, aching shrieks of the vampires. They were no longer on top of me, but instead were collapsing one-by-one, bodies writhing into the ground as they desperately searched for an escape.

I looked around, trying to gauge where the fire was coming from. Had I died? Was I in hell?

My pulse beat wildly in my veins as if desperate to escape my body, until my eyes caught on Max. The girl in front of me was unrecognizable, like she'd been a shadow of herself before.

Her normally warm, brown eyes were now black as night, the pupils completely eating away the whites of her eyes. Her long, dark hair was floating around her as if it was being caressed by a heavy and invisible wind. She was mesmerizing. And terrifying.

Was this her? Was she doing this? My thoughts flew back to the conversation I'd had with my father. Was it only weeks ago? Months? Time felt so slippery lately. There was so much I didn't know about her. What were my father and Cyrus keeping from us all?

Then, as fast as the flames started, they fell silent. The five vampires surrounding me were still and lifeless, bodies burnt to a terrifying crisp. The chaos around the room resumed, and I knew that Declan and Atlas were still fighting their way out of the bodies. Had they seen what happened? Did they know that the strange power and energy sizzling in the room had come through Max?

The blacks of Max's eyes slowly receded until all that was left was her devastating but typical stare, her eyes clouded with a heavy fear—not of the monsters crowding into the hotel suite, but of herself.

She collapsed into a heap, the fucking force from a few moments ago now just a pile of awkwardly entangled limbs.

"Max!" Darius screamed, and I watched in my peripheral vision as he rushed towards her, finally free of his restraints. We shouldn't have locked him up again when we'd come back. He might've been able to help sooner if we hadn't.

My breath stopped as I watched for an agonizingly long moment while the vampire searched for a pulse. When he found it, he let out a relieved exhale, glancing at me—a silent nod passing between us.

She was alive, yes. But what the hell *was* she?

23

DARIUS

Max lay collapsed in my arms, her eyes rolling back in her head as the energy drained from her. My limbs were shaking as I searched for a pulse and I almost pissed myself in relief when I finally felt one. It was slow, breathy. But it was there.

The room was chaos around me, and I recognized a couple of faces from the bar earlier.

We shouldn't have gone there. I shouldn't have taken her. Rage built up in my chest like a snowball, my wrists still aching from the fresh wounds incurred while freeing myself. The metal had been weakened and bent from my earlier attempts at loosening the bindings, but that didn't mean getting out had been easy. I was weak. So much weaker than I should've been.

And my fucking brother snapped my neck. I should've known what I was getting into. I was naive to think we stood a chance of convincing him to actually take us to the hell gate. I was fucking naive and now we'd all end up dead because of it. There were too many, even with the strange fire magic Max used on the guys trying to take down Eli.

I set her down in a corner of the room. I wouldn't be able to make sure she was okay, not really anyway, until the rest of these dickheads were gone.

A smile ghosted across my face. It'd been too long since I'd had the opportunity for a good fight. I was almost excited by the prospect of one. I glanced around, not noticing any weapons except for the long dagger lying on the ground where Max fell. I picked it up, muscles freezing when the boy—Eli—rested a hand on my calf. He inched towards me, trying to pull my attention in his direction.

I glanced down at him, half expecting that I'd have to remove his head from his neck, that he'd try to stop me from taking on the rest of the room.

His normally cocky expression was absent, fear mobilizing his features instead. I watched as he studied Max and realized that it wasn't that he was afraid of dying, rather he was afraid of her dying. The vampires did a number on him before Max took them on with those flames. The wounds in his neck were leaking so much blood that I was surprised he was still alive. The scent of it coated the air.

"You have to get her out of here," he breathed, voice laced with such acute pain that it was hardly more than a whisper. His body was covered in so much blood that he looked like an extra in a zombie movie.

How did she manage to eviscerate all of those vampires but not burn him to a crisp as well? Clearly she was built of some sort of strange magic. But it wasn't like anything I'd ever encountered before. And I'd seen a lot in my relatively short life. It made sense—especially since I was so drawn to her. I could never be drawn to a mere protector like that.

Whatever she was, she was magnificent. And fucking terrifying.

I shook my head, as if I could somehow just dislodge her from my thoughts. My life would be so much easier if I could just turn around now and never look back—leave her and the rest of her friends here to die. It would be my only chance at a head start. And if I wasn't dragging her along, I'd get much farther before anyone caught up to me.

I looked back down at the boy. She cared deeply for him, though I had no idea why. Other than the occasional one-liner, he was a bit of a bore.

Still, he seemed the least likely to kill me in comparison to the other two. His bites were bad. I didn't know much about what determined how easily or not a protector could survive the venom, but this kid didn't look good.

I frowned at that, thinking about how upset Max would be if he died.

Why the fuck was I so focused on the little protector's feelings? What the fuck did they do to me down there in that lab? Clearly a screw or two was loose in my skull. Pre-Guild Darius was a fucking force. Now, I was no better than an overgrown labrador retriever. Albeit one with extra-pointy canines and a raging thirst for blood and violence. But domesticated all the same.

Rolling my eyes, I dragged his body towards hers, placing him in front of her and propping his blade upright in his right hand. Was he right-handed? I shrugged. Probably.

"Live up to your namesake, kid. Protect her." I said, words monotonous as I glanced around the room. The wolf and girl were taking on an impressive number of the remaining ten or so vamps, but they'd fall eventually. The room reeked of blood and guts which meant they probably disemboweled quite a few of them already. I cringed, thankful that they hadn't saw fit to do the same to me just yet. "Anyone comes within three feet of her, scream for me. But they are here for me and you're as good as dead. So you should be fine." As soon as I said it, I knew it was true.

Eli's brows furrowed in concentration as he studied me, studied the room. He sat up, pressing his free hand against the gaping hole in his neck and kept his blade raised. He nodded, understanding my point. If he really was dying, he didn't seem too concerned about it.

If I ran, if I took her with me, this nest of vampires would come for me eventually and she wouldn't stand a chance. Here, at least, we had the wolf and girl as backup. We needed to take them out here and now. They followed us from the bar and I had no doubt in my mind that they'd follow me wherever I went, hunting me until they had my head. I'd brought protectors into the most popular vamp bar in the state. That was unforgivable. I would probably never be welcomed by my own kind again, if my actions spread beyond this room. And they wouldn't rest until I paid.

I ran behind a large, burly asshole right as he reached for the girl. I didn't have a weapon, but I didn't really need one. With a hand on each side of his head, I used the benefit of a surprise attack to twist and rip the asshole's head clean off his spine.

His body fell to the ground in a grotesque clunk, his blood shading my outfit in a sticky, warm red. Four sets of eyes turned in my direction, only one of them friendly.

The girl, Declan, nodded in thanks before jumping back into battle with one of the few females still alive. Climbing over a stack of vampire limbs, I swung out at a guy with long, lean muscles and an unreasonable amount of hair on his face. If I didn't know any better, I would think he was actually a werewolf.

He ducked before my fist could reach his face, using my momentum against me to knock me to the floor. There was enough blood on the carpet that I could feel it soaking through the back of my shirt as I rolled around trying to shift my weight long enough to flip the guy on top of me.

"Precarious position, my friend," I said, flashing the guy with a wink. "You're just my type."

Surprise crossed his ugly-ass features and I used the single moment to deck him in the face, my knuckles drawing a steady stream of blood from his nose. He lifted a hand to stem the flow, which was a big mistake.

I punched my hand clean into his chest, a move that would leave me with some temporarily bruised fingerbones, but nothing worth losing sleep over.

"Fu—" he started, realizing his mistake just as my fist closed, squeezing his heart from within his chest cavity until I could feel it tear and shrivel in my grasp.

With a dull weight, he fell on top of me. Dead.

Another one down.

I took a momentary breath, wishing I'd had a proper few meals before I had to take on a room of creatures almost as powerful as I was—only in way better condition. I glanced up at the werewolf briefly. He was flinging pieces of flesh from his teeth, so I had a feeling he and Declan had taken one or two down on their own since I'd joined in on the foray.

Our odds were looking better, but they still weren't great.

And now that the remaining vamps realized that I was awake and ready to get in on the fun, they started shifting their focus and moving towards me. I was the real prize. They hated protectors, sure. That was nothing special though, they always hated protectors. It was practically encoded in our DNA. But I was the goal here, the reason they'd bothered showing up in the first place.

I was the one who brought the protectors to them, I was the traitor. I could see their hatred mirrored in the six pairs of beady eyes shifting closer and closer towards me, inch-by-inch. They wanted to rip me limb-from-limb and they wanted to make it last.

I could take on two, maybe three of them if I was in my prime. But I wasn't. I'd been locked up in a hellhole for years, starved, and only returned to consciousness less than five minutes ago.

If the wolf and the girl could take out two more, we might stand a chance, but it wasn't looking great.

With a heavy sigh, I shoved the dead man off of me and stood up. Without waiting for another beat, I charged at the vamp nearest to me, not even bothering to catalogue his features. I clawed and ripped. A loud crack told me that one of us had broken a bone, but the adrenaline was so high that I couldn't tell which.

One of his buddies joined in, not waiting for a fair fight, and I flung fist over fist, trying to wrestle a dagger from one of them to give myself more leverage for getting a clean heart stab in.

Just as my fingers closed around the hilt of a blade, my mouth edging into a cocky smile, a thick sharp object lodged itself into my ribs.

With a sharp breath in, eyes wide in shock, I turned to my right side as an annoyingly pretty vamp next to me stabbed into me again. A large grin stole over his face as he glanced at his friends in triumph.

I stood still, expecting to fall over any second, dead. But after a single breath, I realized he'd missed my heart. Judging by the look and feel of his hand against my chest, he probably only missed by a few centimeters at most.

My hand snapped as the vampire whose blade I was lobbying for used my distraction against me. Pretty boy on my right realized his mistake only a second after I did as he pulled the blade out ready to strike again.

Another pair of hands wrestled my other arm away from me, leaving me no way to defend myself against Pretty's next blow. Which meant this was it. I was as good as pinned and as good as dead. No referee needed for the count.

Turning, I watched the boy's face as he shoved his blade back towards my body and watched as his expression turned from glee to wide-eyed shock. An excruciatingly long second drew out as I waited for his dagger to pierce deeper into my chest but, instead, it fell away, landing on the ground with an anticlimactic clunk as the boy's body followed it down.

Dead. He was dead. And I was...alive?

I looked up, expecting to see Declan and reluctantly thank

her for saving my life, when I was met with an unexpected face instead.

My own.

"Claude," I said, the word little more than a whisper.

His eyes were a steel wall, revealing nothing more than anger as he used the element of surprise to wrestle my arm away from one of the guys pinning me, until suddenly that vampire was dead too.

Claude was...killing his own. Not waiting to question the surprising turn of events, I followed suit, picking up Pretty's dagger with my good arm, following my twin's lead. He was stronger than I was—much stronger—and I felt the tide of the evening turning in an instant.

The werewolf and girl seemed to recognize it too. One body dropped, then another, then another. Until, suddenly, the dirty hotel suite was nothing but an unofficial graveyard, a mess of limbs and corpses and more blood than any vampire could drink in a day.

Breath heaving heavy and thick, I turned from the werewolf to Max—still unconscious in the corner, behind the kid—to my brother.

"I am the only one with permission to kill you," he said, words monotonous and only slightly winded.

He nodded his head back towards Max and I realized that she was being cocooned by a large furry creature. A moment's observation revealed it to be the hellhound from the lab, the one bonded to her.

"He came bounding into the bar looking for me," Claude said, surveying the battle scene with little interest, "caused quite a stir and wouldn't leave me the fuck alone until, eventually, he pulled me here."

"Ralph?" Declan whispered, walking over towards the misleadingly cute and fluffy creature.

"Clearly they followed you from my bar," he said, shaking his head with his lips turned into a small frown. "Damn shame. These weren't bad men, not really."

I still couldn't quite process the fact that he'd willingly killed his own. Vampires were a violent lot, but Claude had always prided himself on rising above it whenever possible. It was why his bar was so popular—people could expect a modicum of safety and respite under his roof.

As if reading my mind, he shook his head. "Told you little brother," he said, causing me to bristle. The guy was born ten minutes before me and that apparently qualified him for a lifetime of 'little brothers.' "I'm the only one allowed to kill you. When it's time, your death will come by my hands."

"What now?" The wolf asked, now shifted back into his surly protector form. He looked around, likely trying to find clothes, but I didn't think he'd find them anywhere in this massacre. And if he did, they wouldn't be worth wearing.

"Now?" Claude asked, lifting one brow in challenge. "I do the only thing that will get you all out of my sight and out of my town for good. I take you to hell."

HELL AND BACK

Grab Book Four in The Protector Guild series:

Max and the members of Team Six have finally found their tickets into Hell. But the journey to cashing them will be anything but easy; and every decision along the way will come with a sacrifice...sacrifices they might not be willing to make.

Darius's creepy brother, Claude, is determined to push Max and her team out of his city, as soon as he possibly can. And they are definitely ready to leave him, and the city, behind. But, unfortunately for them all, hitching a ride to hell will have to wait.

On top of dealing with the fang twins' turbulent relationship (and, wow, is that putting it lightly), Max has to navigate Declan and Atlas's suddenly chilly demeanor towards her. Something happened that night in the hotel suite that changed things between them all, but nobody will talk to her about it.

And something changed within Max too, something big that she doesn't quite know how to deal with. A strange power is starting to build, and she must find a way to harness and accept it before it destroys her and everyone she cares about. Unfortunately, that means coming to terms with the increasingly real possibility that everything The Guild—and her family—has told her is a lie.

The monsters are coming for her, that much is clear—but it just so happens that she may very well be a monster herself...

ACKNOWLEDGMENTS

This book wouldn't be possible without the support of my family and friends. You know who you are, and I couldn't be more grateful to have you in my life. Thanks for always encouraging me and pushing me to chase after my writing dreams.

Special thank you to my early readers, editor, Kath, and my cover designer, Michelle. This book is so much better because you've all contributed a piece to it. Thank you.

And to my very own 'Ralph,' thanks for keeping me company while I wrote this series for hours and months on end.

Printed in Great Britain
by Amazon